MY NAME IS MAGIC

Xan van Rooyen

Tiny Ghost Press

ISBN:
E-book 978-1-7399834-3-7
Paperback 978-1-7399834-4-4
Hardcover 978-1-7399834-5-1

Cover artwork by: Alex Copeman
Illustrations by: Susan Campbell

To find out more about our books visit www.tinyghostpress.com and sign up for out newsletter.

*For those who doubt their worth and their place in the world—
please know that you are needed, you matter, and it's okay to not
have it all figured out yet.*

And to Mark, always.

AUTHOR'S NOTE

I was fifteen when I fell in love with Finnish heavy metal. Thanks mainly to Nightwish, but also to Children of Bodom, Ensiferum, Sonata Arctica, and Moonsorrow, I very quickly became obsessed with all things Finnish. So obsessed, in fact, that when I discovered my university had an exchange program with the University of Jyväskylä, I changed my major so I'd be eligible for the program.

I went on exchange and as soon as I stepped onto Finnish soil, I knew I was home. It might sound a bit OTT, but as someone who had always struggled to fit in, had never quite felt like they belonged, I arrived in Finland and everything just felt right: the nature, the people, the culture, the music—everything! Suffice it to say, I have loved Finland for a very long time and while I can only ever lay claim to the smallest smidgen of Nordic ancestry courtesy of my Viking ancestors settling in England, I am extremely proud to now be a Finnish citizen and to call this wonderful, if at times strange and seemingly inhospitable, country home.

It is from a place of love and respect for Finnish culture and mythology that I began writing this book. Finland's ancient pagan history has been eroded and even actively suppressed by oppressive forces throughout the centuries. As a result it's difficult to find references to Finnish mythology beyond the national and well-known epic, *Kalevala,* especially in English. Much of what was compiled by Elias Lonnröt for the version of the *Kalevala* known today was borrowed from local folklore shared in the oral tradition, stitched together, altered, "corrected," and sometimes embroidered with Lonnröt's own interpretations as well as a liberal dash of Christian influence. I have done my best to include older, more authentic, pre-Christian mythology in my story.

While my hunt for Finnish paganism led me to various corners of the Finnish and English Internet, to websites, blogs, personal Instagram accounts, and beyond, I did make extensive use of Risto Pulkkinen's *Suomalainen kansanusko: samaaneista saunatonttuihin,* a book I know is an imperfect resource but one of few regarding traditional Finnish mythology. In *My Name Is Magic*, I have tried to stay true to the essence of the mythology and be fair to the many creatures living in the Finnish forest that peacefully coexisted with the earliest Finns before later being labeled as devils by Christian interlopers. But, this remains a work of fiction, and so I have certainly taken some liberties with the mythology—like adding runes from Norse folklore as well as my own—and it should therefore be seen as a story "inspired by" rather than "based on" any particular aspect of this rich, if lesser-known, mythology.

There's magic in the world. All different kinds, seeping into the veins of people across the planet. Sometimes it soaks an entire family tree, flowing up from the roots and extending out through every branch.

Sometimes it prefers those with a sprinkling of fairy blood or a smattering of troll genes, and sometimes it ends up in a person with entirely human DNA. From Longyearbyen to Cape Town, Los Angeles to Suva—there's no escaping it.

And then there's me—a tiny leaf at the end of a twig shooting off a long branch of the giant, sprawling, epic Turunen family tree, making me a descendant of some of the most powerful *tietäjät* in Finland. Potent lineage, right? Bet you think that means I'm guaranteed to be a total badass, right?

Wrong.

Fact is, I don't have magic at all. Not a drop, not a sliver, not one single quark of the stuff and, to be honest, I'm a little bit bitter about it—especially considering my name.

Taika. It *literally* means magic. So, thanks, Mom and Dad for naming me the one thing I'm not.

It's not fair the week starts with the worst subject in the world: Practical Thaumaturgy. *Theoretical* Thaumaturgy, now that would've been just fine, but anything involving actually doing magic only makes me want to puke.

Trudging through the soggy fallen leaves, I drag my feet to first period. So far my morning is going great. I slept through my alarm and had to eat cold porridge, then I forgot my mittens and when I rushed back for them, I slipped on the porch steps and tore my favorite jeans—skinning my knee in the process. Now, as if all of that wasn't bad enough, the clouds have started spitting sleet into my face.

A typical Monday really.

Worst of all, I still don't have any good ideas for newspaper articles. There's a measly six hours until our next Journalism Club meetup and I'm fresh out of inspiration.

Familiars in School: Why Magical Animals Are a Distraction in the Classroom

Snoozefest.

Conjured Candy Not a Healthy Lunch Choice

Most kids wouldn't agree.

Is PE Really Necessary at a School for Magic Wielders?

Hm. How do I convince the other ninth graders to ditch sports in favor of an extra library period? Who wants to run around a field when you could be reading?

The late bell is ringing and I pause, wobbling between choices. It's not like I want to be one of *those* kids who skip class, but I'm so tired of being the one who sucks at pretty much everything. This class is pointless for me anyway. It's an argument I've had before, but when your mom's school principal it means having to attend all your lessons even if you have "gross ineptitudes," as my sixth-grade conjuring teacher put on my report card. He doesn't work at the school anymore.

So, *inept* it is today, which is only questionably better than *tardy*. I skid-run up the path toward the entrance of Myrskyjärvi International School—*for the Magically Gifted*. I try to ignore the last part of the school's name the same way most people ignore me.

I'm about to slip through the doors and instead end up body-slamming Emmi Lehtinen , who's on her way out.

"Ah, there you are. We're having class outside today," Emmi says. Her robes, better suited to the thirteenth century, swirl as she turns. Other teachers wear jeans and sweaters beneath sensible jackets. Not Emmi.

Does Emmi Lehtinen LARP 24/7, or Is She the Victim of a Chronomancer's Evil Prank?

Would the editor of the *Myrsky Messenger* let me write that? Probably not.

"Sorry I'm late." I ignore the snickers from the rest of the class.

"You arrived precisely when you needed to. Here, you can help." Emmi winks as she hands me a black velvet bag. No wonder they call me teacher's pet but... I can't really complain. Emmi is one of the few teachers who actually acknowledges my existence and lets me do stuff in her class. I take the bag and head out into the miserable drizzle of Finnish autumn.

While the others amble behind, most of them complaining about having class in the wet, I catch Natalie's eye and give her a tiny wave.

"Hi." She gives me a smile that dimples her left cheek. She seems about to say more when Sini, Aysha, and Ekaterina sweep past.

"Urgh, why are you even here?" Sini says. It's the same question I ask myself pretty much every day. I glance at Natalie, hoping my once-BFF will stick up for me like she used to, but Aysha loops her arm through Natalie's, giving me some serious stink eye.

Natalie mouths "sorry," letting herself get swept away by the others, already chatting about a weekend shopping trip to Stockholm. Natalie hates shopping. Maybe Aysha would figure that out if she ever let Natalie get a word in edgewise.

Off they go, the formidable foursome, leaving me feeling as hollow as the rotten oak clinging to the edge of the path and casting gaunt shadows across the school's entrance. It's barely standing, just a shell of gnarled bark with nothing on the inside but bird poop and an abandoned squirrel's nest. Yip, that's me.

Useless, pathetic, waste of space, the little voice at the back of my mind starts to whisper. I hate that voice, but no matter how tightly I squeeze my fists and will the voice to shut up, its words play on repeat. That voice wasn't nearly so loud back when Natalie was my friend, back when she was still new to the school, fresh and shy from her home in Johannesburg.

All that changed last year, and I mean, I get it. Natalie wants friends like her, friends who share her magical abilities, not some useless, pathetic, waste of space like me. I can't blame her, but it doesn't make the knot of thorns in my chest any less prickly when I think about it.

Studying the muddy path, I keep my head down and hood up as Emmi leads us into the forest around the back of the school, away from the lake.

Ridiculous weather. Ridiculous trees and ridiculous leaves clinging to my boots. I stomp my feet but only succeed in splashing mud onto my ankles. I hate everything about this day. I don't understand why my parents force me to go to this horrible school where no one wants me.

"Right, class. Today we're going to practice sourcing and storing natural energy," Emmi begins and everyone groans. "Divide into your houses."

The others grumble even as they gather in their elemental groups. I study my hands, imagining what it must feel like to control electricity the way Ekaterina does. Well, technically it's lightning thanks to her great-great-great-times-infinity-grandfather being Perun, the Slavic god of storms. All I can do is watch as Ekaterina and Natalie join the other fire mages in House Fajro.

Natalie straightens her shoulders in her red jacket with white faux fur on the hood. She tugs her matching beanie down over her hair. My cheeks heat as I remember how she used to let me help her tie it in puffs and how she used to braid mine back before I cut it all off.

"Right, Fajro, let's do this." Natalie assumes leadership given she's the most gifted fire wielder in the whole school. And we're not talking some ordinary pyrokinesist here, but a genuine fire mage thanks to Muspellian genes from her Norwegian mom. Natalie controls elemental fire as easily as others breathe.

She catches me staring and I look away, face as hot as the flames Natalie conjures from her fingertips.

"Out of the way." Sini shoulder checks me to join the water kids in House Akvo. Sini's family originates from a Karelian lake goddess, or monster—depending on which version of the story you believe—although I don't see how it can possibly be the former.

With a flick of long dark hair, Aysha sashays over to the rest of House Aero. Her magic is a more mystical sort and not technically even elemental. She controls energy by humming. Since humming requires breathing, she got lumped in with the rest of the air users.

Of course, I'm all alone. Thanks to the school's "Everyone in their element" motto, I've been dumped in House Tero with the rest of the earth elementalists. Mostly it's so I can wear a house shirt when required, but having a green T-shirt doesn't mean I belong.

"Budding mages!" Emmi claps her hands. "Today each of you will receive a simple amulet." She gestures to the bag I forgot I was holding. "Your task is to imbue your amulet with pure elemental energy."

"Why?" Juan asks from the back.

"Because your magic is only as strong as the amount of energy you can manipulate. When you're young and healthy, that might seem like a lot, but as you age or if you're injured or need to perform a big spell, you may need more energy than you can muster yourself."

"That's when you can draw on external sources, right?" Aysha asks.

"Some external sources." Emmi nods. "Like amulets, talismans, or natural springs of magic, if you can find them."

"Easy enough here," Sini adds.

"We're lucky in Finland," Emmi says.

"That's why we're here," Juan chirps again.

"And when you're not in Finland, blessed with access to the last vestiges of raw, elemental energy, then what?" Emmi's tone turns serious. "Don't assume you'll always have power. Don't assume there will always be magic, because at the rate we're consuming—" She bites her lip, silencing the tirade—a word my brother Toivo often uses to describe Emmi's lectures on the conservation of natural energy.

Emmi takes a breath, seems to force a smile, and asks, "Tell me class, where else in the world can we still find viable wells of natural energy?" She scans the students. "Yes, Natalie?"

"Mostly remote areas like the Outer Hebrides, parts of southern Chile, areas in Nunavut, Svalbard, the forests of Brunei, Kamchatka in Russia, and—" Natalie blinks, then shakes her head.

"Taika?" Emmi says.

Great, now everyone is looking at me. Why do teachers always pick on me when no one else raises their hand? If only I could pretend not to know, but I do know so of course I have to answer because my brain apparently loves how the others glare at me.

"Namibia." The answer tumbles from my mouth. "The Virunga Mountains in the Congo, and a few oases in the Sahara. And actually, the reserve in Kamchatka was just declared depleted." I saw it on the news last week. It made my parents brood in unhappy silence all evening.

"You're absolutely correct." Emmi looks pleased.

Natalie gives me a crooked smile from across the glade and you know what, that makes all the other daggers thrown my way entirely worth it.

"Right, grade nines, your task today is to find a source of natural energy in this forest and imbue your amulet. Taika, please."

Grudgingly, I dish out the amulets: some wooden, some metal or stone, all of simple design.

"I didn't know mages got personal assistants." Ekaterina sneers, her teeth held hostage by silver wire and red elastic, as she plucks a metal amulet from the bag.

"Hey, maybe one day someone might actually hire you to hold their grimoire while they do magic," Sini says.

"A *know*-it-all, can't-*do*-anything." Aysha chooses a wooden amulet. I'm about to attempt a snarky comeback when Natalie beats me to it.

"Could you not?" She steps between Aysha and Sini, jabbing them with her sharp elbows.

"I didn't know about Kamchatka," she says to me, dipping her hand into the bag. "It's a little scary we're losing so much magic." She holds my gaze and I want to respond, I do, but for some unknown reason all the blood has rushed out of my brain and all I can do is stare at her. How have I never noticed the flecks of gold in her deep, brown eyes?

"As if they could care?" Ekaterina butts in. "They're just Taika the Talentless."

"Katya, don't call them that," Natalie says.

Ekaterina shrugs skinny shoulders in her studded leather jacket and trails after Sini.

"Ignore them." Natalie hovers a hand above my arm that never lands. "You know it's not true."

"Isn't it?" I can't look at her. If I do, I might cry, and the class doesn't need any more reasons to think I'm pathetic.

With a sigh, Natalie follows her new and magical friends into the woods, leaving me alone with tears burning at the back of my nose and a churning in my belly that has nothing to do with the cold porridge I ate for breakfast.

The earth group steps up to get their amulets. If they make any comments, I don't hear them. I can't, not over the voice at the back of my mind now sing-songing *Taika the Talentless* on repeat.

I'll never fit in at this school. I don't know why I keep trying. It doesn't matter that I know the Intermediate Spell-Weaving textbook by heart, that I know all the house runes and how to combine them into sigils better than most of the tenth graders studying Runelore, or that I can recite almost all of the spells Emmi teaches in Advanced Thaumaturgy to twelfth graders. What does knowing any of that matter when I'll never be able to *do* anything?

And, no matter how many textbooks I study, no matter the many hours I spend poring over the tomes in the library, I'll never find the answer to the only question that matters.

Why the hell don't I have magic?

"Feel free to move about," Emmi says. "Just don't go beyond the parking lot or MacCrone's cottage."

The groups spread out, fingers sparking magic as they search the forest for energy.

If you know how to look, magical energy can be found almost everywhere in Finland. Even in urban areas, pockets of the stuff exist and might even be coaxed from cracks in concrete, if you're strong enough. Out here in the countryside it's much easier.

The forest around Myrskyjärvi is old, like ancient, and still resonates with power. Apparently. Not that I can feel even the faintest thrum of magic the way the others can.

The school was originally an old manor house, built some 250 years ago for the legendary Gustafsson family. Hard-core mages—very famous back in the day—who detected and then called dibs on the thick artery of power running right beneath our feet. When Old Man Gustafsson kicked the bucket, he left his estate to the National Board of Mages (his descendants are still ticked off about that), specifically to be used for educational purposes, and so here we are. Now kids come from all over the world to Myrskyjärvi to "develop and hone their craft," or so goes the sales pitch.

An oak towers over me and I gaze up into its branches, hoping to catch a glimpse of...something. All I get is an eyeful of the crows Mom spelled to watch over me. That's right, I've got a murder of babysitters even though I turned fifteen last month. Musti has a smudge of white, Rekku has the ragged tail, and Kamu is basically a football with feathers.

Warily, I pull off my mitten and place my bare hand on the tree.

Rough bark, damp wood, cold air. Not sure why I expected anything else.

Emmi settles on the log beside me. A large tabby with four white socks drops from the branches and curls into Emmi's lap. Kalma, Emmi's familiar, regards me with yellow, unblinking eyes.

"Are you all right?" Emmi's kind face is pinched with concern as she strokes the vibrating feline.

How am I supposed to answer that? Would she even want the truth?

"I know these classes are hard for you," Emmi continues, gently, like she's *handling* me. "I know the other students give you a tough time about all this. Would you prefer a—"

A fist of energy erupts from the oak, blasting into my shoulder in a shower of bark. Kalma yowls and shoots off into the woods. The crows shriek and flap in the branches. I brush leaves out of my hair and check for damage. There's a bubbly sear on the tree and a scorch mark across my jacket. Mom is not going to be pleased.

Was it Sini or Ekaterina? I search the woods, scanning the faces for a smirk. A second fist of energy rises out of the tree, but before it can reach me, it ignites into flame then shrivels into ash.

"Are you all right?" Natalie asks, *tiwaz,* a House Fajro rune, sparking in the air above her right hand.

My heart kicks double time as I try to nod and catch my breath. Natalie releases the rune and slips her hands back into her pockets as if what she did was no big deal. I still can't breathe, and it has nothing to do with being assaulted by magic.

"Who did that?" Emmi's face turns an ominous purple.

Seventeen nervous, expectant faces peer out of the forest in tense silence.

"All of you, come here this minute." Emmi turns every word into a sentence and we all obey.

"This is unacceptable," Emmi begins. "If that was anything more than an accident, the culprit will face serious consequences. And do I need to remind you how precious elemental energy is?"

A few students roll their eyes as our teacher launches into yet another tirade on the importance of conserving magic and not wasting it on what she calls *frivolities*. I'm not convinced attempting to beat up a classmate with magic should count as mere silliness, though.

Greater Disciplinary Action Required for the Misuse of Magic

I start composing the article in my mind as I scowl at Ekaterina. It must've been her!

"Who has successfully imbued their amulet?" Emmi asks. No one raises their hand. "I see. You can't find enough magic to charm a necklace, but you'll waste it on nasty spells." Her voice is steely and calm and terrifying. We all look down.

"Everybody, put your hand on a tree."

We do.

"Do you feel that?" Emmi's own hand rests close to mine on the injured oak.

Most of the others nod, a few frown or even grimace.

"A faint thrum, a gentle crackle, very little even at this time of year," Emmi continues.

Rough bark, damp wood, cold air, and an itchy tingle in my palm. Great. Seems I'm developing an allergy to lichen.

I wish I could feel you, I think at the trees. *I wish I had magic.* Not that wishing will achieve anything. That's not how magic works at all. The itch only gets worse, lingering even after I rub my hand on my jeans.

"Fifty years ago, these trees pulsated with energy," Emmi says, her words suddenly choked with sorrow. "A hundred years ago, this area was so rich in elemental energy, no mage could wander these woods without becoming overwhelmed by the magical forces here. And now, this is all we have left. What happens when it's gone? What happens when we've used up all the natural energy?"

"We turn into Taika." Ekaterina's comment earns a chorus of snickers, which die a sudden death as Emmi scowls.

"Release whatever energy you managed to store in your amulets, pay your respects to the forest, and line up at the birch. Ekaterina, with me."

While the others drop their energy-free amulets back into the bag I'm still holding, Emmi takes Ekaterina aside. I wish I could hear what's being said, because whatever it is makes Ekaterina's face turn red and her hands ball into fists, but she nods before marching over to me.

"I'm sorry," she says as if the words cause her physical pain.

I hope they do. She tosses her amulet at my feet.

Mercifully, the bell rings, and we follow Emmi back to school. I'm only paying attention to my feet, so I actually jump when Natalie's voice sounds close to my ear.

"I don't think it was Katya or Sini. Probably someone in Tero," she whispers.

I bite the inside of my cheek, stifling all the angry words I want to fling at her. Of course Natalie would defend her friends! But I don't want her to go. It's been ages since we've talked, just the two of us.

"Are you sure you're okay?" she asks.

"I'm fine. Magic can't really hurt me." My voice sounds as croaky as Kamu's.

"Yes, it can," Natalie says quietly.

"Well you would know, wouldn't you?" The words are out before I can help it. No! Why? Why do I say these things?

Because you're useless. You're pathetic. You can't even do non-magical stuff properly, the voice screams in the back of my mind, and for a moment I think maybe Natalie hears it too, but no, she's wincing at the words I said.

Her face crumples before she stomps away, leaving me scrambling for an apology. When I need them most, words desert me, drowned out by that other voice yelling inside my mind.

"Taika, one moment." Emmi beckons me closer.

Reluctantly, I go over, annoyed when Aysha pretends to retie the shoelaces of her designer sneakers only to eavesdrop. The others have already gone on ahead.

"Have you given any more thought to the camping trip?" Emmi asks. "We need to confirm numbers."

Seriously? This still. "Um, I'm not sure." Truth is, spending a long weekend away from school doing unmagical things with unmagical people doesn't sound half bad. The only problem is that the annual camping trip intended as "a break from the magical and a return to the natural" will be yet another example of why Taika the Talentless doesn't and will never belong at Myrskyjärvi.

"This year we'll be joining a local school from Helsinki. It might be good for you to meet students more like yourself." Emmi's words are a knife through my chest. It hurts far more than any magical sucker punch could.

"More like me?" I wonder which aspect of me she's referring to.

I feel Aysha looking at me with her laser beam stare, and I don't even have to turn around to imagine the smug expression on her face. The tips of my ears burn. There's a nasty, sour taste rising at the back of my throat as Emmi stumbles over her answer.

"Um, students like...er, the less magically inclined. But there might be other LGBT-plus students there too." Her smile doesn't make me feel any less awkward or embarrassed.

"I'll think about it," I mumble.

"Let me know as soon as possible," Emmi says before sweeping into the school, escaping all the awkward.

How nice. Wish I could escape it too, but kind of hard to do that when it's who I am.

"I hope you do go," Aysha says. "And never come back."

Gods, how I wish that too. There's nothing I want more than to be free of Myrskyjärvi, free of the disappointment in my parents' faces every time they look at me, free of asswipes like Ekaterina and Aysha, free of Natalie and the hole she's left in my heart, free of the constant failure.

A deep exhale rattles the tears off my eyelashes, and I swat them away before forcing my feet across the threshold and back into the school. Just five more periods to go. It couldn't possibly get any worse.

2

It's gotten worse.

And it's not only the unappetizing contents of my lunch tray. Can't believe they're still serving this stuff. I wrote a whole article about it last month giving pretty specific suggestions on how to overhaul the menu, and yet here I am with lukewarm boiled potatoes, mushy casserole with questionable meat content, and the saddest sludge of vegetables. This shouldn't be legal.

Lucky for me, I'm sitting alone at a corner table near the bins, so no one notices when I scrape it all into the bio waste. Chewing on a hunk of rye bread, I survey the cafeteria. My gaze searches for Natalie. Remnants of a habit, I guess, or maybe because I still want to thank her for saving me from the magical fist this morning. It's what I should've said in the first place.

She's always in the same place, at a table over by the window—the one we used to share back when we spent lunch obsessing over *Sailor Moon* or the latest dystopian novel, complaining about the gag-inducing food, and coming up with headlines for my articles.

These days she's surrounded by a group I can never be a part of. Maybe it has less to do with my lack of magic and more to do with the other thing that makes me different from them. Sighing, I scan each of the faces wearing various quantities of eye shadow and lipstick. Natalie should be there, but she's not. Her seat is empty.

Ekaterina meets my gaze and I look away, swallowing the sudden lump in my throat. Without Natalie there to look at, there's no point being in the cafeteria. I mince my way toward freedom, eavesdropping as I pass the popular tables in case some golden nugget of gossip falls out of a careless mouth. I have got to come up with something juicy for the *Myrsky Messenger*. Sadly, the conversations are irritatingly dull.

"What are you wearing this year to Kekri?" The question rises from a table of tenth graders.

"Guess it'll be a sari for me again. Maybe I'll add some blood splatter or cobwebs to it this time."

"Why does it have to be cultural dress? Why can't we ever dress up properly for Halloween?" another kid gripes, then grimaces as he nibbles at a potato.

"Properly like what? A vampire?" a girl asks, and the others erupt in laughter as they cast snide glances at the table farthest from the windows.

Sorin Popescu and two girls with Strigoi blood sit talking softly. No one wants to share a lunch table with the vampires. No one wants to watch them eating raw meat or slurping on bloodshakes. Except, my brother is walking over. When did Toivo learn to swagger? Mildly curious, I keep watching. The girls get up to clear their trays, and Toivo slides in next to Sorin. Odd, but whatever. I wish I could hear what they're saying, but their heads are tucked in conspiratorially close.

Maybe I could spin something about students wanting a Halloween free of Kekri tradition. Not that Mom would ever swap the traditional harvest festival for something "commercial and meaningless," which is how she describes most of the non-magical holidays.

I stalk out of the cafeteria and nearly knock Emmi off her step stool. She and Mr. Fotsios are tacking Kekri posters to the noticeboard. The volunteer sign-up sheets for the traditional Kekri buck building go flying, and I scramble to gather them up.

"Sorry," I mumble, face heating as I collate the pages.

"No harm done," Emmi says. She's ditched her rain cloak and looks as if she's recently been to a Renaissance fair in her dowdy brown dress complete with poofy long sleeves and a lace-up bodice.

"Taika, shouldn't you be in lunch?" Mr. Fotsios frowns.

"No. Yes. I—"

"Want to help?" Emmi saves me from further humiliation, offering me a poster and some thumbtacks.

"Sure." It's not like I have anything better to do. Despite how silly other students might find the annual dance, I secretly love it. Not that I've ever gone with a date—not really. I've gone with Natalie a few times, as friends—of course. There's an ache deep in my belly. Guess that single mouthful of mush did more damage to my insides than expected. Or—

"Seriously, no one would go if there was like, literally anything else to do here." Ekaterina's voice is like a papercut to the brain. "This whole Kekri thing is ridiculous."

Emmi frowns, lips pursing as if she's just taken a bite out of a lemon. Fotsios shakes his head and grumbles something about entitled teenagers as Sini & Co. file past.

"Hey, where's Natalie?" I ask before I can stop myself.

"Enjoying time away from you," Sini fires back. "Too bad we have to see you in Chemistry."

I close my eyes and suck in a deep breath, hoping it won't— but nope, there's that little voice again, woken from dormancy and chanting: *Taika the Talentless, worthless, pathetic.* No way I'm surviving a seventy-minute lesson making herbal concoctions for everyone else to imbue with magic. *Taika the Tea-maker,* another moniker they've started branding me with. This day can go suck it.

Emmi is saying something about ignoring it all and being a bigger person, but I'm done. I dump the thumbtacks and grab my jacket, already heading for the doors.

Outside, the dark-gray sky still splutters dark-gray drizzle. I flip up my hood and stomp away from the school half expecting Mr. Fotsios to come running after me, but Emmi must've told him I needed space. She knows me well enough to know I'm not going off to sneak cigarettes or sips from a hip flask in the bushes like some of the older kids. Instead, I angle toward the rickety bridge on a trajectory toward true rebellion and delinquency: the library.

Myrskyjärvi isn't a particularly big lake by Finnish standards, but it's big enough to have a handful of islands scattered across it like pebbles tossed in a puddle. The school's on the largest island, connected to the mainland by a proper road bridge. To the west of the school lie the boarding houses: Kivitalo and Pilvitalo. Gods how I wish I could go to a school far away from everyone who knows me.

The rain is falling in stinging sheets now, and for a moment ,I contemplate taking the shortcut past the caretaker's squat little cottage. This day is crappy enough without risking an encounter with a cranky former battle mage and her pet dragon.

Instead, I hurry across the bridge, taking the long way round, squinting through the downpour as if Natalie might materialize at any second.

Stupid, the little voice at the back of my mind chides. Ekaterina's probably right and Natalie is avoiding me, especially after what I said to her this morning.

"Thank you." That's all I needed to say. Was it really that hard?

Stupid, stupid, stupid sings the voice, and I bite the inside of my cheek hard enough to make my eyes water.

I cross the slippery bridge, my crows squawking their displeasure at having to follow me through the rain. Sometimes I think they might be my only friends. Wish I could talk to them, but that's a shamanic specialization not offered at the school.

The National Museum of Magical Artifacts, aka the library, rises out of the murk all granite and steatite. On an island all to itself, it's meant to be impressive, added to the estate over one hundred years ago when the United Council of Magic Wielders—UCMW—decided Finland would be the best place to store some of the world's most ancient magical relics.

Disappointingly, the museum doesn't house anything particularly powerful. Stuff like that is kept in a vault on Svalbard. There they're supposed to be safe, wrapped up in dozens of protection spells and guarded by battle mages, making the vault an impenetrable fortress no one would ever dream of breaking in to.

Until two weeks ago, that is, when someone actually tried it. According to the newsfeeds, the investigation is ongoing. I pitched the *Messenger* with a piece explaining my own suspicions about who could've done it and why, but it never made it to print because kids at this school would only care if someone stole *their* stuff.

Shaking off the rain, I head for the library's side entrance.

And...the day gets worse. Again.

The school's resident Komodo dragon stands beneath the eaves munching on a pigeon. The bones crack as the bird disappears down the gullet of the enormous lizard.

"Hi Fiona." I attempt friendliness. "You're looking rather lovely in your sweater today."

The reptile would look on the more adorable side of monstrous in her yellow knitwear were it not for the smears of dead pigeon down her chest. If Fiona is about, her owner can't be far away.

As terrifying as the dragon can be, Fiona has nothing on Elspeth MacCrone.

The lizard finishes the pigeon and turns her black eyes on me. She lurches forward, waddling on legs ending in vicious claws. Desperate, I dig about in my pockets even though I know they're empty.

"Sorry girl," I squeak out when Fiona nudges my jacket. "I haven't got any blueberries."

Fiona looks disappointed and I'm probably about to lose a finger, but then Elspeth MacCrone comes storming out of the museum, even more furious than usual.

"Can't find the ruddy thing, Fiona. Old sod must've—ah, Taika."

MacCrone—formerly Sergeant MacCrone, a decorated battle mage—claps her mouth shut and fixes me with a single-eyed stare. She lost her left one in battle with a rabid wyvern. An impressive scar knots the flesh down her left cheek.

Hate to admit it, but it's hard not to admire the mage dressed in black combat boots and camo pants as if she's expecting war any minute. Now pushing seventy, with her gray hair hanging in a long braid down her back, MacCrone enjoys semiretirement as the school's caretaker and self-appointed security guard, bringing misery to any students trying to skip class or sneak contraband.

"What are you doing out and about?" MacCrone asks in a Scottish accent so thick you could deep-fry it. "Hope you weren't teasing my Fiona? If you were, you'll deserve to lose a hand and I won't stop her biting it straight off."

"Ah, no," I say. "I was going to the library."

"Well, get on with it then." She fishes several blueberries out of a pocket and feeds them to the lizard, seemingly unfazed by the pigeon gore dripping in thick strands of saliva from her pet's mouth, or the semimasticated feathers sticking to the soles of her boots.

"Or should I escort you to the principal's office?"

"No. Thank you." Plastering on a smile, I sidle around them—avoiding blood and feathers—before hightailing it inside.

***

Ah, the library. I suck in a slow, deep breath, savoring the musty scent of paper and parchment. I start to relax as I ditch my jacket and boots then make my way through the familiar stacks.

The library isn't any sort of architectural marvel—just an enormous hall divided into sections according to my dad's sense of order, which is utterly incomprehensible. Only he understands why books on the Mage Wars in seventeenth-century North America get sandwiched next to fourth-century treatises on Islamic alchemy. It all makes sense to him and no student is brave enough to challenge a tietäjä of his standing. The word *tietäjä* literally translates to *knower*, a fact my dad never tires of citing to those who question his methods.

Except for the periodic grumblings all old buildings make, the library is delightfully quiet this time of the day, and that shadowy corner on the second floor is calling my name. Hardly anyone ever ventures into what Dad terms the "misinformed" section, home to books on alien connections to Atlantis and Lemuria. It's the perfect sanctuary.

Wrapped in the shadows, I pull out my phone and stab at the screen. To send or not to send? Would Natalie even want to hear from me? Do I apologize? Thank her? Why is this so hard? It never used to be this complicated back when being around Natalie didn't make my insides do spontaneous gymnastics.

I hit Send on a message filled with far too many emojis and then wait. And wait, and wait. Nothing. No reply, because the message hasn't even been read.

A cacophonous clatter rips through the silence, making me drop my phone. With heart still racing, I tiptoe between the shelves. Perhaps MacCrone and Fiona have returned in search of delinquents.

Another clatter-crash, this time followed by a string of cursing.

There, right between the reading desks, someone is trying out skateboarding tricks. And failing. What the hell? In the library?

I'm content to observe for a moment as they attempt to balance. They look up and catch me staring. I start so hard I crick my neck.

"Shouldn't you be in class?" they ask. They're tall but drowning in an oversized sweater the color of week-old scabs. Their eyes are framed in smudges of dark eye shadow.

Morgan O'Connor.

"I—I, um—"

Useless, pathetic, you are such an embarrassment, the voice supplies, and I bite my tongue so I don't say any of it out loud.

Why does it have to be an O'Connor? Only the family with one of the most potent druid pedigrees, said to be direct descendants of the Connacht Kings. I've never paid much attention to the three sibling newbies who arrived back in August, brought to Finland when their mom, Caitlin O'Connor, got voted into office with the UCMW. Suffice it to say, they're all-powerful magic wielders—even Hannah, who's only nine. None of them have ever bothered much with me either, until now. Morgan stares up at me, eyebrows lifted as if he expects an answer.

"Shouldn't you be in class too?" I manage to whisper, pulse still pounding.

"Yeah, but I don't do boring and school today—" he gives an exaggerated roll of his eyes, a hint of a smile quirking up his mouth as he rolls closer on his skateboard.

"You're an O'Connor." I state the obvious. So smooth.

"And you're a Turunen. Taika, right?" Morgan's Irish accent adds soft *r*'s in the names where *r*'s have no business being, but I don't hate it.

"Yeah, Toivo is my brother."

"Nice to meet you—officially I mean." Morgan pulls out two chairs at the nearest desk.

Warily, I sit, tucking my knees up under my chin and wrapping my arms around my legs. I pluck at the loose threads where my clumsiness has left a dirty tear across my knee. It's weird being spoken to by one of the most magical kids at school, and in a way that makes me think he might not mind sharing oxygen with me.

We're supposed to be in the same grade, but Morgan—being a wunderkind—got bumped up two grades in all magic classes. Rumor has it he can even combine opposite elemental runes like water and fire or earth and air into totally unique sigils. It's a super rare ability, which means we only share two periods a week. I've tried to stay off his radar and so far it's been working.

"Hungry?" Morgan is already tracing a conjuring sigil in the air with his index finger capped by chipped black polish. He mutters a few words I think might be Irish and produces two shiny red apples. The air is notably colder, tickling my nose like winter when I inhale.

"That's impressive." I examine the offered fruit, searching for the worm, or rotten spot—trying to find the trick in it. Aysha gave me an orange once only to hum it into a lemon the moment I took a bite.

"It's good. Promise," he says.

Tentatively, I take a nibble. "Oh wow." I take another bite and another.

"Thanks." Morgan stretches out long legs clad in deliberately torn black jeans and props his dark-red boots with purple laces on the desk. He's got six rings in his left ear and four in his right, and there's a stud in his nose in the shape of a triskelion.

"So are you mostly a conjurer?" I ask because I have no idea what else to say to him.

"Actually, I'm a part-time rock star." Morgan crunches through his own apple. "Part-time bookworm." His grin makes me doubt the veracity of that claim. "But mostly I'm allergic to tomatoes. Do you know what my life is like without pizza?" He pouts. "Do you know how disgusting hot dogs are without ketchup?"

Involuntary laughter bubbles through my nose and out of my mouth. I snort, trying to stop myself from spraying apple everywhere. Cool, real cool.

"Thanks for the sympathy," he says.

"Hey, I'm lactose intolerant. I can't eat most pizza either."

"Dude, I feel your pain." He raises a fist and I bump it.

Dude. Even though I know it probably means nothing, it still gives me a rush of the warm fuzzies. Guess the baggy button-downs and chest-flattening sports bras are working the way I want them to.

"We have math together, right?" he asks.

Oh gods, he's noticed me. I nod, struggling to breathe, waiting for him to realize I'm a waste of space he shouldn't bother with.

Dark curls fall across his eyes and he flips them away with a jerk of his head. "Here to do some silent reading?"

Okay, here it comes—the snark, the jibes. I knew it.

Taika the Talentless, the little voice coos at the back of my mind.

"Why are you here?" I bite out instead.

"I love libraries. All that knowledge." He takes a deep breath. "I'm hoping I might absorb some of it just by being here, like how some sea creatures suck in food from the water without having to eat."

"Um, you mean like osmosis?" I say because my treacherous brain doesn't know how to not be a know-it-all.

"That's it!" Morgan claps his hands. "Such great acoustics. And osmosis. Such a cool word. Imagine being able to learn like that." He pulls over a discarded book—*Ancient Norse Sorcery*—and rests his forehead on the cover while making slurping noises.

"Is it working?" I ask, still not entirely sure whether this interaction is going to leave me bruised.

"Nope." Morgan pouts again. "But the acoustics *are* awesome, and the wooden floors are brilliant." He swings his feet off the table to kick his board back and forth, apparently appreciating the noisy echoes. "So, why are you really here in the middle of the day?" He narrows his eyes. He must be wearing mascara too; his eyelashes are so long and full.

I take a moment, appreciating his makeup skills while searching his gray-green eyes for any sign of malevolence.

"Today's been all kinds of awful," I admit, still wary. "I thought coming here might help." That and maybe I'd be struck by inspiration and figure out the perfect story for the *Messenger* that'll see Sini stuck on the back page.

"And has it?" he asks.

My phone shrills and I grab it, hoping it's Natalie. It's not—just a message in the journalism chat reminding everyone about the meeting this afternoon. As if I could flipping forget.

"Bad news?" Morgan asks.

"I need an article for the school paper."

"Hm..." He drums his heels on the skateboard. "Hey! I could be your story."

"No offense, but I think everyone already knows everything there is to know about the O'Connor ubermage."

"So, my reputation precedes me." He does the hair flick thing again like maybe it's a nervous tick and not just an attempt to look cool. "But there's a lot more to me than that."

"Yeah, like what?" I'm genuinely curious.

"Like, back in Ireland, I was in a band. We did some gigs in the summer, started to get some decent attention, and then I had to move." A shadow flits briefly over his face.

"Let me guess: you play drums?"

"And I sing, backup mostly. You should listen to our stuff, but only if you like good music."

"I like bands that can play their instruments."

"Shots fired." He makes a popping sound with his fingers. "You know Nirvana?"

"Duh."

"Like them?"

"Their *MTV Unplugged* show is the greatest live recording by any band ever," I say, surprised by my own vehemence. Guess I have Dad to thank for my taste in music. He used to jump up and down to rock music when we were little kids and taught me how to headbang. My memories are hazy, but I'm sure Mom joined in too sometimes.

Morgan's smile broadens. "What about Jimmy Eat World, or Green Day, or Blink, or hey, you know any of the prehistoric bands like The Exploited or Sex Pistols?"

"Know *of* them sure, can't really say I'm a fan. The others I like, though." And I don't know what possesses me to do it, but I mumble-sing the chorus from "All the Small Things."

Morgan starts playing the drums with his fingers on the table.

"Seriously, though," he says when I stumble to a stop over half-remembered words. "You should give us a listen. I think you'll like our sound. And if you do, write about us." He shrugs, but I can tell it means a lot to him.

"What's the band's name?"

"The Knock-Knock Jokes."

"For real?"

"Don't diss it till you've listened, deal?" He offers me his hand.

"Deal." We shake. Would he act this way with someone more typically "girlie"?

He jumps up, book in hand, then rolls toward the stacks. He crams the book onto the wrong shelf and I'm about to say as much when he kicks off again, disappearing between shelves featuring Ayurvedic recipe books and medieval hymnals.

"What are you doing?"

"Exploring," he calls over his shoulder.

I follow the racket of the skateboard.

"Hey, keep this up and MacCrone'll be back. Then haul us off to the principal," I warn as Morgan attempts some kind of flip-trick. The board lands wheels upturned, making me wince.

"Didn't think lizards like hers were legal as pets," he says.

"There's a loophole concerning its name. Technically, it's classified as a dragon and can be considered magical. Besides, who'd argue with a former battle mage?"

"She was in here earlier," Morgan says. "Rummaging about and cursing."

"Really? What was she looking for?"

"No idea. But she was after something in there." He nods toward my dad's office, tucked away alongside private reading rooms.

"Are you sure?"

"Oh yeah, I've never heard an old lady use words like those before." Morgan pretends to fan himself and I can't help but smile as a few more knots of tension untangle themselves from my shoulders.

This guy is not how I expected an ubermagical-mensch to be.

"My dad's been out of town. This is his office." I try the door, but it's locked. Of course the caretaker would have keys, but still, something niggles in my belly. No one should be rummaging through his office while he isn't around.

"What's up?" Morgan swerves in beside me.

"It's probably nothing," I say as one of the ancient grandfather clocks Mom refused to let Dad keep at home starts ding-donging the hour. "I should be getting back." I head for the coatrack. Skipping chemistry is one thing, but I don't want to miss history. It's one of the only subjects that doesn't involve practical mageship.

He does that hair flick thing again and pulls on an acid-washed denim jacket covered in band patches and Sharpie-drawn anarchy *a*'s.

"It was nice meeting you, Morgan—properly, I mean."

"Agreed, but I do have a question, if you don't mind." He looks nervous and I'm not sure what to expect.

I nod, braced for the worst.

"What pronouns do you use? Sorry if I'm a jerk for asking, but I didn't want to get it wrong."

I could cry. Right here, right now. Tears are welling up in my throat and burning inside my nose again. No one has ever asked. Everyone just assumes. In Finnish, everyone is *hän*, which makes life easier and less embarrassing. But in English, everyone makes assumptions based on what I'm wearing or the length of my hair or something else completely arbitrary.

"I—" I gulp air and swallow down the happy tears.

"Look, I'm sorry. I didn't mean—"

"No, it's just people don't usually ask. It's nice that you did. Thank you."

He gives me a moment and then says, "So, your pronouns are?"

"Oh, right. I use they and them." My face must be turning cherry red. I look down, not wanting to see his reaction.

"Cool. Kelly, our guitarist, they're a they too."

I look up and he's smiling, the expression softer somehow.

"Maybe we can hang out again sometime?" I ask before my brain can think better of it.

"For sure. I expect a full review from my toughest critic," he says. "If you're on QuikGab, add me. If you want."

"Great, I will." I have no idea why it feels like I just swallowed a mouthful of sherbet.

"I should hurry. Got Emmi next. You know how she is. See you later, Tai." Morgan slams a foot onto his skateboard and glides off down the path as if he's immune to the miserable weather.

"Hey, wait!" I call after him, mentally kicking myself for not asking before. "Do you know Natalie Khumalo? She's a boarder with you."

"Fire mage?"

"That's her. If you see her, could you tell her I say thanks for the thing in Thaumaturgy."

"No problem." With that, he's gone.

I flip up my hood, replaying the conversation over and over as I traipse back to the school, a smile creeping cautiously across my lips. Maybe one person here doesn't completely detest me.

Yet, the little voice pipes up, shattering my hope.

Somehow, I make it to four o'clock, which brings the count up to 1,558 days I've survived at this school. There're over seven hundred left to go before graduation, but it's too depressing to think about.

The corridors are emptying now, everyone on their way to after-school clubs.

I head to the music room, wincing as the orchestra starts tuning their instruments. The violins screech and trumpets blare off-key. With Aysha in Art Club and Ekaterina doing something involving martial arts, this is my only chance to catch Natalie alone.

She's always been a music geek and lives for ensemble. She'd have to be *dying* to miss rehearsal, even if she's been AWOL since first period, which isn't like her at all.

Or *wasn't* like her. What do I know about this new Natalie?

I peer through the open door. No Natalie. Her chair as first flute is conspicuously empty. I check my phone for the millionth time and the message is still unread. I've got to be at the journalism meeting in less than five minutes.

"Taika? Can I help you?" Mr. Fotsios asks.

"Um, I was just looking for Natalie," I stammer.

"She has noro."

"Um, really? She seemed fine this morning."

He narrows his gaze. "She's sick and getting bed rest." He shuts the door.

"Gee, thanks." I turn away, annoyed I didn't ask one of the teachers earlier. Noro has been going around, so I guess it's possible Natalie got sick between class and lunch, but there's a prickle of unease in my belly.

Really aren't smart, are you? the voice seizes the opportunity to chant at me, eroding any thought I might've had to pay a visit to Pilvitalo and check in on her. No, she has other friends to do that now and the house mistress will make sure she's taken care of.

Dejected, I traipse to the newsroom. In a former life, it was two neighboring janitors' closets, now combined and converted into a tiny office, home to both the school newspaper and the headquarters for the Spirit Club. Luckily, the Spirit Club has been less than enthusiastic this year, which means we have the place to ourselves.

Cludd—whose name astoundingly rhymes with *teeth*—is already there. He's slowly being swallowed by a beanbag in the far corner, his laptop perched on his knees. Cludd of House Akvo is the editor of the *Myrsky Messenger* and the one person standing between me and a front-page headline. He's also one of the least gifted magic wielders in the school, which would make him a lot more likable if he'd only publish one of my stories.

I settle into one of the four other chairs and flip open my notebook. The clock on the wall ticks through the minutes and, once again, Joakim Blomqvist is late for his own club.

The three other members saunter in late too—two seventh graders both in House Tero, and Sini. I pretend not to notice her even though she's sitting directly opposite me. She takes out her tablet and starts tip-tapping at the screen with an irritating finger while I gnaw on my pencil.

"Should we get started then?" Cludd asks as Joakim blusters into the newsroom, leaking papers from the pile in his hands.

Tenth-grade tests in various states of grading billow to the ground. I gather up some of the strewn papers and hand them back to the permanently frazzled teacher who clearly subsists on caffeine alone. He shoves the papers into a heap on the desk, not seeming to care how he's crinkling the corners.

I clench my teeth and count to ten while the Blomqvist-hurricane settles into a mild storm: creased shirt, crooked tie, and mussed hair. The man is a walking disaster and doesn't deserve to be called a tietäjä, a fact that should be a front-page feature, but that—for obvious reasons—I know better than to ever suggest.

"Right, let's get on with it," Joakim says. "What's everyone working on?"

My hand shoots up as if it's possessed. It's not like my idea is a great one, but it's all I've got, having not listened to the Knock-Knock Jokes yet.

"Which student had a magical mishap this time?" Cludd yawns, making me bristle.

It's not my fault the paper rejects all my best pitches in favor of gossip.

"Actually, no," I say. "I think this could be big."

"Bigger than last month's lunch meat controversy?" Cludd peers at me from between the fronds of his blue bangs while still tapping away at his keyboard.

"After an event in Thaumaturgy this morning, I thought maybe an article about the school's disciplinary system might be a good idea."

Everyone sighs and Sini grins. I bet she threw that magical punch at me.

"A worthy topic, for sure," Joakim says. "But I think the school's policy is quite clear on this matter."

"What about student familiars not being allowed in school, or why we have PE, or how the Kamchatka Reservoir was recently declared depleted?"

"This is the *Myrsky Messenger*, not the *UCMW Gazette*." Cludd does his best to sound as condescending as possible. "Know your audience, Taika."

"A valid point," Joakim says. "We're looking for content that will engage young readers, and PE is part of the national curriculum, whether we like it or not. Anyone else? Sini?"

Summarily dismissed, I stab my page with my pencil, wishing it was Sini's face. Maybe I should've run with my Kekri idea or interviewing Morgan.

"Given how Kekri is happening soon," Sini begins, and I rip a massive hole in my notebook, "I was thinking of an article about that and how our school doesn't let us dress up, you know, like in *Halloween* costumes. A lot of students want to dress up for real. Maybe the younger kids could even go trick-or-treating in town?"

Joakim nods and Cludd smiles, which all but guarantees Sini the front page with the Kekri story that could've been mine. Seriously, I need this day to end—better yet, for a black hole to open up and swallow this whole stinking school.

I'm so tired of seeing Sini Sininen's byline every time I open the website for the *Myrsky Messenger*. Last week her article about a norovirus outbreak took center stage, meanwhile my piece on the school's poor recycling habits got squashed into a side column on the third page.

Today isn't shaping up to be any different as Cludd assigns the main article to Sini. He'll be writing his usual editorial piece and collating ads for school events, while the seventh graders promise their usual slice-of-life snippets, which amount to taking photos of kids around the school and turning them into memes. There's about as much real journalism happening in this club as in *Magicians' Weekly*. I mean, seriously, *magicians*? They can't even get the mage bit right.

The meeting continues as the others discuss the poetry and short story submissions. Joakim insists we post at least four creative pieces in each issue. Cludd reads the submissions out loud and asks the others to vote for their favorites. I don't bother raising my hand and no one even notices. Almost all the submissions are awful anyway, and even though one poem is slightly less terrible, Sini votes for it, so I sit on my hands.

After almost an hour, the meeting comes to a close and once again, I've been forgotten. I don't know why I bother.

Waste of space, worthless, useless, the voice sings to me. Screw it, what do I have to lose.

"Actually," I say while the others start packing up, "I did have one other idea."

"Let's hear it." Cludd drums his fingers against the back of his laptop screen while Joakim scratches at the scraggly patch of hair still attached to his mostly bald head.

"An interview with Morgan O'Connor."

"That punk kid who's like twelve but a senior?" one of the seventh graders asks.

"How about a weather report rather," Sini suggests, straight-faced.

"Oh, I know Morgan. An interview with him might be interesting. Why not?" Cludd doesn't sound overly excited by the idea. "We always have space for column shorts. Can you get it to me by Friday?"

I nod, vigorously, my hair lashing my ears, and with that, the meeting is over.

"Not to worry–" Sini glances at me on her way out. "I'm sure you'll come up with something good for next month's paper."

I slam my notebook shut and shoulder my backpack, not bothering to help this time when the pile of tests explodes out of Joakim's hands again.

Sini ambles down the corridor, staring at her phone.

"Hei, Sini, odota." I switch to Finnish.

"Tä?" She doesn't even look up.

"Is Natalie okay? I heard she's sick."

"Seriously, would you get over it?" Sini turns around only to give me an eye-roll. "She isn't your friend anymore. She wants you to leave her alone."

Her words pummel my gut. She sashays away, leaving me gasping for breath like a dying fish.

If only you could make people disappear the same way sorrows get burned up during Kekri. Maybe if I write Sini's name down on the paper the twelfth graders feed to the bonfire, she'll vanish— or at the very least leave the school, the country, the continent!

Taika the Talentless, the Useless, the Friendless, the voice at the back of my mind jabbers relentlessly as I leave the school and head down the forest path toward home. It's fully dark now and the streetlights fight a losing battle against the rain and mist.

Taika the Talentless. I can't get my headphones on fast enough, hoping I can drown out that voice with Morgan's music, but before I can find the band, every little hair on the back of my neck stands at attention.

I'm alone on the path. Trees crowd the edges, shadows thick as porridge stuffing the spaces between the birches. A flutter of wings and a harsh croak pull my gaze toward the nearest tree where my crows shift restlessly in the branches. They flap and caw, and then fall silent.

My heart beats faster; my hands slick with sweat inside my mittens.

Sometimes bears snuffle about for berries before hibernation this time of year, but a bear wouldn't upset the crows, nor would it make me queasy with the sensation of being watched. Something screams in the darkness. A fox. It has to be a fox, but I'm running all the same like some terrified little kid. I don't stop until I skid up to the front door of our house, rush inside, and throw the bolt behind me.

The house is warded. I'm safe here, I tell myself, over and over again until my heart stops thrashing behind my ribs. If it was something other than a fox—Nope, that's all it was. But the hairs on my arms are still standing up and there's an itchy prickle down my spine like a spider is caught in my shirt.

"Taika, is that you?" Mom calls from the dining room.

"Yeah. Just me," I say, finally catching my breath.

Mom's in front of her laptop, concentration lines cutting across her forehead. "Dinner's on the stove when you want it."

My stomach grumbles as I approach the pan: *pyttipannu*. Great. More mush. This time a mix of fried potato and onion with cubes of sausage. It's only made marginally better when served with a fried egg on top, but if I want that I'll have to DIY. Mom's culinary skills don't extend much beyond what comes frozen in a bag.

"When's Dad coming home?" I ask as I fry up an egg.

"Tonight. Late." She breezes into the kitchen en route to the kettle.

"Any leads?"

"Fishing for the *Messenger*?" Mom knows me too well. "But no, no leads yet apparently, although your dad isn't allowed to tell us very much. School going okay?"

At least Mom has stopped asking if school's going *well*.

"I think I've made a new friend. Morgan O'Connor. He seems nice."

"He needs a haircut."

"Mom." I sigh.

"But yes, the family is... decent, if highly opinionated." She pulls out a bag of chamomile tea.

"Natalie's sick." I change the topic. "Do you know how she's doing?"

"She's fine. This noro isn't sparing anyone, but I'm sure she'll be back in a few days. You two friends again?"

"Not exactly," I say, and a pall of silence descends between us.

A year ago, Natalie and I were inseparable. She was over almost every afternoon. Mom noticed straight away when it all stopped. If she has any suspicions about why, she's keeping them to herself and doesn't ever push me to come up with an answer.

What would I say, anyway? Natalie ditched me because she finally realized I'm not worth her time? She found better friends? Because she's too embarrassed to be around me since I came out, even though she was the one sitting right beside me when I finally worked up the courage to tell my parents I was a *they* and not a *she*. I absolutely, most definitely would never ever admit the real reason Natalie doesn't want to be my friend anymore.

"Well, make sure you do your homework." Mom shoves a steaming cup of tea into my hands before drifting back to the laptop. That's it, the sum total of parental interaction. Thank goodness.

With my dinner in one hand and my tea in the other, I escape upstairs, pausing outside Toivo's room. None of his regular doof-doof techno vibrates the landing. No sounds of single-person shooters or sword-wielding heroes slaying dragons either. The silence is ominous, but then maybe Toivo has learned to spell his room for privacy the same way the teachers have spelled the staff lounge.

His door is bare except for a bold, black poster with white bubble font warning family members to Keep Out.

Whatever.

I kick open my own door, unadorned except for the nameplate my dad nailed up when I was like five. I should really do something about that.

While I'm eating, I go in search of the Knock-Knock Jokes, surprised when the track explodes in my ears, all power chords and frenetic drumming. I pay extra attention to the drumming, easily imagining Morgan slamming the life out of the cymbals.

The lead vocals aren't great. The singer sounds older, with grit in their voice, but it's punk rock so I'm not sure it matters. I much prefer the backup vocals. Wish I could hear the band do something slower and more acoustic. My foot starts tapping to the beat and I hum along to the supercatchy chorus. It's rinse and repeat with all five of their songs and I can hardly tell them apart, but Morgan was right. They're actually pretty good.

I open up QuikGab and add him. His avatar is—big shock—a skateboard with an anarchy *a* on it. My fingers hover above the keyboard, not sure what to type. I guess he must've gotten a notification when I added him because he gets in first.

So? Are you going to make me famous?

The Messenger isn't Rolling Stone, you know. I type back. This is so much easier than talking face-to-face.

Gotta start somewhere. Did you get the green light for the article?

It takes me a moment to understand what he means before typing back Yes as a smile cracks the corners of my mouth.

Great! Want to hang in the library again? Tomorrow?

My hands tremble, fingers unable to hit the right letters. Hard to believe someone like him might actually enjoy my company.

He doesn't, the little voice pipes up. *He just wants you to write about him. Why do you think he's meeting you in the library where no one can see him talking to you?*

Damn. It's so obvious. Why didn't I see it? I squeeze my eyes closed, wishing the voice inside my head would shut up and stop ruining things, but I can't deny the truth. My phone buzzes again. Another message.

We could do lunch rather if you don't want to skip??

My heart stutters and so does the voice in my head.

Sure. Lunch sounds great! I hit Send before I can overthink it, before that horrible voice can damage this too. Have you seen Natalie at all? I ask after he replies with a string of smiling emojis and a thumbs up. I think she's got noro.

It's been going around, Morgan answers. What are you doing right now?

Homework. Boring. You?
Regripping my skateboard.

I have no idea what regripping a skateboard involves and I'm about to ask but once again, Morgan gets in first.

I gotta go. I'm making a mess of my deck. See you tomorrow. He goes off-line before I can respond, and I deflate.

Dinner sits like a lump of stone in my belly as I reread the conversation, waiting for the voice to pounce on something I missed and tell me all the ways I suck. It's only in rereading I realize he never answered my question about Natalie and she still hasn't even seen my messages.

I'm contemplating calling her when there's a flicker of green in the corner of my vision. I turn toward the window, but as soon as I focus on the spot where I thought I saw the smudge of color, it's gone. Again all my little hairs are standing up, and this time there's no way whatever I saw could've been a fox.

****

Fiona's gnashing teeth snap at my face, her fangs caged in braces with red elastics. Morgan's there, wielding an oversized safety pin like a club, but he misses every time he tries to hit the dragon. There's a clash of guitar chords with every swing of the safety pin. I stare into the face of the lizard and watch, paralyzed, as her eyes turn bright green. When the dragon opens her mouth, it's Natalie's voice calling my name.

I wake up sweaty and breathless. According to my phone it's 1:15 a.m. I draw up the covers, determined to go back to sleep so tomorrow isn't any harder than it has to be, but muted voices drift up from downstairs. Someone's in the kitchen.

In stealth mode, I make it past Toivo's room and perch at the top of the stairs, straining my ears. Mom, Dad, and Toivo are deep in conversation. Of course no one thought to include me. Guess I'm just easier to ignore.

"...really quite bizarre," Dad says.

I'm glad he's home. At least dinners will be edible again.

"I just don't understand why someone strong enough to get past six battle mages wouldn't take anything," Toivo says.

"They broke enough." Dad sighs. "Many irreplaceable relics. I'd almost prefer it if they'd stolen the items instead."

Now here's a story! Even Cludd might be impressed to know someone got the better of seasoned battle mages. Although, that feat is as terrifying as it is impressive considering battle mages only really became a thing during the Chaos Wars, when mages started training in combative elementalism. They were forced to swear a hard-core oath to uphold mage law. Theoretically, no one but a chaos mage should be able to take on a battle mage, but chaos magic was outlawed after the wars when the corrupt mages were imprisoned in special dungeons, if not killed outright. There are no more chaos mages in the world. But then, who could've defeated *six* battle mages? The question knifes through my thoughts.

Someone powerful. Very, very powerful.

I suppress a shudder and keep listening.

"Juha, do you think..." Mom sounds uncharacteristically nervous. "Do you think they're after it?"

"Haven't they always been?" Dad responds.

"It, oh you mean..." Whatever Toivo says next, he says too softly for me to hear.

I drop a step lower, wary of the creaky spot.

"Clearly they didn't know it wasn't in the vault," Toivo says. "So it's safe, right? I mean, we've always kept it safe."

What are they talking about?

"We thought the vault was safe too," Dad says.

"And look how that turned out." Mom's incredulous. "But enough for tonight. Let's get some sleep."

Three sets of footsteps start for the stairs. I scurry back to my bedroom and leap into bed just in time. My pulse is still racing when Dad comes in. He pulls the covers up over my shoulders like I'm four, leans in to kiss my cheek, and whispers, "It's nothing for you to worry about, Taika. You're safe. We'll always keep you safe."

To prove the point, he waves his hand and lights up the wards on my windows. One of them is the *Hannunvaakuna*, a complex knot for protection and good luck. It's also the school's emblem.

"Love you, kulta." Dad smooths my hair before leaving the room.

I reach my hand toward the window, tracing the winding lines of the Hannunvaakuna even as it fades. What good are a few protection charms against someone who could get past the most elite battle mages? My mind instantly conjures up images of shattered sigils and unknown shadows reaching from the darkness.

I pull my headphones on and queue up the Knock-Knock Jokes, hoping angry guitars will drive the nightmares away.

The next morning, I chug back a cup of milky coffee but skip the porridge. Catching Cludd before class is more important than breakfast. Forget the interview with Morgan, I've got a proper story now, one that'll put Sini in some serious shade.

Battle Mage Thwarted by Chaos Mage!

Attack of the Chaos Mage!

Why do all my titles sound so cheesy? I need something clever and attention grabbing, something worthy of the front page.

There's a flicker of green between the trees, and I skid across the path trying to hit the brakes. I scan the gaunt birches. Did I imagine it?

Then I hear it.

It starts out like the wind rattling the skeletal limbs of the trees before morphing into something more guttural, like the croak of a crow. Only, I don't think either the wind or my crows could be saying my name.

A prank. It's got to be. I squint into the woodland, peering through the morning gloom, hoping to catch sight of some asswipe who thinks they're hilarious for scaring me. Musti, Kamu, and Rekku perch above me, still and silent. Their heads are all cocked in the same direction.

"Nyt on vähä jännäpännä," I whisper out loud, hoping the sound of my voice will chase away the heebie-jeebie weirdness I'm feeling. My words are shaky and brittle and do nothing to make me feel less creeped out.

And there it is again: another wisp of green. I whip my head around, following the darting glow toward the lake. The murky water mirrors the steel gray of the October morning, and above it, a green light flits back and forth as if beckoning me closer.

Okay, this is beyond strange, but I can't help myself; I have to know what it is. Is someone messing with a laser, teasing me like a cat? It seems a little elaborate to be a prank, especially for this early in the morning.

The entire lake has taken on an eerie glow as if blanketed in a spreading, neon mist. Blinking my eyes does nothing to clear away the acid-green mirage. If anything, it burns brighter now, the mist flickering like ribbons or tendrils of flame.

Taika!

Definitely my name. A layer of frost grips my insides in a frigid fist. The voice is louder this time and so very not a figment of my imagination. I want to scream, but I'm barely breathing.

The green ribbons writhe and knot into a ball of fire, swishing closer against the wind.

Taika, please. The voice resonates from the approaching fireball, a high-pitched whine.

Please! Help us!

The flames whip left and right in a frantic dance, closer then farther away, almost as if it's beckoning me to follow. Part of me realizes this can't possibly be a prank; another part is still waiting to become the punch line of this joke.

I've read about marsh flames, so-called *ignis fatuus* or will-o'-the-wisps caused by the breaking down of certain swamp gases, but as much as I want a perfectly logical explanation for what I'm seeing, the literature never mentioned will-o'-the-wisps *speaking*. Possibilities swarm like yellow jackets inside my skull. One buzzes louder and stings harder: *liekkiö*.

Taika, please please please—the flames swirl in a frenzy. *Taika, please.* The way the wisp says my name—I don't want to, but I recognize that voice.

"Help you? How, why?" Despite my better judgment, I follow the fireball along the shore where it cuts a zigzagging trail through the trees. It darts away from the water and into the forest where the spruce and birch, juniper and maples tangle together like metalheads in a mosh pit. Branches snag at my hood as I push my way through the undergrowth. Musti, Kamu, and Rekku follow too, keeping pace above me, silent still, but their presence is reassuring.

We haven't gone far before the green light stops its chaotic flight, hanging suspended between blackened branches.

"What now?" I ask, but there's no response, only a dimming and brightening of the light.

It pulses like a star, bobbing higher and lower.

"I don't know what you want."

Something crunches under my heel: the remains of a cell phone. One I know far too well considering I'm the one who bought the case for Natalie's birthday last year.

The colors of the South African flag are streaked with ash and mud . It must have been here for hours. Wow, so Natalie's still using the gift I gave her. I assumed the others would've given her something better by now—that they'd want to erase every trace of me from Natalie's life. But maybe this is proof Natalie doesn't completely hate me and that she might be able to forgive me for what I did.

I pluck the phone from the muck of fallen leaves, inspecting it for damage. The screen is shattered beyond repair. No wonder Natalie didn't respond to my messages. But when did she lose it? During

Thaumaturgy? After? What was Natalie doing this far from the path anyway?

Carefully, I pocket the phone, trying not to touch it too much in case I smudge away fingerprints or other evidence.

Evidence? Of what exactly? Natalie dropped her phone in the woods after class, that's all. And she's been so sick, she hasn't noticed it's missing.

Yeah right—I don't need the little voice in my head to tell me how ridiculous *that* is.

Instead, I study the damage on the trees. The burned branches and trunks could mean Natalie was out here practicing her magic. Or... They could be signs of a struggle—that's what the cops call it in all those TV procedurals.

There's a flutter of red in one of the low-hanging branches. A snag of wool, the fibers frayed and soot-stained. Now that really is evidence. My leg bones turn to marshmallow as I carefully pry the threads from the twigs and fold them safely away in my pocket along with the phone. I realize I might be messing with a crime scene and consider putting everything back where I found it, but the green light weaves through the branches, leading me out of the thicket and back toward the lake. It swishes left and right across the water.

"What are you?" I call out to it, my voice quavering a little less this time. "Why did you bring me here?"

The flames don't answer. They grow smaller, fading until the wind snuffs them out, leaving me shivering on the shore with the first bell ringing in the distance. I step back, yelping when I hit a solid body I didn't realize was standing right behind me.

"You should get to class," Toivo says with all the authority of a big brother, plus a generous dollop of the arrogance he's developed since turning seventeen.

"Did you see it?" I stammer.

"See what?" he answers with a glare that could douse a bonfire.

"Don't be like that. You must've seen it. The liekkiö." There, I say it out loud.

"Taika." Toivo turns my name into a reprimand the same way Mom does. "You're going to be late." But he doesn't take his gaze off the lake, his eyes filled with shadows.

"If you're too scared to admit what you saw—"

"Stop it. You didn't see anything because there was nothing to see."

His hands curl into fists and his shoulders hunch. Fear or anger? I can't tell, but it can't be anything good if it's making him even more of a jerk than usual. He turns and trudges down the path without saying another word, thinking he's won.

I shove my hands into my pockets, clutching Natalie's phone. Whatever the green light was, it led me to the phone. And that voice—it called my name and asked me for help. *Me!*

Of all people, why me? I don't have a lick of magic. What could I possibly do? Why not speak to literally any other kid at the school, or better yet, one of the tietäjät? The lack of answers curdles my thoughts.

It doesn't make sense.

Grudgingly, I follow Toivo's footprints along the path, glancing back at the water with every other step, willing the voice to call my name. I need to be sure that I'm not losing my mind, that what I heard was real, because I'm like ninety-five percent sure the voice coming out of the green ball of flames belonged to Natalie.

Everything is normal. Kids chat at lockers, hang about before class, finish up homework, or make final adjustments to hair and makeup with a snap-crackle of magical fingers.

All I can think about is Natalie. Her voice. And that ball of flames.

"Hey, you all right? You look like you're gonna be sick," Morgan says when I stumble into math.

My usual spot is up front but he heads to the back and I follow. He pulls out a chair for me and I crumple into it, trying to ignore the looks I'm getting from Sini & Co., who are sprawled across the second row. Natalie isn't with them. Her absence makes me feel woozy, as if all the blood has decided to puddle in my feet instead of making my brain work.

"Tai, you really don't look good." Morgan peers into my face.

"I—I'm—I think..." The words get all netted up in my throat, my thoughts tangled in knots. I know what I saw, no matter what

Toivo says. I know what a liekkiö is and I know I heard Natalie's voice.

"Wanna skip?" Morgan keeps his voice low.

The final bell rings. Any second, the teacher will arrive and there'll be no escaping after that. I think I manage to nod because Morgan grabs my hand and hauls me to my feet, saving me from an hour of parallelograms.

I let myself be led through the emptying corridors until Morgan ducks into the student lounge reserved for eleventh and twelfth graders.

"Not supposed to be in here."

"It's cool." He closes the door. "Aoife lets me hang out sometimes. Should be safe from teachers for a while. Want to tell me what's wrong?"

I collapse onto the couch. It groans under the weight of my newfound delinquency but doesn't buckle. I pull my knees up to my chest, sitting scrunched into the corner so I'm protected on two sides. Morgan sits backward on a chair, so effortlessly cool it would be annoying if he wasn't being so kind.

He's in the same ripped jeans as yesterday, this time paired with a distressed stripy sweater that somehow manages to hang down past his fingers despite how long his arms are. He might as well have PUNK skywritten in neon above his head. He's only missing a Mohawk.

I breathe, focusing on the house banners dangling from the walls as I attempt to make sense of the jumble in my brain. House Fajro, Natalie's house. My hand slips into my pocket and clutches the phone.

"I saw something this morning." My voice comes out thin and whispery. "I think something's happened. Something bad."

I'm worried he'll laugh at me—that any moment now his earnestness will dissolve like nail polish in acetone, revealing his pretense at friendship as part of some elaborate joke.

Instead, he leans forward. "What did you see?"

"You'll think I'm an idiot."

"Don't say that. Like, for real, Tai. I would never think like that and you shouldn't either." His forehead is puckered, face pensive. "You can tell me, but only if you want to."

I do. I need to tell someone, someone who'll believe me. So I start speaking, stammering at first until the whole story tumbles out of my mouth. Almost the whole story—I leave out the bit about recognizing the voice as Natalie's. I'm not ready to admit that and make it real. At the end, I pull out the phone like an exclamation point.

"Whoa, but what is a liekkiö exactly?" He struggles with the Finnish word.

"Sort of like a ghost. The spirit of a person who's been"—now it's my turn to struggle with words—"a person who's been murdered."

He's quiet for a bit, a muscle in his jaw clenching and relaxing while he taps a finger with chipped polish on the back of the chair. "And you're sure that's what you saw?" he asks, kindly though, and not like he doesn't believe me.

"Yes. No. I don't know." I retreat farther into the sagging cushions of the couch. "I want to be wrong, I do, but I don't think it could've been anything else."

"Guess you won't be needing the interview with me anymore then."

"Oh—"

"I'm joking," he says quickly, and drags a hand through his hair. "A crappy joke. Sorry, I do that when I'm nervous."

"No, it's okay. It's just—thank you for believing me."

"Toivo should've too."

I shrug. I really don't want to get into a discussion on family dynamics.

"You want to go to the police?" Morgan asks, words frosted thick with skepticism.

Slowly, the fear and shock loosen their vise grip on my chest and I manage to take a deep breath. "For a broken phone and some thread? Besides, my mom wouldn't like it. If it was a liekkiö, then that's magic, and anything magical is tietäjä business. The school doesn't like involving outsiders."

"Think she'll believe a swamp fart spoke to you?" He nudges

my right foot with his own, offering me a grin.

"She'll probably tell me Natalie lost her phone and everything's fine. Have you seen Natalie at all?"

"Nope, sorry."

"We could go now. If she's sick, she'll be in her room. You okay with skipping more class?" I ask, surprising myself. As much as ditching school puts my insides on a spin cycle, thinking about all the awful things that could've happened to Natalie is infinitely worse.

"What do you think?" Morgan swings his leg off the chair and offers me a hand up.

I take it before leading him out of the lounge and tiptoeing down the corridor. The coast is clear and we swing past our lockers to get our jackets. I'm shoving my arm through a sleeve when my heart stops.

"Hey! You two!"

Joakim Blomqvist. He starts toward us and I freeze, doing the whole deer in headlights thing. My mouth is dry, palms sweaty. I'm so not used to breaking the rules.

"Come on." Morgan grabs my hand again and starts running.

My feet follow as I struggle to keep up with his longer strides. The outside air is a slap of cold and a frenzy of sleet, but we don't slow down, skidding across the courtyard and angling onto the path that'll take us to Pilvitalo.

"We're going to be in so much trouble." I spit the words between ragged breaths.

"Think we could get expelled?" he asks like he's excited by the idea and not appalled.

Why did I never think to try and get *myself* expelled? All this time I've been wanting to get away from this place. But now's not the time to solve for hypothetical x where x is the amount of rule-breaking my mom will tolerate before kicking me out.

"I have no idea," I say.

"Just have to try harder then." He keeps running.

We slow down once we reach Pilvitalo, both of us needing to catch our breath. It's not like Joakim could've kept up even if he'd tried.

"Ready?" I ask and Morgan nods, more out of breath than I am.

I key in the access code, suddenly aware of how long it's been since I last visited—since I last had a reason to come to this house at all. Inside, I hesitate.

Is Natalie even in the same room this year? Would she still have the same posters of our favorite anime on her wall? Did she keep the framed photo of the two of us at our seventh-grade Kekri dance? I'd cried getting dressed that night, not wanting to wear the dress my mom had bought me and not really understanding exactly why yet.

It was only when Natalie spelled real flames along the hem that I didn't hate it and had managed to go. The magic lasted barely long enough to make a grand entrance, but it was awesome and it left holes charred in the fabric which, meant I never had to wear the thing again. Actually, I think that's the last time I wore a skirt at all.

"Going up?" Morgan shatters the memories misting up my thoughts.

"I don't know. Maybe this is silly. We're not friends anymore. Maybe that thing at the lake was all some sort of joke."

"You don't actually believe that," he says.

With a sigh, I summon the elevator and we ride it to the fourth floor, still reserved for Fajro members.

Nothing here has changed, all rosy-pink wallpaper and worn wooden floorboards with the Fajro crest stenciled onto the wall graffiti-style. Room 422 still has Natalie's name tacked above the number, the letters curly and individually laminated. I knock, but there's no reply.

"Maybe she went to school." I'm desperate and grasping because the alternative means admitting the contents of my pocket really are the signs of a struggle.

"She wasn't in math."

"Maybe her schedule changed."

"I can open it." Morgan waggles his fingers.

"Maybe she's sleeping?"

He raises his eyebrows at me.

"Okay, fine. Do it," I bite out.

Morgan carves the fire rune *kaunaz* across the wood with his fingers and mutters the spell to activate the more destructive aspect of the rune. The spell works instantly, and I'd be impressed if I wasn't suddenly battling freezing nose hairs and rime-coated eyelashes as his magic sucks energy from the air. The door pops open, old hinges creaking.

Her room doesn't look any different: same lilac bedspread and matching curtains, same posters of *Sailor Moon* and *Death Note* on the walls, and fairy lights strung around the headboard. Natalie's desk is a mess of social studies papers, and above it on the wall is a large collage in the shape of a butterfly made up of photos. Mostly selfies of Natalie and her BFFs.

There, right in the middle of the butterfly's body, is the Kekri photo of the two of us. A fist squeezes tight around my heart and I can feel the blood vessels bursting between those clenched knuckles. I'm not sure why seeing it hurts so much. We're standing with our arms around each other, both smiling. What we had was so good until I destroyed it.

"That's you?" Morgan says from behind my shoulder.

"In seventh grade." I'm weirdly self-conscious about him seeing me with long hair and wearing a dress. I don't want him to stop calling me *dude*.

"She's clearly not here," he adds.

I scan the rest of the room: neatly made bed, laptop sitting closed amid the papers, orchestra folder sitting under her flute case on the shelf, and a nest of hair ties sitting on top of her chest of drawers.

"Her backpack isn't here either." But it's the only thing missing. What did I expect? Charred marks on the wallpaper and broken furniture? Morgan sneezes violently, and rubs his nose. His eyes are watering, leaving eyeliner tears down his cheeks.

"Allergies?"

"Tomatoes, cats," he says. "And certain kinds of magic. Does Natalie have a cat?"

"No pets allowed and only twelfth graders get familiars,

usually around graduation. Emmi's the only tietäjä with a cat."

"I think I'd rather have a dragon." Morgan stifles another sneeze in the crook of his elbow. His face looks like a Rorschach test.

"Let's go. Not going to find anything more here." We creep out of Natalie's room and head back to the elevator.

Before we can press the button, the doors open.

"Oy, what's you lot doing in here?" MacCrone looms, her face contorted in a scowl. Her one good eye laser-sears right through me. Fiona stands beside her, tongue whipping in and out of her mouth between fangs that could rip my arm off.

Morgan curses under his breath beside me.

"Playing truant again, are we?" She continues to glare at me and I imagine this is what it must feel like to be incinerated by a solar flare. "I didn't expect you to succumb to bad influences." Her attention wanders from me to Morgan.

Morgan? One of the best mages at school, a *bad* influence?

"We just wanted to check on Natalie," I stammer. "We thought she had noro because she wasn't at school, but she's not here either."

MacCrone jams her boot against the closing elevator door and sifts saliva through her teeth.

"That noro's doing the rounds," MacCrone says without her usual amount of drill sergeant conviction.

"If she was sick, she'd be in bed." Morgan slips his hands into the pockets of his patched and safety-pinned jacket.

"She's not, and her backpack's missing too," I add, wondering if MacCrone might be the one to tell about the liekkiö.

"Breaking and entering, are we now?" MacCrone raises a single eyebrow, causing the scars down the other side of her face to pucker in an even sterner expression.

Busted.

"We—um—"

"We were just concerned about her." Morgan saves me.

So pathetic, the little voice seizes the moment. *Can't even get delinquency right.*

"I've no doubt Miss Khumalo is quite fine, so best you two be on your way." MacCrone steps out of the elevator. "Or should we pay a visit to the principal?"

"We were just leaving, Sergeant." Morgan nudges forward.

Fiona stands belligerently blocking the hallway, her hulking body forcing us to squeeze along the wall into the elevator to avoid her blueberry-stained fangs.

"That was weird," he says once the doors are closed and we're both breathing a little easier. He's still rubbing at his nose and eyes.

"I'll bet Natalie doesn't have noro." A bad feeling cinches around my insides. This would've been easier if Natalie didn't care about me anymore, but the photo on her wall makes me think maybe she doesn't hate me as much as I thought.

"But where the hell is she then?" he asks as we step out of Pilvitalo.

"And why am I the only one who seems to care?"

"Me too, now," he says between another set of sneezes. "Dammit."

He rests his hands on his knees for a minute, recovering. My crows circle above us, croaking from the eaves to let me know they've got their eyes on me. It's not much comfort. They didn't do much when the liekkiö showed up, and now Nat's missing. I need a bloodhound, not a mangy murder of crows.

Missing—the word hisses through my mind. That happens to other children in other places. Not in Finland, and certainly not in Myrskyjärvi.

"Who else supposedly has noro?" A dark suspicion scratches at the back of my mind.

"I know Manami in Hannah's class has been sick for a while," Morgan says. "She and Hannah are pretty close. And Elijah has been absent. He missed our test with Joakim last Friday."

I don't know Manami well since she's in House Akvo, but Elijah is in Tero with me. He's a powerful earth wielder from the US, capable of complex transmutations like turning coal into diamond with a snap of his fingers.

"There's supposed to be a lot of kids sick. You'd think we'd have noticed more people absent."

"It's a big school." Morgan flicks the curls out of his eyes.

"Not *that* big."

"What are you thinking?" he asks between sniffs.

"I don't know, but something isn't right. If what I saw this morning was a liekkiö, then something really awful might've happened. And with what's going on in Svalbard, I just don't know."

"You mean the break-in thing?" He scuffs his toe across the gravel pathway.

"Yeah, I overheard my parents talking." I give him a quick summary of what went down. "Worst of all, I think my parents know who did it, but they're not saying."

"Didn't think anyone but a chaos mage could take on a battle mage." He swallows hard.

"Scary, right?"

"Chaos magic doesn't exist anymore. Whoever got into the vault must've just been lucky, or maybe battle mages don't take their training as seriously as they should."

I want to believe it. I want to believe in incompetent battle mages rather than a resurgence of chaos magic.

"Besides," Morgan continues, "if whatever they were after wasn't in the vault, then it can't be all that powerful, so why would they even want it?"

"That's a good point and makes the whole thing even weirder." I take a deep breath and exhale noisily through my nose, realizing it's exactly what my dad does whenever he's stumped by some magical problem.

"Think you've got everything you need for a front-page story," Morgan says.

"Supposition and false claims aren't great journalism."

"Then that means the Knock-Knock Jokes still stand a chance? Did you listen to us?" He glances up at me, looking genuinely nervous.

"I did and yeah, not bad." I feel myself smiling. "The

drummer's pretty good."

"Told ya," he says with a flash of a grin. "Anyway, back to bigger issues: what are we going to do?"

"I think I should speak to my mom."

He groans and I get it. It's not like I want to involve the school principal in this.

"You got another idea?" I ask. "It's not like we're detectives."

"No, but you're an investigative journalist, right?"

"Thought I was a music critic."

"That too. You could be like Steve Morse or something." His eyes are bright, hands waving as they paint imaginary pictures of crowds and stages. "Go to hundreds of gigs a year, get all the inside scoops, hang out with the hottest bands."

"Not sure that's the kind of journalistic approach we need right now." I've always wanted to be more like Jane Mayer or Martha Mendoza.

"Fair enough." He deflates, shoulders drooping like a basset hound's ears. "So, your mom then?"

"It's our only option."

Morgan starts down the path and I stride along beside him, driven not only by the icy wind slicing around the edges of my jacket, but by the tornado in my belly telling me something is truly, terribly wrong.

"Your mom's a little busy right now," Markus says before I can even say good morning to the school secretary. "She shouldn't be disturbed."

"I'll only be a minute." I go with the flow of momentum, letting it carry me past Markus, and I knock on Mom's door.

It's yanked open a moment later.

"Taika, I'm in a meeting."

With Emmi, Joakim, and Aleksi who's equal parts PE teacher and conjurer extraordinaire. A secret gathering of the school's tietäjät? Their expressions are the dictionary definition of grim, and only Emmi offers me the weakest hint of a smile.

"This really isn't a good time," Mom says. "Shouldn't you be in class? Is everything okay?" She looks tired, her blouse stained on the cuffs and her skirt creased. In fact, I'm pretty sure she's still wearing yesterday's outfit. That is so not a good sign.

"This *is* really important," Morgan pipes up behind me as if he can sense I'm about to wilt under my mom's glare.

Mom mutters apologies to the others before placing a heavy hand on my shoulder and guiding me out of the office.

"What is this about then?" She already sounds bored and annoyed. "And what happened to your jacket?" She brushes her fingers across the scorch mark I'd been hoping she wouldn't notice.

"That's nothing. Listen, I think something bad happened," I say quickly. "To Natalie."

"Taika." Mom pinches the bridge of her nose and closes her eyes for a moment.

"This morning, I saw a liekkiö down by the lake. It led me through the forest and I found this." I hold up Natalie's smashed phone and the snatch of wool.

"A liekkiö?" Mom's eyes flash open. "I really don't have time for this."

"But it asked me for help, I heard it, and it led me to Natalie's phone. And she's missing. She's not in class, not in her room. I'm not making this up."

"What do you mean, you *heard* it?" Mom's face scrunches up in confusion.

"The liekkiö, I—I heard a voice." My own quavers and Morgan leans closer, his shoulder momentarily brushing mine.

"This isn't funny." Mom switches into stern, principal mode. "I don't know what you're playing at but—"

"I'm not playing at anything. This is Natalie's phone. What was it doing out in the forest? Where's Natalie?" This was a mistake. Mom is never going to believe me, and even if she does, she'll tell me to go back to class and forget all about it. To let others handle it, others with magic.

Useless, pathetic, worthless, my personal vocalist starts up again.

"She has—"

"Mrs. Turunen, sorry to interrupt," Morgan says, all lilt and charm and polite formality, "but we checked and Natalie isn't in Pilvitalo. She's not in school either. We wouldn't have come to you if we weren't really concerned."

Gods bless him. He might need a haircut, but as a magical wunderkind, his words carry the kind of weight mine never will. I can see Mom's opinion changing, her expression flitting back and forth between concern and aggravation.

"Everything all right out here?" Emmi peeks her head around the door.

"Natalie is missing," I say. "And I saw a liekkiö this morning by the lake."

"Missing?" Emmi pales a little, a frown line slicing her brow. "Oh my, that does sound serious."

"Natalie's supposed to be sick, but she wasn't in her room."

"Perhaps she's in the infirmary?" Emmi says.

I want to facepalm so hard I'd give myself a black eye. How could I have not thought of that!? But why didn't MacCrone tell us that's where Natalie was when we ran into her earlier? It doesn't add up.

"The infirmary, yes. That's exactly..." Mom trails off as her gaze seems to lose focus.

"That doesn't explain the liekkiö though, does it?" Morgan chips in.

"I'm sure there's a perfectly rational explanation for what Taika saw. There was a regrettable incident in our last Thaumaturgy class," Emmi says. "Perhaps there are some residual effects."

"What incident?" Mom's gaze sweeps over me and I feel my spine buckling, my whole body wanting to pretzel into itself.

"An accident, we think," Emmi says. "But Taika has been bullied before, and in their...situation, it's hard to know what the lingering side effects might be after they interact with magic."

Did she have to say this in front of Morgan? I want to die. Please Void, open up and swallow me whole. Right now.

"Bullying?" As if a switch has been flipped, the stern expression melts from Mom's face. "I'm so sorry, Taika. I didn't realize."

She steps forward as if about to hug me and I back away. Any other day I might've been grateful for it, but right now I only want to escape. My whole body is a giant blister of mortification.

"It's whatever. It doesn't matter."

"Of course, it matters," Mom says. "I want to know who the culprits are."

"Mom! I just want to know where Natalie is."

"And I'll look into it," Mom says. "But we need to have a proper conversation about all this later."

Finally, she seems to notice Morgan again and how my cheeks are burning. They're on fire and must be flashing bright as lighthouse beams.

"I'll see this gets returned to Natalie." Emmi plucks the phone from my fingers, causing the threads to drift to the floor. I snatch them up and tuck them back into my pocket.

"Shall we get back to our meeting now, Meri?" Emmi gestures to the door.

"Yes, sorry." Mom pauses before returning to her office. "Tonight, Taika. We'll talk tonight."

I can't move, even after the door closes and the muffled voices resume beyond.

Taika the Talentless, the little voice chants, *and now Morgan knows just how pathetic you really are.*

Tears burn at the back of my nose. Crying now would only make everything worse.

"Well, that went great," Morgan says with a hard edge to his voice.

I really didn't want Mom knowing how Sini and the others treat me. It'll only make things worse if Mom gets involved, and now she definitely will. I scrub a hand over my face, tugging at the dangling points of my bangs as if I could hide behind them.

Maybe Emmi was right and what I saw was some lingering effect of being punched in Thaumaturgy. Maybe I imagined hearing the voice, but I didn't imagine finding Natalie's phone or those threads snagged on the branches. There's more to this, I know it.

"Not sure why I thought she'd help." I'm surprised by the

bitterness in my words.

"Because she's your mom and it's supposed to be her job," Morgan says. "But adults tend to suck and never listen when they should."

I'm not entirely sure we're talking about my mom and Natalie anymore, but I'm too upset to get into whatever he's got going on right now.

With frustration roiling in my belly, I stomp away from the offices and slam into Sini. She clutches a bunch of Sigils and Systems worksheets in her hands and must've been making copies for Miss Kaneda next door, which means she probably heard everything.

"Did you—"

"Oh yeah, I heard." Sini folds her arms, awkwardly because of all the papers.

"Unless it was you who hurt me, you've got nothing to worry about."

"Well, it wasn't." Sini's gaze flicks to Morgan. She straightens and tries to brush a lank strand of yellow hair behind her ear. She only succeeds in giving her cheek a papercut.

"That's malfeasance. Not how I roll." She clears her throat. "And that's—I mean—I heard what you said about the liekkiö, and Natalie." The papers spill from her trembling hands, the worksheets spreading out like a tsunami across the scuffed linoleum.

Morgan immediately crouches down to pick them up.

Sini doesn't move. She holds my gaze and smooths her hands down the frothy skirts she's wearing over stripy tights. When she speaks, her voice is a gossamer-thin whisper.

"We haven't seen her since Thaumaturgy. I don't know why it took me so long to realize it. I mean, what I said to you after Journalism Club. I'm sorry—I just..." She hooks a finger under the blue elastic bracelet at her wrist, letting it snap against her skin three times before she clears her throat. "It's like I didn't notice she wasn't around, or something. I don't know, it's been weird. But you're right. I think Nat's missing."

"She's probably in the infirmary, just like Emmi said." I want it to be true. I rub at my wrists, wishing I could reassure Sini so she'd stop hurting herself, but it's not my place.

"She's not, I mean—Aysha and I, we took Katya..." Snap, snap, snap goes the bracelet. Sini clears her throat and tosses her head back. "We had to see the nurse, okay, and we would've noticed if Natalie was there."

"None of this makes any sense! And why are the teachers dodging our questions?" I start gnawing on a fingernail—a bad habit I ditched over a year ago.

"Maybe they just don't want to admit they're clueless," Sini says.

"Hey, you wrote that article about the norovirus, right?" Morgan asks as he hands back the sigil papers.

"You read it?"

"I did, but do you know how many people are actually sick? Your article didn't list names or anything."

"Joakim thought it was better I didn't since people would want to blame a patient zero, you know." She lifts a thin shoulder in an approximation of a shrug. "I know a few like Elijah and Qendresa got sick. A sixth grader called Peter." She taps her chin with her index finger. "Also Risto, he's your brother's friend, right?" She looks at me.

"Yeah, he is." Or at least he was the last time I bothered to pay any attention to my brother's social life.

"Do you know who got sick first?" I ask.

"No, by the time I wrote the article, there were already a lot of kids puking, apparently. That's why I was asked to write it in the first place."

"You were *asked* to write it?" Morgan frowns. "By Joakim?"

"No, by—" Her face goes blank. "I can't—I don't think it was Joakim. I'm sorry."

Weird.

"But why? Five sick kids isn't exactly a pandemic," Morgan says.

"Why lie about something like that?" Sini asks.

"Exactly." Morgan makes that popping sound with his index fingers again.

"Something strange is definitely going on. Did you notice *anyone* in the infirmary?" I ask. "Risto, Peter, Qendresa, Manami?"

Sini shakes her head. "Only one of the Strigoi picking up iron supplements. I don't think any of the beds were occupied."

"So the others might be missing too. We really need to find Natalie," I say.

"If you need help, I mean, if you wanted—I care about Natalie too, you know," Sini says.

"Thanks. But we've got this." I nod toward Morgan, knowing Sini isn't going to argue with me in front of him.

"Will you let me know if you hear anything about Natalie?" she asks.

"If you promise to do the same."

Sini nods and adds an "I promise" as the bell rings. Cursing, she hurries back to Kaneda's classroom.

"What now?" Morgan asks.

"Honestly? I have no idea, but I should probably go to class."

"Really?" He seems genuinely surprised.

"Not all of us can afford to skip every period." I force a grin, but the words come out more barbed than I mean them to. "Sorry—it's just...I hate feeling this useless."

Taika the Talentless, Taika the Talentless, the voice blasts through my brain. If only it came with volume control or a mute button.

"I need some time to think," I add. "Can we still meet at lunch?"

"Of course."

"See you then."

He gives me a salute and I watch him amble down the corridor, hands stuffed in the pockets of his jacket, clearly in no hurry.

I can only imagine what it must feel like being that powerful, knowing you're so naturally gifted you don't even need to try, and people will still treat you like a god. It must feel amazing knowing you'll end up a successful mage one day, leading a division of the UCMW or taking over your parents' empire.

Every time I think about my future, as much as I dream about winning a Pulitzer, I know I'll probably wind up creating "What kind of pizza topping are you?" quizzes for people bored on social media. At least, that's what Toivo tells me every time I mention wanting to be a journalist. It's not fair.

And it's not fair Natalie kept that picture of the two of us. This would be so much easier if she hated me and I could pretend I didn't care what happened to her.

I expect to find Morgan surrounded by a group of friends, all with ripped jeans and skateboards, chatting, laughing, and generally enjoying their status as school royalty.

Instead, he sits alone at a corner table by the window, his gaze on the courtyard where the younger grades are having recess. Milky sunshine seeps through the clouds, grazing the windows and illuminating his face as he pushes the day's insipid bolognese around his plate with a fork.

I take a moment to scan the cafeteria, wondering once again if this is some sort of joke. Are his friends all going to pounce the moment I sit down? A few stray glances wander my way from the other tables. Of course, Natalie isn't here, and I look away when Ekaterina notices me staring.

"Hey." I slip my tray onto the table but don't sit down yet. "This seat taken?"

"Hey, tervetuloa." Morgan smiles. His Finnish pronunciation

is awful but I appreciate the welcome nonetheless. "And no, it's completely free."

"Where are your friends?" Still nervous, I'm tempted to look over my shoulder.

"You're it." There's a weight to the way he says it that makes me think maybe he isn't as popular as I thought.

I sidle in opposite him. Musti, Rekku, and Kamu caw from the gutters and flap their wings to let me know they're there, right outside. It's weirdly comforting having three feathered shadows.

"Had any revelations since this morning?" he asks through a mouthful of spaghetti.

"Not really." Honestly, I still have no idea where to start, despite spending the last two periods racking my brain. "But I've been thinking maybe we should check on all the kids who are supposedly sick. If they aren't in their rooms and aren't in the infirmary then that proves they're missing."

"I think we should get Sini to help," he says and I almost choke. "Or not. I sensed some tension there. What's up with you guys?"

"It's a long story." And not one I want to share. It might make him realize how useless I really am.

"I'm listening." His eyes glitter in the ray of sunshine cutting across his face.

"You heard what Emmi said. I get picked on sometimes."

"Bullied," he says, but I hate that word and how small it makes me feel.

"Whatever." I shrug, not wanting his pity. "Sini, Ekaterina, and Aysha have never liked me. Ekaterina shocked me so badly once, I still have the scar." Slowly, I roll up the sleeve of my gray hoodie and show him the pale zigzag where Ekaterina branded my wrist. "She claimed it was an accident."

"You don't believe her?"

"I don't know. I mean, it's possible, but Aysha gave me an orange once only to turn it into a lemon when I took a bite so, it's not like I trust any of them not to be jerks."

"What about Natalie?" He looks up at me like he knows he might be picking at a scab. "She ever been a jerk to you?"

"No, never," I say. "But she did take Ekaterina's side, saying it was a mistake and I shouldn't be so mean about it." I've caught a glimpse of similar scars on Ekaterina's arms, though she almost always wears long sleeves, even in warm weather.

"Accidents do happen," Morgan says. "I'm not defending her, but not everyone has perfect control of their magic. It's hard, especially when we're first coming into it."

"I guess." I tug my sleeve back down. "It's not like magic can really hurt me anyway. Spells never stick for long."

"Can I try?" He holds out his hand across the table. "I won't hurt you, promise. Just going to try to paint your nails."

"Go for it." I put my hand in his, even though my palms are a little sweaty. At least my nails aren't the ragged mess they used to be.

"What color?"

"Purple," I say, remembering the times Natalie and I did this, only with polish instead of magic.

A tingling begins in my fingertip as Morgan mumbles some words. Again, I feel the sudden snap of cold in the air around me as my nails turn metallic purple one at a time. Morgan releases my hand, his gaze on the paint-job. It only takes a few seconds for the color to start fading.

"Huh." His mouth twists as if he's pondering a particularly complex math problem. "So, you're like *immune* to spells?"

"Not immune exactly, maybe more like I have a high tolerance for it? Like spells just don't stick and affect me a lot less than they should. I guess you could say I'm *resistant* to magic."

He regards me from across the table with narrowed eyes. "That's a kind of magic power in itself, you know."

"What, having *anti*magic? That's not an ability."

"It could be useful."

"I'd rather have regular magic, like you," I say.

Morgan leans back in his chair as if my words have physically shoved him away. I'm about to ask him why, but he cuts me off.

"So, I was thinking," he says. "If Natalie is truly missing, you have any idea who'd want to hurt her? I'm guessing you're not the only one getting it from her friends?"

"Her friends are jerks, but not Nat. She's loved by everyone." Oh gods, my cheeks are burning. "I mean, she's really popular and besides, she's descended from fire giants. I don't think anyone *could* hurt her even if they tried."

"There's always a way. Even the most powerful mages have vulnerabilities." His words send ants scurrying beneath my skin.

There's one kind of magic that can hurt anyone. It doesn't matter if chaos magic has been outlawed for centuries—and for good reason—someone must be using it, or how else were the battle mages on Svalbard defeated?

"I'm guessing Natalie isn't the type to run away or get herself in trouble either?" Morgan asks.

Before I can answer, the sound of a breaking window splinters the drone of lunchtime conversation.

"Look out!" a teacher shouts as glass showers into the courtyard right in front of the cafeteria.

My crows squawk, taking to the air in a frenzy of feathers.

A ball of white light hurtles across the yard. It tears after a group of kids, who scream and cry as they run for cover. Morgan and I push up close to the window to watch. We've got front-row seats as everyone in the cafeteria gathers at the glass.

Tiny arms extend from the ball of light, tinier hands grabbing at beanies and ponytails as the light-ball zips back and forth, slow-morphing into a toad with wings and a long spiky tail. This is nothing like a liekkiö.

Musti, Rekku, and Kamu dive at the unknown creature when it gets too close to my window, managing to keep whatever the thing is at bay.

"Quick, everyone inside!" Joakim yells, beckoning students toward the doors. "Don't let it into the school!"

Joakim, of course. His classes are notorious for their mishaps.

Another Blomqvist Blunder

My brain automatically starts composing an article for the *Messenger*, but my thoughts derail when Morgan jumps to his feet.

"Hannah!"

A third grader wearing purple jeans stands frozen as the conjured critter dive-bombs straight toward her. We both watch, numb and paralyzed.

Hannah raises her hand, carving the water rune *isa* into the air. It's such a delicate gesture and yet the puddles scattered across the courtyard respond immediately. The muddy water forms a barrier of dirty ice at least two meters tall to protect Hannah and her classmates.

No third grader should be able to draw so much energy so easily. In fact, most high schoolers would have a hard time doing the same, but Hannah does it effortlessly. The creature slams into the barrier, razor-sharp claws gouging at the impenetrable surface before my crows launch an assault with beaks and talons.

Hannah releases the spell and the ice shatters. Morgan's already on his feet, elbowing his way through the cafeteria crowd. I rush to follow, not caring when he breaks the rules and shoves open the emergency exit to get into the yard faster. He races toward his sister, skidding across frozen puddles. I follow, wanting to protect them both even though I know that's ridiculous. Maybe if I had a baseball bat I wouldn't feel so useless.

"Are you okay?" Morgan tugs Hannah into his arms before she can answer.

"It's coming back." I point at the shrieking creature.

Hannah pulls free and sends up another wall of ice, smaller this time, but the creature shatters it with a flick of its morning star tail.

"Use *uruz* too," I shout over the cacophony of the courtyard. An earth rune would be much stronger.

Morgan frowns, considering, then flicks his fingers. Breath wrenches out of my lungs as he crafts earth and air runes into a powerful sigil. The spell takes effect, and Morgan raises pillars of earth, sod erupting from the ground at our feet He wields the pillars like hockey sticks while the creature tries to slalom past.

Sweat beads his forehead and rolls down his temples as he strains to maintain the spell. Binding earth and air magic together is beyond impressive, but I'll marvel at that later when we're not under attack.

Rekku swoops low, knocking the creature from its trajectory. The thing shrieks in anger and tears after the crows. With an exhausted exhalation, Morgan releases the spell and the muddy pillars crumble.

"Go!" he yells, already running for the doors and dragging Hannah along behind him. I don't need to be told twice. All the younger kids are inside. A few teachers and seniors remain in the courtyard trying to contain the creature with bouts of fire, bursts of icy air, and slabs of earth. Cludd attempts a water spell using *laguz* and only manages to soak himself and the girl standing beside him, dousing the flames in her hands.

"Out of the way the lot of you bairns!" A voice full of gravel barks the order.

The squash of bodies at the doors separates as Elspeth MacCrone and Fiona come running out of the building. Despite her squat legs, Fiona is fast. MacCrone isn't too bad herself, surprisingly spry for an almost septuagenarian. Turns out, it's a good thing MacCrone maintains her combat readiness.

Fiona's armored scales ripple over impressive muscles as she darts about the courtyard doing lizard parkour after the creature. MacCrone wields something resembling a butterfly catcher, only this one is made of iron netting and its wooden handle is littered with runes.

We watch, awestruck, as MacCrone and Fiona chase the screaming creature. Emmi follows in their wake, hands raised at the ready.

"Ah, ya wee bogle. You'll not get the better of us." MacCrone evades an attack. A bogle! Of course. I should've recognized it, but I'm a little rusty when it comes to Scottish folklore.

Emmi carves a sigil in the air using the *tiwaz* fire rune and something else I don't recognize as the bogle darts toward her. The sigil blocks the bogle's flight with a curtain of fire, but the creature slashes its tail through the flames and splits open Emmi's sleeve. Blood gushes and we all take several steps back, Hannah tucked behind Morgan.

"Stay back, Emmi! We've got this," MacCrone orders Emmi out of the way.

Emmi obliges, clutching at her arm.

Not Even Thaumaturgists Can Avoid Injury—not the most inspiring title.

Blomqvist Bungling Results in a Bogling—that's a bit catchier.

"Are you all right?" I shout over at Emmi.

"I'm fine. Worry about yourself, please." Emmi ushers us into the school.

We turn and press our faces against the closed doors.

The bogle dashes toward MacCrone and, at the last moment, when I'm sure MacCrone is about to earn some fresh facial scars, Fiona leaps, catching the bogle by the tail. She flings it to the ground and MacCrone deftly slams the net over it. With practiced precision, MacCrone transfers the squealing, squirming bogle from the net into a small containment jar she produces from her utility belt.

Like that, it's over, and it took under five minutes.

Joakim shoulders his way past us and into the courtyard as MacCrone screws on the lid. She gives the jar a good shake and the bogle flings itself at the warded glass in rage, its tail flicking back and forth like an angry cat's.

Students start clapping and whistling, shouting admiration for MacCrone.

"Och, stop it. It's our job." MacCrone offers Fiona blueberries from her pocket. "What you been teaching them, Joakim? Summoning a bogle, indeed. Nasty critters those."

"Yes, quite. My apologies." Joakim turns several shades of pink as he accepts the containment jar.

"Come on, Hannah, let's get you back to class." Morgan loops his arm around his sister's shoulders.

My gaze lingers on the jar as Joakim traipses sheepishly through the throngs.

"Hannah! Morgan! Are you all right?" The oldest O'Connor

rushes over to us. Aoife flicks her gaze over Morgan before she kneels down, eye level with Hannah.

"We're fine," Morgan says.

"Truly?"

"Truly," Hannah whispers and accepts her sister's hug. I don't think Toivo has ever hugged me, certainly not willingly at least.

The three of them look a lot alike, except Aoife has grown her curls out long where Morgan's are cut into a bushy halo. Aoife's eyes are a little more green than gray. She's tall, a bit taller than Morgan even, with long legs I can't help but envy given how I'm barely five foot one on a good day.

"Hannah was a star out there. What you did was really brave." Morgan winks at his little sister and Hannah beams. "This is my friend, Taika," he says. "They and them pronouns, please."

"Oh, like Kelly." Hannah is totally accepting.

It sets off a bath bomb of fizzy warmth inside my chest.

Friend. He called me his friend.

For now, the little voice quips. I bite my inner cheek hard enough to hurt in an attempt to shut that voice up.

"Taika, nice to meet you," Aoife says. "I have Thaumaturgy with your brother."

"Poor you," I say and Aoife laughs, a warm and infectious sound that makes me like her immediately. "You have Joakim for conjuring, don't you?" I ask, still needing to iron out a few details in my germinating plan.

"Yes, but not today. That critter came from the other class," she says, her accent making all the consonants soft and round. The other class being Toivo's. "Someone must've got their summoning spell backward," Aoife continues. "Bogles are graylisted."

"Why?" Hannah asks.

"On account of their being wicked little creatures with very nasty intentions. They're very good at creating chaos. Not for an amateur summoner." Aoife glances around the hallway, scanning faces as they pass.

"You looking for someone?" Morgan asks.

"Sorin. Haven't seen him today. We were supposed to meet—I mean, we had a potions test in chemistry this morning and he seems the diligent type." Aoife's freckled cheeks blotch bright pink.

"I'll bet he is," Morgan says with a knowing grin quirking up the corners of his mouth.

"Think it's noro?" Hannah pipes up.

"A vampire with a stomach bug?" Aoife screws up her nose in an expression that holds no disdain as she shakes her head.

Hannah giggles. Gods, why couldn't I have had siblings like this instead of the irritable asswipe I'm forced to share DNA with.

"Actually, I'm not sure there's a stomach bug outbreak at all." I'm afraid to say out loud what's only been a nasty suspicion gnawing at the back of my mind. "I think it's a cover-up."

"Sounds dramatic. A cover-up for what?" Aoife asks, but Morgan flicks his gaze to Hannah and back, giving me a little shake of his head.

"Maybe it's just a vampire thing," he says. "Maybe Sorin ate some garlic yesterday." He pulls a face, making Hannah giggle again.

"Yeah. Let's hope it's that." Aoife doesn't sound convinced.

The bell rings, signaling the end of lunch.

Aoife tosses her hair over her shoulder and straightens to her full height. "Come on, I'll walk you." She bumps her hip gently against Hannah then tousles Morgan's hair before sashaying down the corridor, her arm draped protectively around her little sister.

Morgan turns to me, his smile instantly melting off his face. "I did some digging. Peter, Elijah, Qendresa, Risto, Manami, Natalie, and now Sorin," he says. "They're all really good at magic."

"Everyone's good here."

"Yeah, but they're better than good," he says. "Each of them is pretty exceptional in their own way."

"So, all the allegedly sick kids also happen to be ultratalented with magic?" A queasy feeling ripples through my belly.

"Think we should check the dorms and infirmary? Make sure they're not being quarantined somewhere Sini wouldn't have seen?" Morgan asks.

Part of me really wants to believe this is all some big misunderstanding, but I saw the liekkiö. I heard Natalie's voice and she asked for my help.

"No, screw that." My vehemence takes me by surprise. No more skulking about where we could run into MacCrone. Despite Morgan's attitude, if either of us get caught skipping any more classes, we're going to be in serious trouble.

"I think I have a better way to figure this out," I say. "Can you meet me after school at the bridge?"

"Why not go right now?"

"I've got some prep to do. See you later?"

"You sure?" He eyes me uncertainly.

"I've got this. Promise. Just meet me after school, okay?"

"Okay. Later, Tai," he calls after me as I hurry toward Miss Kaneda's class.

For the first time, Sigils and Systems might actually be useful. If this plan's going to work I'll need to steal a containment jar and bend a few school rules.

Break them, the little voice says at the back of my mind. Somehow, I don't think Morgan will mind too much.

Except, you could get him expelled, the voice says, punching me in the gut with a fist of guilt and anxiety. I'm not going to let that happen. Morgan might not be too concerned by the idea of expulsion, but, selfishly, I wouldn't want him to get kicked out, not when it feels like he might be becoming a friend.

Besides, when we succeed—because we will—it won't matter how many rules we had to break because we'll be heroes, the ones to figure out what's really going on here and what happened to Natalie.

"No." Morgan stares at me, his eyes steel discs in the fading light.

It's drizzling again and we both have our hoods up as we make our way through the forest to a clearing near the bridge. The rain leaves graffiti splatter across his head and shoulders.

"Would you at least try the containment spell?" I hold up the book of sigils I borrowed from Miss Kaneda. I guess *borrow* might not be entirely accurate, but Morgan doesn't need to know the details.

"I don't need that." He gestures to the book with hands plunged deep into his pockets. "Besides, containment is a piece of cake. It's the summoning."

"You make it sound like something bad." As if he got a mouthful of salty *salmiakki* when he expected sweet licorice.

"It can be," he says. "Especially if—"

"It's not necromancy." It can't be, because otherwise that would mean Natalie is dead and there is no flipping way I believe that.

And also because that would be teetering precariously close to chaos magic.

"Tai." He looks up through the thatch of wet curls plastered across his brow.

"Technically, it's sciomancy. We'd be summoning a ghost, not the dead, if that's even what I saw. I mean, maybe it wasn't even a liekkiö."

"That's worse!" His gaze is radioactive. "First rule of summoning, don't ever call up something unknown. There are far more dangerous things than bogles."

"I know, but this'll be fine," I say, willing myself to believe it.

"I'm not doing it."

My jaw clenches and knuckles turn white where I clutch the book. I'd give anything to be able to do this on my own, but without magic I'm...

Useless, the voice supplies with glee.

Mom said I have to be patient, that magical abilities manifest later in some people. For years I believed I might've been a late bloomer, that maybe as I got older my latent talents would finally show up. Instead, all puberty has given me is monthly cramps and gender dysphoria. No magic, not now—probably not ever.

"What if we don't summon it then?" I'm not giving up, not yet. "We wait for it to appear again and then we trap it. Does that sound better?"

"You sure it'll turn up again?" Morgan's voice loses its flinty edge.

"No, but if you don't want to summon it, what else can we do? In the meantime something terrible might be happening to Natalie, but I guess we just have to wait because...because— *You're too scared to help me!* I manage to bite back that last part. Morgan is right to be wary even if it's infuriating.

"I know you care about her, but messing with this kind of stuff is dangerous," he says, and I know he's right about that too. Not that it helps.

"I have to do something." I swat a tear off my face.

Morgan takes a deep breath and pulls his hands out of his pockets. "Let me see the book."

I hand it over, watching nervously while he fans through the pages filled with runes.

Every element has five basic runes, which can be combined for different spells. When combined, the runes become sigils. Every element has combat runes too, but only battle mages are allowed to use those. Still, combining the basic runes in clever ways can create any number of sigils for any number of purposes. And with Morgan's ability to combine runes across elements, the sigil potential is near infinite.

After a minute, Morgan finds what he's looking for.

"I'll give this a shot, but for the real thing we'll have to have a warded jar." He kicks aside rotting leaves, smoothing the damp earth with his foot.

I pass him a stick and he grumbles a thank-you as he begins carving a circular sigil into the ground. It's made up of four runes: *ansuz, jera, dagaz,* and *eiwaz*—one for each element. Together, we measure the angles, squinting along the radius of our spell circle and pacing out the circumference until we're sure it's perfect.

"I should warn you," Morgan says softly, "this is going to need a bucketload of energy."

"There's plenty in the forest." What we're about to do definitely doesn't count as a "frivolity."

"It's still a lot for me to handle by myself. It would be better if I had help."

It takes me a minute to realize what he's trying to say. "I do not want Sini and the others involved. Don't you have friends who could help us?"

The look he gives me is a weird one. "No," he says.

"No, you don't have friends you want to ask or...?" I'm letting my curiosity get the better of me.

"No, I don't have friends, period."

I find that impossible to believe and I guess my skepticism must be showing.

"You wouldn't get it." He sighs.

"Because I'm Mx. Popular."

He smirks at that. "Think about it? I'm new and got bumped up two classes. Think the eleventh graders like getting shown up by a punk kid who doesn't even want to do magic? Think the ninth graders are going to be my friends when they all think I think I'm better than them?"

"You are better than them." Wait, did he say he doesn't *want* to do magic? Those are words my brain cannot compute.

"Doesn't win you friends." He sounds a whole lot more dejected than I would've imagined for someone with his power.

It's oddly comforting to know we're both rejects, even if it's for entirely different reasons. My thoughts snag again on that bit about him not wanting to do magic, but considering the spell I've just asked him to complete, I'm not going to bring up the not-doing-magic thing right now. Definitely time to change the subject.

"Okay. If you do this alone, will you pass out?" I ask, half joking, although it has been known to happen during spellweaving.

"Probably." Morgan shrugs. "Or worse." He doesn't elaborate and I'm not sure I want to know.

"Even for the test?"

"Guess we'll find out." The look he gives me skewers me like an insect pin through a dead bug. Am I asking too much of him?

"Just need something to contain now." He quirks up a brow and I point to the branch above us.

"Which one?"

"The big one. He's not the sharpest." Making Kamu the easiest of the crows to coax into the circle.

"All right, let's do this." Morgan cracks his knuckles and clicks his neck left then right.

I pretend to fish treats out of my jacket, tossing pocket lint instead of crumbs into the circle. "Tule tänne." I sing-song up at the crows, pretending to scatter more food. Musti gives me a rather disapproving look and Rekku isn't paying any attention at all, but, as I predicted, Kamu flutters down. He lands in the circle and starts pecking at the pocket lint.

Morgan is already chanting, a look of intense concentration on his face, eyes glazed as he kneels and digs his fingers into the soil.

The sigil rises from the ground in a layer of mist and the air turns cold. My breath comes out in steaming white clouds. Frost cakes a thick crust along the edge of Morgan's hood as he continues the incantation, burying his hands up to his wrists. The sigil responds, the curls of mist forming a net over the crow, who's too busy picking at nothing to notice.

Musti and Rekku squawk alerts from above. Kamu flaps, trying to heave his heavy body to flight, but the trap is sprung and the magical net holds him in the circle.

"It's working. You did it!" My joy is short-lived when I look over at Morgan.

The sweat on his face is turning to ice. His hands are shaking, the sigil dissipating.

He slumps to the side and Kamu bursts free of the circle, croaking his indignation before joining the others up in the branches again.

"Oh crap, oh crap. Morgan! Are you okay?" I catch him before he face-plants in the mud. I try not to think about the forest muck seeping into my jeans.

"Come on. You're okay. Please be okay." This happens, it's normal. He warned me. There's no need to panic, I tell myself as I take shallow sips of air, counting the seconds and keeping a finger on the pulse in his neck.

Never mind getting him expelled, you're going to get him killed, the little voice interjects, helpful as always.

After precisely three minutes and forty-eight seconds, Morgan opens his eyes.

"Thank the gods!" I help him sit up. The relief crashing through my veins makes me dizzy. "Are you all right?"

"Been better." He dusts off his hands before massaging his temples.

"It'll be easier with a jar," I say.

Morgan gives a tired shake of his head. Before he can say anything, another voice slices through the forest.

"Urgh, it's *her*," Aysha says as Sini & Co. make their way into the clearing.

"I'm not sure what an O'Connor is doing with Taika the Talentless." Ekaterina's words are as sharp as scalpels. She casts her dark gaze on me and once more I find myself appealing to the Void to swallow me whole.

Taika the Talentless, Taika the Useless, Taika the Pathetic— the voice at the back of my mind thinks it's time to belt out a punk-rock chorus. The verse is just as good, it goes *her her her her her. She she she she she she.*

I swallow hard, darting a glance at Morgan as I surreptitiously smudge leaves and soil over the runes with my toe while my cheeks ignite with a mix of anger and humiliation.

"Seriously? Are we in kindergarten?" Morgan shoots back. "And don't be a jerk. Get Taika's pronouns right. It's really not that hard."

I want to throw my arms around him, but I restrain myself, not wanting to give the others more ammunition. I absolutely appreciate him coming to my defense, I just wish he didn't need to do it at all. I should be standing up for myself.

Ekaterina purses her lips, sparks dancing along her fingers. She folds her arms, trying to look tough and mostly succeeding given the black leather jacket she wears. It's the one with silver spikes on the collar.

"What are you doing out here?" Sini asks.

"What are *you* doing here?" My voice quavers far more than I want it to.

"We were looking for Natalie." Aysha smooths her bangs beneath her beanie which, like the rest of her designer clothes, has its brand label on the outside. "Sini told us you found her phone out here. We thought maybe you missed something else."

Of course they did.

"What's this?" Ekaterina points at the ground where one of

the runes is still visible.

"Nothing," Morgan says too quickly as he scuffs it out with a foot. Gingerly, he plucks Kaneda's textbook from the dirt where we abandoned it before the spell.

"You're up to something," Sini says, eyes puffy as if she's been crying. "You promised you'd tell me if you heard anything."

"We don't know anything new," I say, entirely the truth.

"A containment circle?" Aysha asks with a swish of her long dark hair. Rain beads on her cheeks like rhinestones. "I doubt Kaneda would approve of this."

"Containment for what?" Ekaterina asks before either Morgan or I can deny the accusation.

"Nothing, just an experiment." I do not want to get Morgan into trouble and I absolutely do not trust the others not to run straight to Principal Turunen.

"Oh please." Aysha gives an extravagant eye roll.

"We looked up liekkiö, you know," Ekaterina adds. "We know it's some sort of ghost." Her voice wobbles a little, showing a crack in her hard exterior.

"You think you can trap this ghost?" Aysha's eyes are wider now and her face less pinched.

These girls are Natalie's friends, and even though they're awful to me, they are clearly concerned—same as me. Maybe not entirely the same as me. I bite my lip and look down, not sure how to answer. Morgan gets in first.

"We were planning to try," he says.

"You strong enough for that?" Ekaterina asks.

Morgan hesitates.

"Even with the elemental energy in these woods..." Aysha lays a hand on the nearest birch. "That's still a lot of magic for one person. Especially if you're doing a summoning as well."

"Who said anything about a summoning?" I ask.

"You going to just wait for this thing to show up?" Aysha looks unimpressed.

"They're too chicken to do a summoning," Ekaterina says.

"If you don't appreciate the danger in magic, you have no right meddling with it." Morgan tosses damp curls from his eyes.

"Oh bite me, O'Connor, you're not the only powerful conjurer in this school," Ekaterina all but snarls in response.

Electricity flickers along her fingers in white-blue sparks, sending a static charge rippling through the air. My insides contract with memories of pain, the scar on my arm burning. Morgan takes a protective step forward.

"Don't, Katya," Sini says. "Do you want to get expelled—or worse, end up in another of Taika's articles?"

Over the last year, I've written quite a bit about Ekaterina. She's an easy target what with constantly, if accidentally, damaging school property. It felt good seeing somebody else's shortcomings out there for everyone to laugh at, but I have to admit, it wasn't the kindest thing I could've done.

"Do you want to find out what happened to Natalie or not?" I ask and Ekaterina's sparks fizzle.

"Of course, we do," Sini says. "You really think this ghost, this liekkiö, will tell us what happened to Natalie?"

"Maybe." I shrug. "If we can catch it."

"Does it have to be a summoning?" She hooks a finger through the blue bracelet on her wrist.

"If you're too scared, we can do it by ourselves."

Beside me, Morgan clears his throat, and I will him not to disagree.

"You sure about that?" Aysha asks.

No, not at all.

"We could use some help." Morgan glances at me a little sheepishly, but I don't argue. Not when the practice containment left him unconscious.

The summoning and containment of the liekkiö would be even more difficult for Morgan to do alone. Like it or not, we need magical assistance.

"You could've just asked," Aysha says.

"You would've said no out of spite." I fold my arms and

suppress a shiver. It's getting colder out here.

"Whatever, when do we do this?" she asks.

I turn to Morgan. He's gone even paler, his freckles standing out like brown paint spatter across his nose and cheeks.

"Soon as we get a containment jar," he says. "Shouldn't be too hard. Aoife can probably sneak one out of class for us next week. Or…"

"Next week? That's too far away!" I say. "We have to get it sooner." A week? Is he joking?

"Guess we could steal one." A smile creeps across his face.

"Some of us could actually get expelled," Ekaterina adds.

"What about Friday night?" I remember the posters Mr. Fotsios and Emmi were pinning to the noticeboards.

"Kekri building?" Sini says. "It could work."

"You already know I'm in," Morgan says.

I glance around the rest of the group and gradually, they all nod.

"Friday then." Ekaterina jams her fists into her pockets.

"Just don't forget, we're doing this for Natalie," Aysha adds.

"Yeah, we're in this together now." Sini's glare is for Aysha, not me. "And we have Taika to thank for coming up with this plan."

Her words hit me like that first bite of ice cream, skewering my brain. Is she being nice to me?

"Fine." Aysha flicks her hair before she and the others stalk out of the woods.

I exhale the breath I've been holding, my shoulders shuddering with relief and more than a little confusion. Did that really just happen?

"Okay, I guess we're doing this then," Morgan says quietly.

"And with the worst people imaginable." I take my feelings out on the remains of the containment circle with my heel. "But hey, students seem to be disappearing so maybe one of them will be next."

"I know they can be asshats, but you shouldn't joke about stuff like that," Morgan says, and an unpleasant hollow yawns open inside my chest.

"We don't know what's going on," he adds. "Any of us could

be next."

11

The gym is way more crowded than I expected. Almost all of the boarders are here since it's compulsory for them, but a bunch of day students are too. I scan the crowd but of course Natalie isn't here, and neither are any of the others who're supposedly down with noro. All the students are busy, hands clumsily tying up bundles of twigs and kindling to add to the frame preconstructed by the twelfth-grade art students.

Not even half done, the Kekri buck already looks pretty impressive. With its stance and the enormous horns curled over its back, the buck looks like a mythical forest chimera rather than a wood-and-thatch art project. Too bad it's destined for destruction. Every year, we spend hours building the thing, only to watch it burn to nothing in a matter of minutes. I'm sure there's a metaphor in there somewhere.

Despite the crowd, the vibe isn't exactly festive. Students gather in their houses beneath their banners, all sporting house shirts.

Usually, the buck building includes house competitions. Last year, Fajro brought their dragon emblem to life in curls of blue-and-red flame. This year though, Emmi and other teachers decided the conservation of natural energy was more important than showing off conjuring skills.

So here I am. I've got the T-shirt too. It's not a bad design or a particularly vomitous shade of green, but I still hate the tree emblem of House Tero sitting above my heart. It's a lie, and everyone knows it.

"Nice to see you here." Emmi greets me with a too-big smile and a wave of twigs. Kalma the cat perches on her shoulder, eyes narrowed into golden slits. "I'll need to know your final decision about the trip before Monday."

Urgh! I'd completely forgotten about this awful camping expedition.

"I probably won't be going," I say.

"You've still got a few days to think about it."

"Is your arm okay after the bogling?" I ask.

"Just fine. Nothing but a scratch. Oh—Mr. Fotsios, we need to talk." Emmi hurries off to join the music teacher.

"Hey," Aoife says. "This spot taken?"

"All yours." I brush a pile of twigs out of the way so Aoife can plonk down beside me.

Aoife is in House Tero, not that she's ever talked to me before now. I glance over at the students in yellow and find Aysha getting cozy with Morgan. He must feel me staring. He looks over and his scowl smooths into an almost grin as he gives me a salute. Somehow, he manages to look punk rock despite the yellow school shirt, wearing it over a black long-sleeve tee with self-cut thumbholes in the cuffs.

"You doing okay?" Aoife asks.

I clear my throat, nervous in front of this older girl who radiates grace and power even while weaving twigs.

"Yeah, just worried about Natalie. Did you find Sorin?"

Aoife knots the string around her bundle and bites off the excess. "Yeah, I did."

So much for our theory about all the most magical kids going

AWOL.

"Was he okay?" And, as if my words are a summoning spell, a long shadow falls over us.

Sorin.

Unlike everyone else in House Aero, he isn't wearing his yellow house shirt. He doesn't seem the sort who'd ever wear yellow given his black-and-white attire. He shouldn't be in House Aero at all. Technically, vampires are shape-shifters and they all belong in House Aithyr along with shamans, 'mancers, and the like, but Myrskyjärvi doesn't offer those subjects. Too dangerous, apparently, and teetering too close to chaos magic.

It means the six shape-shifters at our school get lumped in with air elementalists and House Aithyr simply doesn't exist. Aithyr runes are still included in runelore textbooks, but no one really bothers with them since they're mostly useless, unless you can combine elements like Morgan.

"Didn't think you'd show," Aoife says, her words so sharp I wonder how they don't leave her lips bloody. Her hands tighten on the twigs, snapping them in half.

"Can we talk?" Sorin asks.

"Oh, so now you want to talk?"

"Please." Sorin's voice is low and resonant, like it's been biologically programmed with reverb.

I don't know much about the guy except he's one of the most gifted shape-shifters *in the world* thanks to his pure Strigoi blood. All the vampires—even the half-blooded ones—tend to be good-looking, and Sorin is no different, even if he tries to hide it under baggy sweats and messy hair. His eyes are so dark they're almost black, catching the light as if he's got tinsel where the rest of us have pupils.

Sorin offers his hand to Aoife. Slowly, she accepts.

"I'll be back soon," she says. "Keep my spot, okay?"

I nod, watching as the power couple stalk around the edge of the gym, Sorin steering a course away from the teachers who are busy making sure we don't stab each other with scissors.

Toivo detaches himself from the wall where he's been

standing at the back of House Fajro and follows. Weird. I mean, Kekri is one of the few school events Toivo doesn't consider beneath his participation, but what's with his sudden Sorin obsession? It's not like they've ever been anything close to friends.

"Guess he's not missing then," Morgan says. His sudden appearance makes me startle and earns me a few frowns from fellow green-clad Teroans.

"Guess not."

"Think it's a love triangle thing?"

"With my brother? Gross!"

"Sorin is really pretty, I mean, I get it." Morgan glances at me sideways.

It takes me a moment to catch what I think he's trying to tell me.

"You think he's pretty?" I ask gently, not entirely sure how to navigate these waters. The only person I've ever talked to about this stuff is Natalie and that went *fantastically*.

"Don't you?" Morgan shoots back.

"I guess, but I'd never want to date him, or any boy for that matter." Each word sounds more strained than the one before it.

Morgan doesn't respond straight away and for a moment I think I've shattered yet another friendship with a confession I should've kept to myself.

"I would. I mean, I think I'd be okay dating a boy or a girl or anyone actually," he says it so quietly I have to lean in close to hear him. His freckles disappear beneath the pink glow splotched across his cheeks and he swallows hard. "You're the first person I've told that to. Here at least. Back home, Kelly knows, but not even my parents do. Not yet."

"I won't tell anyone, promise." I pat his frayed knee in a gesture that is super awkward, but hopefully also reassuring.

"You're out, right?" he asks.

"Yeah. If I want people to use the correct pronouns, I have to be."

He picks up a bundle of twigs and I do the same. "Were your

parents cool with it?" he asks after a minute of silence.

"A bit unsure at first. Lesbian they could understand. Being nonbinary was a bit harder for them to get, but my parents were still pretty supportive. The pronouns only matter in English anyway, so it wasn't such a big deal. Not even with Toivo. He's a jerk, but never about that."

"That's good," he says, and then adds, "you're lucky."

I haven't really thought about it much, but he's right. I am lucky. I know there are kids like me who end up getting kicked out of home for being their true selves. It's hard to imagine what I would've done had my parents refused to see me as *they* instead of *she*. Maybe I should cut Mom and Dad a little more slack.

"You think your parents would react...differently?" I ask.

His fingers tighten around the bundle in his hand and a muscle ticks along his clenched jaw. "You could say that. They have really set ideas about who you should be as an O'Connor, and they don't like me not fitting that mold."

I'm about to say how much that sucks and ask if that's what he meant about not wanting to do magic when Sini & Co. show up.

"So, when are we going to make our move?" Aysha asks.

"There's a hot chocolate break at seven thirty," I say. "They're sending the Pebbles to bed after that."

"We could volunteer to walk Hannah and the others back and then sneak off," Morgan suggests.

"Sounds like a plan," Aysha says. "We'll be ready."

***

At seven twenty-six, Aleksi blows the whistle. Everyone tosses aside their bundles of twigs and stampedes toward the trolleys bearing thermoses of hot chocolate and platters of cookies.

Seventeen excruciating minutes later, Emmi finally announces it's time for the Pebbles to head to bed. We all volunteer to chaperone the younger students back to Kivitalo, and Emmi gives us encouraging nods as if this one group activity suddenly makes us BFFs.

Together, we usher the first to fifth graders out of the gym and down the first-floor corridor until we reach the doors leading outside.

Hannah clings to Morgan's hand, looking up at him with enormous eyes like a real-life anime character when he pauses at the doors. "Night, Hannah."

"You're not coming?" she asks, and guilt needles my gut.

"We're going to wait here and make sure there aren't any stragglers. You'll be fine," Morgan says. "You just follow Cludd. You'll be fine. Remember how you kicked that bogle's butt? Nothing out there can hurt you." He offers her his fist to bump, and she gives him a megawatt smile.

"That was easy," Aysha says as we peel away from the group and head for the stairs.

"The next part might not be," I say.

"Why are you even coming?" Ekaterina asks in a harsh whisper. "Not like you can do anything."

"Hey, this was Taika's idea," Morgan says. "So, unless you have a better one, they're in charge."

Once more I'm caught between feeling grateful Morgan doesn't see me as Taika the Talentless and ashamed that I've failed to stick up for myself yet again.

Shelving those feelings, I lead the way up the stairs to Joakim's classroom. It's dark, but the light from our phones is enough to stop us from tripping over each other. Before we go in, we pause to catch our breath and listen for sounds of being followed.

Hearing nothing except the moans and groans of the pipes in the walls, we slip inside. The phone flashlights turn all our faces into horror masks, but we need the light to navigate the clutter and don't dare turn on the main overhead ones.

Containment sigils, protection charms, wards for wood and glass, metal, ceramics, and even plastic are all daubed on pieces of paper and haphazardly stuck to the walls with no sense of order.

"I've never actually been in here," I say.

"Me neither," Sini adds.

"What a shambles." Aysha's nose puckers in disgust.

"If Joakim teaches the way he decorates it's no wonder bogles end up being summoned." Ekaterina is wearing her usual sour expression.

"Joakim is all right, if a bit disorganized," Morgan says. "Containment stuff is back here."

He moves toward a door marked Storeroom, except the only visible letters are *st* and *oo* courtesy of screeds of incantations printed and stapled to the door. Not even stuck, *stapled*. Can't help wondering if my mom knows Joakim is damaging school property.

Morgan closes the door behind us and flips on the storeroom lights.

"How on earth does he find anything in here?"

The storeroom is a disaster. Jars of various sizes teeter on lopsided shelves, inexplicably sharing space with homework assignments from two years ago, which have yet to be graded. Outdated textbooks lie back-to-back with current ones. There are even damaged books—some clearly singed by spells gone awry—nestled alongside several broken jars.

"Where do we even start?" Aysha's mouth hangs open as she surveys the mess.

"We start from the door and move along each shelf." My gaze slides from one hideously shambolic shelf to the next. My fingers itch to sort and straighten, but the last thing we need is Joakim knowing someone has been snooping.

"What's that up there?" Sini points to the topmost shelf.

"Bingo!" Morgan smiles, and I catch Aysha staring at him with a look I hope I never ever gave Natalie. It's so obvious she's into him.

"Glass would probably work best, and those jars look like they haven't been touched in years. Joakim won't notice one of those missing," he says.

Even from the floor, I can see a thick layer of dust coating the shelf, turning the clear jars grimy.

"Are they warded?" Ekaterina asks.

"Won't know till we touch one." Morgan takes advantage of his height, stretching his arm to full extension, but he doesn't quite manage to reach.

"Let me. Help me up," Aysha says, and Morgan obliges, letting her use his hands and then shoulders to clamber onto the shelving. She reaches the nearest jar and shakes her head.

"Good for jam, not for ghosts," she says, earning a chuckle from Morgan. I think I might be sick.

"Maybe the slightly bigger one then." I point to a jar two over from the one Aysha is holding.

She stretches even farther with Morgan holding her waist to keep her steady as she grapples along the shelf. The ominous sound of splintering wood heralds the shelf's collapse.

Morgan scrawls the *raido* air rune with a finger and exhales a string of words I don't understand. The six containment jars bob above my head, cushioned by Morgan's magic.

"Jeez, it's freezing." Sini shivers and rubs her arms vigorously.

"You should try to use less energy, be more conservative," Ekaterina's tone is fully chastising.

"That's rich coming from you," I say, rushing to catch the books sliding off the collapsed shelf while Morgan plays hero to Aysha's damsel in distress.

The book in my hands doesn't have a speck of dust on it, despite sliding out of a particularly cobwebby corner. The others prop up the shelf and return all but one of the jars to their former places. I'm still staring at the book.

"What is it?" Morgan asks while securing the jar in his backpack.

I blink. Words are impossible. This *book* is impossible.

"Is that...?" Sini swallows the rest of her sentence with a terrified gulp of air.

"It can't be." Ekaterina backs away, her fingers sparking with nervous energy. The last thing we need is Ekaterina starting another fire.

"Tai, drop it. You don't want to touch it." Morgan tugs on

my shoulder, pulling me away.

"I'm magic resistant, remember," I say. "And someone has to pick it up, otherwise Joakim will know we were here."

"Clever, hiding it behind all the jars," Aysha adds. "All the wards on the jars were masking its energy."

"It is what I think it is, right?" I scrutinize the symbol on the cover emblazoned in white.

"That's a chaos star," Morgan whispers.

He's right, but it's different from the chaos stars I've seen before—all jagged and messy. This one has eight points of equal length neatly arranged around a central circle.

"It's a book on chaos magic." He stifles a sneeze and rubs at his eyes, which are already turning red and puffy. Mascara and eyeliner smear down his cheeks.

"I'm not going near it." Sini wraps her arms around her chest.

"I didn't know the school had books like this." Ekaterina takes a curious step forward even though tiny bolts of lightning still flicker off her fingers.

Aysha grabs her arm and jerks her back. "Careful, Katya. Don't get too close."

"You seriously don't feel anything?" Morgan asks, and his words are wasps, driving their stingers into my skin.

"No, nothing at all. To me, it's just a book." I gather up the pile. There's no way I'm reaching the top shelf, even on my tiptoes.

"Here." Aysha drags over a broken chair from a shadowy corner, and I wince out a "Thanks" at her before climbing up and sliding the book back into its hiding place.

For a moment, curiosity gets the better of me. I crack open the cover to peek inside. There are notes in pencil in the margin and several Post-its covered in a sloppy cursive I know all too well.

Morgan sneezes violently behind me and my heart jackhammers against my ribs. Why on earth does Joakim have a book on chaos magic? And why is it full of notes in Toivo's handwriting?

"I'm sorry, I've got to get out of here," Morgan manages between sneezes.

"Come on, Taika," Aysha whines from below.

Quickly, I flip to the page marked Preface. Several words have been circled and underlined, words I don't really understand like *Tumultua* and *egregore*.

"Seriously, what the hell are you doing?" Ekaterina shouts from below. "We need to get out of here!"

They're right and Morgan is still sneezing. I slam the book shut and clamber down with Aysha's help.

Together, we rush out of the classroom and run down the stairs, taking two at a time. None of us see the two shapes slinking into the stairwell before it's too late.

The overhead lights flick on, dazzling all of us. I squint through the glare. Yup, we're screwed.

"Care to explain yourselves?" MacCrone stands dressed for battle as usual, except she's traded her signature camo pants for an all-black ensemble. Fiona stands beside her, forked tongue flicking between her teeth.

"We were...um...just getting more supplies for the buck building," Aysha says, and Ekaterina's sparks flare.

"Is that so?" MacCrone peers at us with her only good eye. When no one responds she chortles victoriously. "Right, you lot are coming with me then."

I cast quick glances at the others. Morgan grips the straps of his backpack and stares at the battle mage defiantly. It doesn't last long before he's racked by sneezes again.

Sini has a finger hooked under her bracelet, snapping relentlessly at her wrist, and Aysha has started humming faintly, her left hand gripping Ekaterina's right. One by one the tiny lightning bolts dancing along Ekaterina's fingers snuff out. She nods at Aysha, who releases her slowly.

"We were looking for supplies, honest," I say.

MacCrone stares at each of us in turn, her wizened lips twisted in disbelief. "Oh, I'll bet. Best you tell the truth right fast, or it'll be grounds for expulsion."

She's exaggerating, trying to scare us, and it's not like getting Sini & Co. kicked out is an unpleasant thought. If only Morgan wasn't standing right beside me, caught just as red-handed.

Sini tugs at the elastic band on her wrist, the sound of the snaps like firecrackers echoing down the quiet corridor. Aysha closes her hand over Sini's wrist and a tense silence falls over all of us.

"You've no business being up here tonight," MacCrone says.

"And you had no business snooping in my dad's office." The words are out of my mouth before I can catch them. Sini & Co. gape at me. Morgan grins through his sneeze-induced tears and gives me a thumbs-up.

"I'm pretty sure riffling through a high-ranking tietäjä's things would be grounds for dismissal." I have no idea if that's true or not, and I might've sounded more threatening if my voice didn't squeak up at the end of my sentence. Still, my words seem to have hit their target.

MacCrone's grin slides into a frown as she scratches at the welter of scar tissue on her cheek.

"Maybe if you were doing your job," Aysha starts. "Maybe we wouldn't have to go sneaking about trying to find out what happened to our friend. Natalie's missing, but I bet you knew that already."

"Missing, is it?" MacCrone says through gritted teeth.

"You know she is," I add. "You saw us at Pilvitalo. You know Natalie's not sick and she's not at school. Don't try to tell us she's in the infirmary."

"And she's not the only one, is she?" Morgan adds. "Do you know where Risto, Qendresa, and the others are?"

"You'll be getting yourselves mixed up in all sorts of business you know nothing about," she says, every word carefully measured.

"Like what exactly?" I glance at Sini, who looks as if she's trying not to vomit instead of taking mental notes for an article. What kind of journalist misses an opportunity like this?

"You three." MacCrone gestures to Sini & Co. "I won't report this matter as long as you head on back to where you belong this very instant. Do you understand?" She glares.

"We understand, Miss MacCrone," Sini says, the image of polite obedience.

"That's Sergeant MacCrone to you."

Sini gulps and snaps the bracelet again until Aysha grabs her hand, already tugging her toward the stairs.

MacCrone mutters a command in what I assume is Scottish Gaelic. The dragon seems to understand. Aysha mouths a "later" to us over her shoulder as Fiona shepherds the three of them down the stairs.

"As for you two..." MacCrone turns her attention back to us. "Are you all right?" she asks Morgan, who's mopping his face with his sleeve.

"Allergies," he says.

MacCrone purses her lips and draws a sigil in the air so quickly I don't have time to decipher it. With a puff of breath, she blows the sigil toward Morgan, and it hits him square in the face. He coughs a few times, then takes a deep breath. His swollen eyes stop running, although his face remains a mess of smeared makeup.

"Neat trick," he says. "I need to learn that one."

"There is much you need to learn." MacCrone straightens her shoulders and regards me with a steely eye. "Now, about your accusations."

"This whole norovirus is a big lie, isn't it?" I feel a whole lot more courageous standing next to Morgan.

MacCrone's gaze gets extra squinty, but she doesn't deny it.

"It's got nothing to do with you." MacCrone leans against the wall, so casual and unperturbed, I'm surprised she doesn't whip a machete off her utility belt and start paring her fingernails.

"You're supposed to be protecting us, but considering there's a bunch of kids who haven't been seen in days, it doesn't seem you're doing a very good job of it." Morgan goes for the jugular.

"And you were poking about in my dad's office," I add. "What were you looking for?"

"For Truth, child. You think I'd have a key to your father's office if he didn't want me in there? Kids these days, think they know everything. Do you even know why your dad was away?"

"Svalbard, of course, and whoever broke in got past six battle mages and managed to do a lot of damage. Not that they got what they wanted." My words seem to have a pretty big impact since MacCrone releases a long, low whistle.

"It's safe, then. Good on the Turunens," MacCrone says. "But six. Six is a lot. Six is too many." She seems to be rambling to herself. Her right hand traces the black ink running up her left arm, pushing up the sleeve of her black sweater. MacCrone doesn't have dragon scales on her arm, just tattoos, symbols like none I've ever seen before. Morgan stares, transfixed by the ink.

"What is it?" I ask. "Why will no one tell us what's going on!?"

"If students are going missing, we deserve to know the truth." Morgan sounds as frustrated as I feel.

"The truth?" MacCrone snaps from her reverie and rolls down her sleeve. "The truth is that whoever got past six battle mages is not to be trifled with by recalcitrant children—unless they want to end up as swamp gas."

I have no idea what *recalcitrant* means, but it sounds like an insult, one I'll be sure to look up later and add to my own verbal-weapon stash.

"Wait," I say once my brain has processed what MacCrone said. "Swamp gas. Like a liekkiö?" Maybe it's connected. It has to be. Why else would MacCrone bring up swamp gas?

"No idea what that is." MacCrone shifts from foot to foot.

"It's chaos magic, isn't it? Someone is practicing again—that's why no one wants to talk about it," Morgan says.

"Don't be daft," MacCrone says far too quickly.

"How else do you defeat a battle mage?"

"No one's dabbling about with any of *that*, little druid, and if anyone was, we'd know." She taps the device clipped to her utility belt.

"Is that a Zeiger counter?" There's a hint of awe in Morgan's voice.

"Designed by Arch Mage Zeiger, founder of the battle mages," I say. "They're used to trace chaotic energy."

"Oh, I know. Just never seen one before," he says.

"This is what I was looking for in your father's office, if you must know." MacCrone rests her hand on the magical multimeter. "Few of these left in the world. Not much for it to detect though. And *nothing* for it to detect here."

It makes sense for Dad to have one considering his job authenticating relics. Wouldn't want to accidentally put a chaos relic into a museum when the UCMW has issued an edict to destroy all such artifacts.

"You sure about that?" I ask.

"Yes," MacCrone says. "So put the matter clear out of your heads and return to doing whatever it is kids your age do best."

"Anarchy and rebellion." Morgan deadpans. "And you still haven't told us about Natalie or the others."

Concern creases MacCrone's wrinkled face and lingers a little too long before morphing back into her typical scowl. "Trust the grown-ups to handle this."

Morgan makes a derisive scoffing sound.

"Now off with you before I let Fiona eat your fingers."

The lizard has returned, surprisingly silent despite the length of her claws. She nudges my pockets and flicks a forked tongue at my empty hand.

"Off with you," MacCrone says. "Best we all forget about what happened this night."

I feel so close to uncovering the truth. "But, we—"

"Not another word unless you'd like to have this conversation with Principal Turunen," MacCrone directs her words at Morgan and points to the stairs.

"Please, just tell us. Natalie is my friend. I need to know if she's all right." Emotion turns my words into spiky sea urchins on my tongue. Maybe it's my tears or the way Morgan takes my hand and mutters a comforting "It'll be all right" that finally softens MacCrone's shriveled prune of a heart.

"Natalie will be fine. She's got the blood of fire giants in her veins. Them all's made of fierce magic and will be right as rain if you leave me to do my job."

Her words don't make me feel better, but they do confirm some of our suspicions. Unless the battle mage has had a drastic change in job description, I doubt she means emptying puke buckets and making chicken soup for sick kids.

Grudgingly, we head back to the gym where buck building is winding down amid a chorus of yawns.

"Well, that went to gingerbread," I say.

"Gingerbread, what?" Morgan looks at me quizzically.

"You don't say that in English? I mean, it didn't go the way we wanted it to."

"Didn't go as planned? You think?" He scrubs his hands over his face and tugs on his curls. "Think we should've mentioned Joakim's book?"

"It's better we didn't. Either MacCrone is telling the truth and there's no trace of chaotic energy, which means the book is harmless, or she lied about that, which means she's in on it."

"In on what?" Morgan asks.

"If only we knew, but what she said about Natalie and the others—at least now we know there's definitely something going on."

"I guess." He scissors his teeth across his bottom lip.

For a moment I consider not mentioning what I saw in the chaos book, but Morgan needs to know. "Also, I think my brother might be involved somehow."

Morgan raises his eyebrows and I hurriedly explain about the notes in the margins. "Don't tell the others," I add. "Not yet. Please."

Sini & Co. are heading toward us.

Morgan mimes zipping his lips. "But why would your brother be interested in that kind of magic?" he whispers. "Doesn't it go against everything a tietäjä stands for?"

"Yes, it does." I kick a pile of twigs, earning a disapproving look from a nearby teacher.

"That was scary," Sini says.

"At least we got the jar." Aysha flashes a grin at Morgan. "We're still going to do the summoning, right?"

"Tonight," I say. "Now."

"Now?" Sini sucks in a breath, looking all kinds of queasy again. "No, I can't. Not after MacCrone. Do you want us to get expelled?"

I give her a look that says *You really want me to answer that?*

"Then go back to Pilvitalo if you're too chicken." Ekaterina flings her words at Sini.

Part of me is grateful I'm not the only one in Ekaterina's crosshairs.

"Katya." Aysha turns the name into a reprimand. "If Sini doesn't want to do it, that's fine. I mean, it would be better if we had you with us, of course." She turns to Sini. "Because we need you and you're our friend and we're doing this for Natalie, right? She'd do the same for us, I'm sure. But if you don't want to, we'll understand."

"Oh fine!" Sini throws her hands in the air. "Fine, I'll do it."

"Let's go." I'm already on my way out, passing beneath the enormous blue-and-silver banner hanging above the doors.

A convoluted Hannunvaakuna embroidered in black thread adorns the center of it. I doubt the old symbol for luck and good fortune has any chance of protecting us from chaos magic. And the sigils on my windows certainly won't do much if the threat's already inside my own home.

Contrary to what many of the less magically inclined believe, summonings don't require a Ouija board, incense, or candles of any specific color. All it takes is someone willing to channel a ton of energy and then use that energy to form a bridge between the worlds. It's that magical bridge that whatever you're summoning will temporarily use to cross over. Emphasis on *temporarily*. Sounds simple enough—and it is, but being simple doesn't mean being safe.

Trying to pull anything permanently across the veil disrupts the natural order of things. Same as trying to bring someone dead back to life. That's chaos magic.

What we're doing is absolutely *not* chaos magic. Not even close. Not even if a liekkiö is technically a ghost.

Sure about that? The little voice pipes up as I lead the way through the forest.

Aysha illuminates our path, humming the sparks from Ekaterina's fingers into glowing orbs above our heads. The light is enough to navigate by, but hopefully not bright enough to draw any unwanted attention. At this time of night, no one should be hanging out in the woods anyway. I shudder, remembering the scream I heard the other afternoon. I take a surreptitious step closer to Morgan.

Musti, Rekku, and Kamu flit between the branches, croaking in disapproval.

Ekaterina plays with the pendant dangling around her neck. The metal glints in the flickering light above our heads, the emblem of her thunder-god ancestor Perun barely visible. It's as much a symbol of protection as it is a declaration of her genetics.

"Are the crows really necessary?" she asks and drops her hand when she catches me staring. "They creep me out."

"You have your pendant, I have the crows." It's not like I can do anything about the birds anyway.

"They're spelled by their mom," Sini adds.

"Your mom?" Morgan asks.

"You know how some people have familiars," Sini answers before I can. "In Finland, the tietäjät have *apueläimiä*—animal helpers."

"Our family has always had crows," I say as we approach the lake.

"Mine has salamanders," Sini says.

"Salamanders are cool." Morgan smiles, and I swallow the desire to point out how slimy and gross amphibians are and how much smarter crows are—Kamu not included.

"Urgh, we're going to get filthy." Aysha grimaces as she toes the soggy ground.

"Terrible things might be happening to Natalie, but it would be a real tragedy if your jeans got muddy," I snap.

Aysha glares at me as she drops onto her haunches. It's hardly my fault she's wearing white pants. The back pocket has a skull on it, stitched in black sequins.

"You sure you know what you're doing, druid?" Ekaterina crouches down, clearly less concerned about the mud showing on her all-black attire.

"If you don't want to be here, don't be." Morgan starts gouging the requisite runes into the ground with a stick.

Again, I help make sure the geometry is correct, eyeballing the angles. When that's done, I place the containment jar and the woolen threads in the center of our circle.

"Wait, are those... You think the liekkiö is Natalie?" Ekaterina asks, gazing wide-eyed at Aysha and Sini.

"Hope not." I don't want to think about Natalie being a ghost, about Natalie being anything other than absolutely fine. "But if it is, this might help."

"She's not—she can't be." Sini shakes her head.

"Hey, it'll be okay." Aysha pulls Sini into an awkward hug. "This is just in case, right?" She glares at me, and I nod.

"It certainly can't hurt," Morgan adds. "Helps to focus our energy, that's all."

And with that we take up our positions at the five terminal points, ready for what comes next.

"But like, you do know how to do a summoning, right?" Ekaterina asks, her brow furrowed with concern.

"I just need you to channel the energy. I'll direct it where it needs to go." Morgan takes off his fingerless mittens and rolls up his sleeves. It's the first time I've seen his tattoos. Matching Celtic knotwork in blue-black ink form thick bands around each wrist. It must've been so painful having those done.

The others peel off their gloves and I do the same.

"I'm scared," Sini says. "What if we summon something we're not supposed to?"

"I'll zap it." Ekaterina sends a bolt of lightning zipping into the ground.

This seemed like a good idea at first, an easy way to get information, but now I'm not so sure. What if Sini's right and we call up something worse than a bogle? What if *I'm* right and what we summon is the ghost of Natalie? I'm so not ready for Natalie to be...to be—

"Don't waste energy on the light," Morgan says, and Aysha

stops humming. The lights fizzle out, leaving us in sticky-thick darkness.

He closes his eyes and presses his hands into the wet earth beneath his knees, burying them up to the ink. The others hold their hands up as if they're cupping water; sparks dance wildly between Ekaterina's fingers.

Morgan begins the incantation and Aysha adds a quiet hum to the chant. I know the words of the summoning and lip sync along with Morgan.

The temperature drops as the spell takes effect. My breath steams in cumulus clouds and I blink frost from my eyelashes. The chant continues, punctuated by the creaking, groaning tress around us. Beneath my feet, the mud freezes and cracks. A branch drops, shattering into icy fragments on impact. It's too much, we're drawing too much energy from the forest!

Morgan's voice falters for a moment. He glances up at me, a cold-blue light in his eyes as he reaches for my hand. The tattoo on his wrist glows too, like bioluminescent plankton. His grip tightens, his mud-flecked fingers pressing so hard they're going to leave bruises.

My heart hammers against my ribs. This was a bad idea.

I hunch over, trying to catch my breath. It feels as if someone just punched me in the belly.

The sensation changes. Now it feels like I'm being dragged down into the earth. This isn't right. We shouldn't be doing this. The fear I squashed way down inside comes bubbling to the surface like a volcanic eruption. I'm trying, but I can't pry my hand away from Morgan's. His grip is iron, and my skin is burning under his touch.

Drawing energy from other people to work magic is controversial at best. Something actively discouraged because it's way too easy to get it wrong and draw too much. Draw too much and you can kill someone. But that's what Morgan's doing. Right now. To me.

The air is freezing, making my chattering teeth ache. I can't keep my eyes open despite panic raking every inch of my body. If I fall asleep now, I know I'll never wake up.

Green flashes in the corner of my vision. It takes monumental effort to turn my head. Mist swirls around Morgan, enveloping him from head to toe. Finally, his grip relaxes, his tattoos stop glowing, and I tug my hand free. I suck in a deep breath and the exhaustion sloughs off my skin like soap suds in the shower.

The mist flickers with ethereal fire. The voices emanating from the it grow louder, becoming shrieks and screams. I clap my hands over my ears, glancing around the circle. The others all have their eyes open, but they're blank, reflecting the green mist as if they're made of glass. In slow motion, like some creepy puppet, Morgan raises his hand and draws the *ansuz* rune in the air, sending it toward the center of the circle with a puff of breath.

The mist trickles into the containment jar. Maybe it's working.

I peel my hands away from my ears.

Silence.

Nervousness scuttles under my skin like a swarm of beetles.

Musti, Rekku, and Kamu squawk and reel above us, beating their wings at the mist but unable to cross into the circle.

The jar cracks, the sound like a gunshot.

Morgan's eyes roll up white and he topples sideways. Like dominoes, the others follow, leaving me alone in the clearing as the mist coils closer.

*R*un! Every stitch in the fiber of my being screams at me to make an escape, but I'm paralyzed, frozen—literally—where I sit.

Besides, I can't leave Morgan or the others passed out in the darkness without any way to defend themselves. I scrabble through the dirt in search of a weapon, anything I can use to fend off the mist. Cool, a pebble. As if that'll do any damage to a mist demon from beyond the veil.

Slowly, the smudges of green coil together to form arms and legs, and a halo of hair puffs around a featureless face. Then it speaks, and this time it's not a scream.

"That wasn't very smart," it says in Natalie's voice. "You're lucky I got here before something else did."

"Is it really you?"

"It is."

"Prove it," I say, all stuttery.

"I ruined your Kekri dress with a fire spell, which was actually pretty awesome," she says. "And—last winter, you kissed me."

Her words whip the breath out of my lungs. Tears freeze salt tracks down my cheeks.

Sorry, I'm sorry, I'm so so sorry—it's what I should've said when I ruined our friendship. But an apology isn't what comes out of my mouth now either.

"It's really you," I manage to squeak.

"Unfortunately for me," Natalie whispers.

The realization hits me like I just stubbed my toe, the pain intense and mincing up my insides. If Natalie is a liekkiö, we're too late. She's already dead.

"Are you—still alive?" I ask so quietly I'm not sure even a ghost can hear me.

"I think so," she says. "But we're fading. Faster and faster." The green tendrils billow, the emerald turning the sickly yellow of an old bruise before brightening again.

Maybe there's hope then. Maybe we can still save her.

"You said we?" I knew it!

"There are others."

"Risto? Qendresa?"

"Yes. Peter, Elijah, Manami and—" Natalie's voice fades in and out between static, like a badly tuned radio station.

It's just as we thought. This whole norovirus thing is a gigantic cover-up for the most magical kids going missing, and none of the adults seem to be doing a flipping thing about it!

"Where are you? What happened? When—I mean, how— and why? And—" My brain fires off questions faster than my tongue can form them.

"I don't know," Natalie says. "I got jumped from behind. I never saw their face. They had tattoos on their arms though. I tried to burn them, but only burned their clothes. They were too powerful."

Tattoos? MacCrone has tattoos.

So does Morgan, the little voice supplies.

And so do several other students and teachers, most of that ink serving magical purposes if not aesthetic ones.

"Were you taken from school?" I manage to wrangle the deluge of words assaulting my mind into something more coherent.

"I don't remember. My memories are fading. I'm fading. You have to help us. You have to hurry. We don't have much time before—before..." The ribbons of green shiver and Natalie's body expands. Her edges soften and lose focus.

"We need to know where you are."

"I don't know!" The tendrils of mist snap like dancing cobras. "I was blindfolded. I think we hiked through a forest. Not for long though. It was cold and there was snow on the ground. It got in my takkies." She uses the South African word for sneakers. "Then they made me touch some stones."

"What stones?"

"Two big, one smaller, all piled on top of each other. Like this." Natalie's right arm swirls into a formation I've seen before. A *tonttukivi*, literally elf stone. There are at least a dozen of them, dotted all over Finland.

"That could be anywhere."

"You have to hurry." The mist turns milky, already dissipating.

"Natalie?" I step forward as if I can grab her and keep her here in the realm of the living.

"I can't stay much longer," she says.

"Why me?" I ask through the tears clotting my eyelashes with rime.

"There was darkness. Just darkness." Her voice echoes around the circle. "Then there was light, and that light was you. Please, Taika. Help us."

"I will. I promise," I say. "You have to hold on."

"We'll try, but time is running out. By—" Natalie starts to say something else, but whatever power has been keeping the crows at bay evaporates. Musti, Rekku, and Kamu fling themselves at the mist, talons and beaks shredding the tendrils.

"No, wait! Natalie, please. Come back!" I wave at the crows, trying to drive them away. But it's too late. The damage is done and the liekkiö is gone.

Darkness settles over the clearing and the forest falls silent.

"Natalie! We need to know more. Come back!" I slump to the ground, fresh tears spilling acid trails down my face.

"Hello? Anyone there?" Sini squeaks from the other side of the circle.

"Yeah, I'm here." I wipe my eyes and sniff back snot.

"Did it work?" Sini asks.

I only manage to nod.

"Hold on, let's get some light." Aysha sounds groggy. "Come on, Katya. Wake up. There you go."

"Urgh, I feel gross," Ekaterina says. "Give me a sec."

Thirty-three seconds later, lightning arcs from Ekaterina's fingers and Aysha hums them into twinkling lights again, dimmer than before but enough to see each other's faces by.

Morgan is still slumped to the side, eyes closed, body unmoving.

"No, no, no." I rush to his side and start shaking his shoulders.

The others gather close, expressions all reflecting the same fear.

"Is he dead?" Ekaterina asks, and Sini stifles a sob.

"Come on, wake up. Please."

His hands are freezing, and I take them between my own, rubbing them as if that'll somehow jump-start his heart. My fingers brush the tattoos on his wrists, and I feel a jolt through my hands, like the static shocks you get in winter, only this is bone deep and a lot more painful.

Morgan blinks awake and struggles to sit up. He draws his knees to his chest with a groan and rests his face in his hands.

"Are you okay?" I ask.

"Remind me not to do that ever again." He tugs at the curls escaped from his beanie, then looks up at me, his eyes no longer glowing with magic. "Really. I came so close to crossing the line." He shakes his head and straightens up a bit. "I'm sorry, Tai. I shouldn't have done that. Did it even work?"

"I spoke to the liekkiö. I spoke to Natalie."

Sini doesn't manage to stifle the sob this time as she crumples into Aysha's arms.

"But she's alive, right?" Ekaterina grips the pendant around her neck again.

"For now. She's running out of time though. The others too. I think I know where she was taken." I tell them everything Natalie said—minus the bit about the kiss. I fold up that memory and tuck it into a pocket for later contemplation.

"How come you're the only one who heard or saw anything?" Ekaterina asks. "You don't even have magic."

"Which is why they were the only one not passed out," Morgan says. "Are we really going to argue about this when we could be coming up with a plan to help?"

"We should tell our parents," Sini says. "They'll know what to do."

"Like mine would even care." Ekaterina's voice is all metal spikes and snarl.

"I already tried talking to my mom," I say. "It did not go well."

"But we summoned a liekkiö. The school has to believe us now," Aysha says. "Especially if Morgan's the one who tells them."

"You overestimate how much teachers like me," he says.

"The tietäjät will help. They have to!" Sini says. "We'll just tell them—"

"What, exactly?" Ekaterina interjects. "'Hey, Mrs. Turunen, I broke every rule doing this summoning spell and chatted to a liekkiö of my nearly dead friend.' How do you think she'll deal with that? I know we don't all share the feeling, but I, for one, like being at this school. I do not want to get expelled, thanks."

Ekaterina's right. There's no way we can tell my mom about the spell, not without getting everyone into serious trouble.

"Besides," Aysha says, "we don't know who took Natalie—or why—or who else might be involved."

"Not my mom," I say.

"Not the tietäjät," Sini adds. "A tietäjä would never hurt anyone. This is the work of a chaos mage."

"Oh please. They don't exist anymore except in stories to scare little kids." Ekaterina rolls her eyes so hard I'm amazed they stay in her head.

"Tell that to the six battle mages defeated at the Svalbard vault." My words leave the others in stunned silence.

Aysha's lights flicker as she blinks. "That can't be true."

"My dad was investigating it. And you saw that book in Joakim's room."

"If chaos mages can take down battle mages, then what good is a tietäjä anyway?" Ekaterina's fingers spark blue and white where she clutches her pendant.

"Better than just us, that's for sure," Sini says.

Morgan remains quiet, rubbing at his wrists. It's hard to tell in the dim light, but the skin around his tattoos looks red and raw.

"Fine," Aysha says. "Taika, talk to your mom if you can without telling her about all this, and see if you can find out which stones Natalie was taken to. We'll see what we can find out about MacCrone and the other teachers with tattoos."

"Students too," Ekaterina adds, giving Morgan a weird look.

"Meet us at Pilvitalo tomorrow after breakfast," Aysha says.

I do not like the way Aysha is taking charge. It was better when only Morgan and I were doing the investigating. Whether I like it or not though, we're going to need all the help we can get if we want to save Natalie and the others.

"We need to be careful," Morgan says.

"Obviously, druid." Ekaterina sneers as she gets to her feet and dusts off her jeans.

"These are ruined!" Aysha fingers the dark splotches across her butt.

"Oh, dear gods," Sini says, the snap of her bracelet

accompanying every word. She points up to where Aysha's orbs illuminate the trees.

I suck in a breath and Morgan visibly pales.

"Did we do this?" Aysha asks.

"I did." Morgan jams his hands into his pockets, his shoulders hunched, and mouth corkscrewed in a grimace.

I turn in a circle, surveying the damage our spell has caused. All around the clearing, the trees are gnarled, and any remaining leaves have turned black. It's dead and we killed it. The ground beneath our feet is littered with branches that crumble to ash at the gentlest nudge of a toe.

"I drew too much and killed the whole damn forest." Morgan looks like he might be sick.

"Hardly," Aysha says. "You killed a few pines."

"Birch, actually." I seriously can't stop myself.

"It's not the end of the world." Aysha glares at me.

Maybe not the end of the world, but there are so few pockets of magic left in nature, we absolutely should've been more careful. Using magic has consequences. It's a fact I've known but never understood until now, faced with the dead trees and the ash of the glade coating my shoes.

"We should get back before they realize we're missing," Ekaterina says.

Aysha picks up the shards of the containment jar as well as the threads, closing her fist around them. "We have to save her."

"We will," I say, my conviction struggling against the churn of doubt in my belly.

I stumble through my front door at nine forty-two p.m. and attempt to slip into the house unnoticed.

"Where have you been?" Toivo slumps on the couch, his arms folded over a cushion as he flips through the TV channels, not paying much attention to the screen.

"With friends."

"Didn't think you had any of those," he says with casual venom.

This time I don't let it get to me and head instead to the kitchen. My whole body feels like a giant icicle and the spell has left me light-headed. Tea and cookies will help and give me a minute to think about how to talk to Mom about all this. Or maybe Dad. Dad is usually easier to deal with.

"There you are, we were starting to get worried." Mom sails into the kitchen.

"Sorry," I mumble while making tea.

"What on earth is all this?" Mom gestures to the mud and ash I've tracked from the door.

I ditched my dirty boots and jacket, but my jeans are coated in the stuff and shedding spell detritus all over the tiles.

"We were in the forest," I say carefully. "I saw the liekkiö again. I—I spoke to it."

Toivo grunts his derision from the couch but switches off the TV.

"Taika, I thought we talked about this." Mom looks exhausted.

"Hardly, and this is important. I really need you to listen."

Mom looks at me and I take her silence as a cue to continue.

"The liekkiö—it's Natalie. I spoke to her, and she told me someone attacked her. They blindfolded her and took her to a tonttukivi, but I don't know where and they're running out of time, all of them and—and—" I'm hyperventilating, my whole body shaking as the reality of what I'm saying hits home with the ferocity of a sledgehammer.

I can't stop imagining it all. Images play out like a horror movie in my mind. Natalie must've been terrified! What would I do if it were me? Would I fight back? Would I freeze? In my head I can hear Natalie screaming, tearing at her attackers, unable to fight them off.

"Calm down." Mom grips my shoulders, her hold firm and reassuring. "Breathe, Taika. There we go, another deep breath. Good. Now tell me—how exactly did you manage to commune with this liekkiö?" Her eyes narrow as if she already knows.

If I tell her, the others are going to be in massive amounts of trouble.

"Yeah, how exactly did you manage to *talk* to a liekkiö?" Toivo strides into the kitchen. "No way you could've pulled that off alone."

I want to punch him right in his smug mouth.

Mom cocks her head at me the way a hawk sizes up a mouse. "Please tell me you didn't do something foolish."

"All I did is prove Natalie isn't dead yet." I shake free of

Mom's hands. "She's still alive and we can save her, but we have to hurry."

"Taika, please. I need to know exactly what you did," Mom says. "Whatever it is, you can trust me." Her voice has gone all sugary the way it does when she's trying to soften up a student, to get them to admit they plagiarized or performed a spell they shouldn't have. Her tricks won't work on me.

"Like trusting you to secure the vault?" Toivo says. "Like trusting you to keep the Sampo safe?"

Sampo? Is that what the chaos mage is after?

"It is safe." Mom glares, her jaw clenched tight enough for a muscle to twitch near her ear before she rifles through cupboards in search of her own mug and tea bag.

"It's safe"—MacCrone's words echo in my head, bashing at my brain like hammers. Was the Sampo the "it" the old battle mage was talking about too? Does that mean the break-in at Svalbard is connected to what happened to Natalie?

Mom slams the mug onto the counter, making me jump. She's annoyed but she should be shocked. I just told her Natalie appeared to me as a liekkiö and said she was kidnapped. Why isn't Mom freaking out? It's almost as if...

"Wait, you knew?" Anger burns through my veins. "When I came to you the other day, you already knew, didn't you? You've known this whole time the norovirus thing was just some ridiculous cover-up. You knew Natalie and the others were missing. You knew they were being kidnapped and didn't do a thing to stop it?"

"Taika, enough," Mom says softly, and I do, zipping my lips, hoping she'll say more.

The silence lasts all of twenty-three agonizing seconds before I can't contain myself anymore. "Well?" I fold my arms, mirroring Mom's scowl.

Mom sighs and massages her temples. "Yes, we realized something untoward was happening, but we didn't want to create a panic."

"Untoward?" Toivo laughs, the sound as bitter as black

coffee. "Bit of an understatement, don't you think?"

"I don't have to justify my decisions to you," Mom says as Dad stomps down the stairs. There are bags under his eyes and his hair is all messy.

"Adults think they know everything," Toivo says.

"Don't take that tone with me, young man." Mom brandishes her mug.

Toivo and Mom have had arguments before—serious ones inevitably resulting in slammed doors and Toivo doing all my chores for the next few weeks—but this is different. It feels as if a storm is brewing above our heads. I do not want to be caught up in the war that's about to break loose.

"Leave it be, son," Dad says.

"Students are going missing. Risto hasn't been at school for over a week, and you won't even admit what's happening." Toivo's face is turning beet red with rage.

"Why is this happening?" I ask in the sudden silence filling up the kitchen.

"It's complicated." Mom shares a worried look with Dad.

"Then explain it to me."

"Careful, whatever you say might end up in the *Messenger*," Toivo says. "Or is Cludd saving space for Sini?"

"I really, truly hate you, you know that?" I glare at him, but the fire in my veins has been doused with ice water as my brain struggles to connect the dots. The break-in at Svalbard. Chaos mages. The most magical kids kidnapped and taken to a tonttukivi. "Toivo, that was unnecessary," Dad says. "But your brother's right. We certainly don't need a school-wide panic. I don't want to see a word about any of this in the *Messenger*. Is that understood?"

"But if students are being kidnapped, maybe we should be panicking," I say.

"You cannot possibly comprehend the gravity of this situation." Concern has etched deep furrows at the corners of Mom's eyes and mouth.

"I would if you explained it, but you treat me like a little kid.

Like I don't even exist."

"This isn't about you," Toivo says.

"You're right. It's about Natalie. She asked *me* to help her. Why won't you believe me?"

"Right, because you're a budding necromancer," Toivo says. "Who helped you? Was it that O'Connor kid?"

"Leave him out of it."

"Taika the Talentless—"

Whatever Toivo was about to say gets vaporized as Mom explodes.

"Enough!" Mom detonates and turns on Toivo. "Go to your room this minute."

For a moment I think he might argue, but even he knows when to back down. Silently, he trudges out of the kitchen.

"Please, Mom—"

"You too." Her glare leaves me singed. "To your room. Not another word."

I swallow my protests and slink out of the kitchen, padding slowly up the stairs. Toivo is waiting for me on the landing.

"Whatever you and that O'Connor kid are up to, best you stop," he says. It's not anger in his voice this time, it's fear. "Seriously, I don't think you realize how dangerous this all is."

"At least I know better than to mess around with chaos magic," I snap back.

Toivo reels away from me as if I slapped him. "What did you say?"

"You heard me." Maybe I said too much, but it feels good to see him being the one to flinch for a change. Except, I should be careful. For all I know, Toivo could be involved. He might not have tattoos, but that doesn't mean whoever attacked Natalie didn't have help from others.

"Is the break-in on Svalbard connected to Natalie?" I ask instead. "Whoever broke in wanted the Sampo, right? But they didn't get it—so they started kidnapping kids?" Saying it out loud doesn't make it sound any more logical than when it was all jumbled together in my head. "Come on, you have to tell me."

"Perkele, you need to drop this." Toivo runs a hand over his buzz cut.

That's his tell. Before he shaved his head, he was a compulsive hair-tugger. Now he only ever scratches at his scalp when things are starting to get to him. He's rubbing his head so hard right now, he might actually leave a bald spot. That, combined with the irritation on his face, lets me know I'm on to something.

"If you don't fill me in, I'll tell Mom and Dad what you've been up to." I'm precariously close to pushing the big red button that'll make my brother go nuclear, but I really need to know.

"You have no idea about anything." The frown on his face makes him look an awful lot like our mother.

"I only want to help Natalie," I say. "What's your excuse?"

"There's nothing *you* can do for her."

He's right, you're useless, pathetic, worthless, the voice tells me as if I don't already know it.

"I hope you're next," I fire back. Remorse instantly knifes through my belly, but I'm not apologizing.

"You know, I just might be." He jerks open his door.

The hallway light illuminates a sliver of his bedroom, and my eyes go wide at the dozens of sigils scrawled across the walls—sigils like the ones I glimpsed in the book on chaos magic.

"You should be grateful," he continues. "For once, your lack of magic might actually be a good thing." With that, he slams the door in my face.

All things considered, it could be worse. Being grounded sucks and is absolutely not fair at all. The worst part isn't being housebound all weekend, it's that Dad switched off the Wi-Fi and confiscated our phones.

Toivo argued and had his laptop taken too, so when Dad asked, I handed over my phone and didn't say a word. This way at least I still have access to my downloaded playlists. I've been playing the one called *Bad Day* on repeat, turning up the volume on all the tracks by the Knock-Knock Jokes until it feels like Morgan's drumsticks are battering my brain.

What sucks the most is not being able to message Morgan and explain why I can't make it to Pilvitalo as agreed. Instead, I pour all my energy into studying the assortment of books I've got stashed under my bed and trying not to think about Natalie or the attempted kiss that messed up everything.

Half of the books I'm not even supposed to have as a ninth

grader. Not that any of them have proven particularly helpful yet. None of the tomes on runelore contain anything close to what I glimpsed on Toivo's wall. Makes sense. Chaos runes wouldn't be in an eleventh-grade textbook.

So far, this is what I do know:

1. Chaos magic is entirely rune-based, using sigils that combine elemental runes (like what Morgan can do—I try not to think too hard about that connection).

2. Chaos magic is usually represented by a chaos star, a sigil of sorts with eight jagged points of differing lengths pointing in all different directions, but it's entirely useless without knowing any of the base runes.

I wonder why the chaos star on Joakim's book looked so different. Anyway...

3. Chaos magic has been used by sects or cults all over the world. In Finland, the most infamous of these is called the Order of Louhi. The Order's emblem is a stylized chaos star with flame-like wings. The Order supposedly ceased to exist after the wars. But what if it just went dormant instead?

4. Louhi is a superpowerful witch-queen and the alleged daughter of Death itself, with all kinds of magical powers—like being able to shape-shift into the massive Kokko eagle with fire for wings. She has a serious obsession with the Sampo, which led to her having major beef with the legendary Väinämöinen.

5. The Sampo is the most powerful artifact in Finland—actually, in the whole world! No one can agree on precisely what the Sampo is. It seems to appear as different things to different people based on what they want to use it for. It's been described as a tree, a coin, a treasure chest, a compass, an astrolabe—which was something used in the olden days to navigate by the stars—or a quern. I have no idea how a quern works, but apparently it can grind gold out of thin air. And that's one of the Sampo's less impressive qualities. All sources say it's super powerful, super dangerous, and a good thing no one knows where it is.

6. So, a great tietäjä, Mervi the Magnificent, used to be the

official custodian of the Sampo and is allegedly responsible for its mysterious disappearance. Also, Mervi the Magnificent was Mervi *Turunen* before she earned the epithet, making her my great-great-great-something-grandmother. According to some sources, she's a descendant of Väinämöinen, which I guess makes *me* his descendant too!

I'm not so sure about being related to the most epic hero of heroes. Being related to a possibly incompetent mage who misplaced a magical relic—now that is something I can believe.

Althought there's not much about the Sampo's disappearance, I guess it somehow eventually ended up in Svalbard—at least that's what Mom and Dad clearly believe. Perhaps the custodial duty was passed down through the generations to my parents. The book doesn't say anything about that, or give an official list of artifacts hidden in the vault. There are mentions of things like the Holy Grail, the Book of Thoth, and the Cintāmani Stone, but it doesn't seem anyone has published an actual inventory. I guess no one wants the wrong people to know for sure what relics the vault contains, especially not if there are chaos mages running around again.

As for *Tumultua* or that word *egregore* I saw in the book in Joakim's room, I'll have to wait until I have an Internet connection again to find the answers.

At some point in the morning, Mom pads down the hallway, her Reinos chuffing across the floorboards. I'm grateful the scruffy old slippers always announce her presence even if they're a fashion offense. She pauses a moment outside my door. I brace myself for a sweeping entrance and another lecture. But, after a minute, my mom's steps recede, and I release the breath I've been holding.

Back to my list:

7. A tonttukivi, or the so-called elf stone, consists of a pile of rocks used to mark the locations of wells of elemental energy, sacred sites reserved as powerful resources not to be used except under the most extreme circumstances. Also, they're allegedly doorways to the space between worlds. How the logistics of this might work is vague at best.

So why would anyone take Natalie, or any of the others, to a bunch of elf stones? Sure, magic has been growing weaker in the world and these might mark the last remaining sources of pure energy, but I just don't get the connection—especially not how the kidnappings are connected with some rogue mage hunting down the Sampo. I'm missing something.

Frustrated, I shove aside the textbook and rub my eyes as if I can massage my brain through my eye sockets and fit the puzzle pieces together.

Natalie. Her face fills the blank canvas behind my eyes. I replay what she said to me in the clearing.

"And—last winter, you kissed me."

Thing is, when I play it over, she doesn't sound angry or annoyed about it. I've tried to bleach the moment from my brain, but now I riffle through my mind in search of the memory.

It was right after I came out—we were sitting here on my floor. She leaned in close to give me a hug and our faces were so close, already almost touching. It was so easy to close the gap between us. For a moment it felt right, and her arms tightened around me, but then she pulled away and pressed her fingers to her lips and shook her head as she mumbled something about needing to leave. That's the last we ever spoke about it, or at all.

A week later, she went away for the winter break, and when she came back to school, it was clear we weren't friends anymore.

The knock on my door makes me jump and I quickly shove the books under my bed with fingers I've accidentally chewed bloody, before calling out "Come in." Dad brings me a cup of tea and a *korvapuusti*. Warily, I accept the cinnamon bun peace offering. I shift over so Dad can join me on the floor.

"Something new?" He points to my speakers. The Knock-Knock Jokes are playing again.

"That's Morgan O'Connor on the drums. Did you know he was in a band back in Ireland?"

"I'm not surprised," Dad says with a hint of a smile. "They're not half bad, actually. Reminds me of the Offspring." He bops his head along to the beat for a bit while I sip my tea, remembering the photos I've seen of Dad as a teenager. He had a bright-blue Mohawk when he met my mom, while Mom sported Chucks and chokers.

Now Dad's hair is gray and rebelling against Mom's attempts to keep it sensibly trimmed, and there are hard lines cutting down his cheeks from a lifetime of smiling.

I'd ask what's wrong, but tea and a pastry aren't going to make up for the fact he took away my phone and Internet for asking questions he doesn't want to answer.

"I'm sorry," Dad says, and I almost choke on my tea. "Sometimes we don't treat you fairly."

Understatement of the freaking year!

"I only wanted to know what's going on," I say. "I'm worried about Natalie."

"I know." He scratches at the untidy tufts of his thinning hair. "It's hard to talk about this for us adults, especially as parents," he says, and I sit up straighter to show him I'm listening. "We're meant to protect children. As teachers and tietäjät, we're especially meant to protect the children at this school, and we failed. That's why it's so important to us to keep the rest of you safe." He clears his throat before continuing. "Your mom feels personally responsible for a lot of this."

"I'm pretty sure Mom didn't kidnap Natalie."

Did she? The little voice adds at the back of my mind.

Dad winces. "No, but children going missing from your mom's school doesn't make her look good. It hurts her reputation and reflects badly on all of us."

"Is this all about hurting Mom then?" I ask. Why? How?

"Your Mom is involved in making decisions that upset quite a few people," Dad says. "Not everyone agrees magic should be so controlled in this world. Some believe people should be free to practice magic as they wish. And the number of people who believe that is growing."

I haven't paid that much attention to UCMW politics considering it'll never be my concern, but I remember reading some articles last year about an opposition faction led by...Caitlin O'Connor.

Morgan's mom!

"So is all of this—the vault break-in and the kidnappings—is this all to show Mom they can do what they want? Is what happened in Svalbard connected to Natalie being taken?" My palms are starting to sweat. "Is it all political?"

"Everything is always political." Dad takes a deep breath and steals a sip of my tea before continuing. "There are powerful objects in that vault that some might wish to use for their own purposes." He's clearly choosing his words carefully and not telling me anything I don't already know.

"Like the Sampo?" I watch Dad's face. His frown deepens, cutting canyons across his forehead.

"Yes, like the Sampo."

"I know about Mervi the Magnificent. I know she was supposed to keep it safe. Is that want Toivo meant? Are the Turunens custodians of the Sampo?"

"You don't need to worry about any of this."

"Because I don't have magic?" Saying it hurts worse than the hot tea scalding my lips. "I'm still a Turunen."

Taika the Talentless, the little voice sings. It doesn't have the same ring to it as Mervi the Magnificent, that's for sure.

"Perhaps one day you'll come to appreciate who you are," Dad says. "For now, leave these matters to us. Please. We don't need any more stress."

I nod because obedience is expected, and I do not want him to walk out with my laptop as well. But there's something niggling at the back of my mind, something I've been too afraid to ask in case it's true.

"Dad?" I start, my voice all quivery like I could burst into tears at any moment. "Do you think the reason I don't have magic... Do you think it's because—could it be because I'm not really a girl or a boy?" I struggle to get the words out.

"Oh Taika, no." Dad pulls me into a hug. "Absolutely not. Magic has never cared about that. There have been trans and gender-nonconforming mages throughout history."

I'm stunned. My mouth is literally hanging open as I stare at my dad.

"You think because I'm old I don't know what these words mean?" He tousles my hair. "No, Taika. You being you has nothing to do with the vagaries of inherited magic, I promise you that."

I'm not sure if I feel better or worse now. At least if it was because of me being *they* instead of *she*, I'd have a reason. The reason would suck big-time but at least I'd know the why.

"Don't worry about it, kulta. We'll figure this all out." Dad places a hand on my back and rubs circles that are anything but comforting. "But given all that's happened, perhaps it's best we don't let your mom see these." Dad reaches under the bed and pulls out four of the five contraband books.

"Dad—"

"We appreciate your concern. But your mom and others are working nonstop to figure this all out," he says. "We don't want to have to worry about you too. Do you understand?"

"I understand," I bite out through gritted teeth.

"Good. Now do your homework and read something more appropriate." He waves at my bookshelf chockablock with novels about brave teenagers defying their parents to save the world. He leaves, taking all my research material with him.

I wait for the sound of Dad's steps to retreat down the stairs before I tiptoe into the hallway. He and Toivo are in the kitchen, and judging by the sound of slamming crockery, they're clearly having a lovely chat.

With Mom out doing who knows what, now's my chance to find out what Toivo is hiding. My pulse thunders in my ears as I hurry into his bedroom. He hasn't bothered to lock the door this time and I leave it slightly ajar behind me so I can hear him coming.

I haven't been in here in over a year because, hygiene. It's still gross, except instead of posters of video games and celebrity mages, his walls are covered in runes and sigils and other symbols I don't know. There's barely a spare inch of blank space between all the printouts and drawings.

Above his desk are a dozen different World trees—a symbol often associated with the Sampo. The trees are surrounded by intricate runes—or maybe sigils—I've never seen before. They have to be related to chaos magic otherwise I'd definitely recognize them. Toivo always talks about how he's going to become a tietäjä, how he's destined for greatness. It makes no sense for him to dabble in chaos magic and yet all this seems to tell a very different story.

I shiver. Being in here is giving me a serious case of the creeps.

Still, I kick aside a pile of BO-soaked clothes before ducking down to peer under the bed. Dirty socks, an old tennis ball, a pair of hockey skates with rusting blades, and a homemade contraption that could be a Zeiger counter. I fish it out, careful not to get contaminated by the filthy clothes. Is this what he's hiding?

Finding nothing more under the bed, I wheel his desk chair over to the bookshelf and wobble my way onto it to search the shelves. There, nestled between dust bunnies and several dog-eared paperbacks, lies the book I saw in Joakim's classroom.

Carefully, I pick it up, half expecting to get vaporized by chaos magic but, once again, being magic resistant comes in handy. Toivo is pretty brave to bring this book home. If Mom or Dad find him with it—but the thought burns away as another sparks into being.

What if Mom and Dad already know? They've been hiding so much from me. I don't want to believe they'd be encouraging my brother's exploration of forbidden magic, but I honestly don't know if I can trust any of them anymore. Not even Dad, considering how well he just managed to avoid answering any of my questions.

If I'm going to get the truth, I'll have to find it myself. And the only people I'm willing to trust right now are definitely not in this house.

The middle stair creaks and I'm out of time. I scramble off the chair and duck out of Toivo's room, only just making it into my own before Toivo stomps along the hallway and slams his door shut.

I shove the stolen book along with the remaining textbook into my backpack before rummaging in my cupboard for my old boots. It's only a matter of time before Toivo figures out the book is missing, and I do not want to be around for that.

Boots on, I shrug into my spare coat and tug on a beanie and mittens before heading to the window. I turn up the music, hoping it'll cover any telltale sounds of my escape. I pause, regarding the oak tree outside my window where my crows are perched, looking sleepy and unconcerned among the last of the autumn leaves. Those branches better be strong enough to hold me.

With trembling fingers, I pry open the window, step onto the sill, and grab the nearest branch.

17

I run to Pilvitalo, pausing to catch my breath and smooth down my hair before tapping in the access code and stepping into the foyer.

It's so quiet. On the weekends, the boarders who don't go home are usually out and about doing various activities involving social interaction. I've never participated for obvious reasons.

Muted voices drift from the common room at the east end of the ground floor, accompanied by short-lived screams and the percussive blasts of apocalyptic explosions happening on the TV. I race up the stairs to the second floor.

I search the names on the doors, systematically working my way up and down the corridor. Morgan's name is done graffiti-style with colored chalk on a blackboard fixed above the number on his door. The *a* in his name is the same spiky anarchy symbol he has patched on his jacket.

I knock.

No answer.

I knock again, harder this time.

Still no answer.

Maybe he's sleeping or out on his skateboard somewhere or downstairs in the cafeteria, but what if...what if—the thought drills holes through my mind.

What if he's been taken like Natalie? the helpful little voice pipes up.

No. I refuse to believe it. Instead, I march up the stairs to the floor occupied by House Tero, hurrying from door to door, searching for Aoife's name. When I find it, I bang hard with my fist.

A bleary-eyed Aoife answers. "Taika. Did you get our messages?"

"No, I've been grounded. My dad took my phone." I look past Aoife to where Morgan lies on the bed clutching a pillow to his chest. Waves of relief crash over me seeing him alive and right here. He turns to face me, eyes red-rimmed, devoid of their usual makeup.

"What's wrong?" I ask.

"It's Hannah." He sits up, still clutching the pillow. "No one's seen her since last night. We can't find her anywhere."

His words land like concrete blocks inside my chest, crushing the air from my lungs.

"When did you realize she was missing?" I sit beside him, resisting the urge to gnaw on my fingernails.

"We went over to Kivitalo for breakfast, like we do every weekend," he says. "Hannah wasn't there."

"Her friends were really confused when they realized she wasn't with them," Aoife continues. "We searched the whole building. Not a trace of her."

"What's weird," Morgan says, "is that no one can remember seeing her after the Kekri buck building."

"She must've been taken on the walk back," Aoife says, and Morgan clenches his jaw.

"That means it has to be someone at school, right?" A bubble of guilt pops inside me. "People would've noticed a stranger lurking about."

"Maybe, maybe not. The path to Kivitalo isn't all that well lit," Aoife says.

"Have you told anyone yet?" I ask.

"Morgan told me all about your escapades in the forest." Aoife glares at me. "I've already given him a lecture about how irresponsible that was. How dangerous and reckless—"

"Aoife, stop. It won't help us find Hannah." Morgan sighs, and white-knuckles the pillow.

"Well, after hearing about all that, when you didn't show this morning, we weren't sure what to think," Aoife says. "We've been trying to decide what to do and who we can trust."

"You're right, I'm sorry." I nibble at the cuticle of my thumb. "We were reckless, but we had to do something, and at least now we have some clues. Does Joakim have any tattoos?" I should be asking if Morgan has heard from Sini & Co. but I don't want to rely on them any more than absolutely necessary.

"You really think Joakim could do this? He can barely tie his own shoes," Morgan says.

"If that were true, he wouldn't be a teacher at this school." Aoife flicks her bangs out of her eyes. "He might be disorder personified, but he's a powerful tietäjä."

"And he did have that book," I add.

"Yeah, Morgan told me about that too. You really have been making some poor decisions of late." Aoife scowls at both of us and the gulf of our three-year age gap yawns wide between us. "I'm just not sure if accusing Joakim is a great idea," she continues. "Not without solid proof."

"I have proof." I rummage in my backpack and haul out the book I took from Toivo's room.

"Holy cow, it's real. Where did you get it?" Aoife backs away.

"My brother's room. He's involved somehow, I just don't know how or why yet."

"Does he know you took the book?" Morgan asks then buries his face in the crook of his elbow to sneeze.

It was the same the last time he was near the book, and just like when we were in Natalie's room. The gears in my mind begin to turn, and finally pins fall into place.

"He might by now. Hey, you obviously checked Hannah's room, right?" I ask and Morgan nods. "Did you start sneezing in there too?"

"Yeah." His eyes are streaming and swelling up as if he's been stung by bees.

"O'Connors can be sensitive to certain kinds of magic." Aoife passes Morgan a box of Kleenex. "I've never seen it this bad before."

"Do you think you could be allergic to chaos magic?" I ask.

"But that would mean someone used chaos magic in Natalie's and Hannah's rooms."

"I bet you'd be sneezing your head off in Qendresa's, Risto's, and the others' rooms too," I say. "Wait. You had the same reaction to MacCrone. And she caught us coming out of Natalie's room." I shove the book back into my backpack and leave it by the door, as far away from Morgan as possible. It seems to help a little.

"You think MacCrone is using chaos magic?" Morgan asks. "But she's a battle mage!"

"It fits. Natalie said the person who took her had tattoos."

"Whoever it is, seems like they're collecting elementalists," Aoife says. "Natalie is a fire mage. Qendresa and Peter are air, Risto and Elijah are earth, Manami and now Hannah are water. They might go after another fire wielder next."

That means Toivo could *actually* be next—if he isn't in on it somehow.

"But why? What are they trying to achieve?" I ask.

We sit in silence for a bit, each of us racking our brains.

"Natalie said they were running out of time... Students have only been going missing in the last week or so though, so why now? What's with the timing?" Morgan asks. "There's no syzygy we're forgetting or some other magical date coming up is there?"

We all look at each other, blink, then speak at once.

"Samhain," the O'Connors say at the same time I say, "Kekri."

"Of course." Aoife slaps her palm to her forehead. "Dammit, I should've realized. And this year, the moon will be almost full. In planetary geometry, we learned…" She trails off and bites her trembling bottom lip. "Whatever it is this person wants with Hannah and the others, it'll all be over by the end of the month. Janey Mack, that's so soon." Aoife presses her knuckles against her teeth.

A little over a week. Kekri marks a time when the veil is thinnest, when it's easier for spirits and energetic forces to cross between worlds. When all magic, particularly chaos magic, is strongest.

"What do you think they're trying to do?" I ask.

"If I knew that, do you think I'd be standing here?" Aoife snaps. "Sorry. It's just, it's Hannah." Her voice cracks and she tilts her head back as she blinks away tears.

Morgan immediately pulls her into a hug, and they cling to each other for what feels like forever while I look on feeling utterly helpless.

Utterly useless, utterly worthless, the voice chimes in so very reassuringly.

Aoife pulls away first and dabs her eyes. "Okay, let me have that book."

"Why?"

"Because it's dangerous and not doing Morgan any good, and because I'm going to talk to Toivo about this."

"I don't think that's a good idea." I do not want to be on the receiving end of my brother's wrath when he finds out I went snooping in his bedroom.

"I won't go alone." Aoife pulls out her phone and starts tapping at the screen.

"Sorin?" Morgan asks, and Aoife nods without looking up. "Sure you can trust him?"

"I think so," Aoife says. "Can I take your backpack? I don't want to touch the book if I can help it."

Before handing it over, I pull out the folklore textbook. Aoife's phone beeps as she shoulders my backpack.

"Okay, he's meeting me downstairs. Wait here, I'll call when

I've got something."

"We can help too," Morgan says.

"Oh no, you two have done quite enough already. Stay here and stay out of trouble, got it?"

Morgan glares but doesn't argue as Aoife ruffles his hair then leaves the room.

We sit in tense silence, listening to the sound of Aoife's fading footsteps. The swelling around Morgan's eyes goes down a bit and he stops sneezing.

"It's my fault Hannah is missing," he says. "I should've walked her back to Kivitalo."

"It's not your fault." I want to hug him, but I'm not sure he'd appreciate it. "It's *our* fault," I say instead, even though the admission blisters my tongue. "Which is why we are absolutely not going to just sit here."

"Oh, I have no intention of doing nothing." He pops his knuckles.

"First of all, students need to know what's happening. It won't take long to draft a couple of paragraphs about the missing students, and Hannah. If you want. Or not, of course."

"You can write about Hannah. I want everyone to know what's happening, but we shouldn't publish it in the *Messenger*."

"Now you sound like my mom," I say.

"I just think we need the students to know without tipping off the teachers. Any of them could be involved, right?" he says. "So we post it somewhere only students will read it." He fishes his phone out of his jeans. "Here." He opens up some gaming-related forum I've never seen before. "Enough students are on here that they'll get the word out."

"What if there are students involved?"

Morgan chews on his bottom lip. "Guess we'll have to risk it. Start typing. Characters are limited so you'll have to summarize." He hands the phone to me. The cursor blinks at the start of a blank post, waiting for my words. "Just say enough to let students know about the danger, not to walk alone anywhere, watch out for their friends, that sort of thing."

"You sure you don't want to write it?"

"You're the journalist," he says.

I start typing, and nine minutes and three seconds later, I get Morgan to proofread what I've written then hit post.

"Now what?" Morgan asks.

"Now we come up with a plan," I say. "Because I think I know how we can find Natalie and your sister."

"Here's the map." I flatten the page so Morgan can see. We're sitting cross-legged on the floor of Aoife's room, both leaning forward to look at the page. The drawing isn't the best, but it's all we have to show us the location of each tonttukivi.

"Joakim has talked about *liminal* realms before," Morgan says once I've given him a crash course on the stones. "We've got portals like this back home too, usually marked by a cairn as well." He taps the map.

The image is recognizably Finland, the dotted borders cutting the country into wonky pizza slices showing areas of magical energy. There are a lot more areas up north in Lapland. The south only has four divisions, with a tonttukivi in the middle of each of them.

"We're here." I point at the tiny dot of Myrskyjärvi almost one hundred kilometers outside of Helsinki. The closest tonttukivi is seventy kilometers to the west. Natalie said there was snow on the ground.

"Hey, can you look up the weather for the last couple of weeks?" I ask. "We're looking for snow."

Morgan taps at his phone and pulls up archived weather reports. Two tonttukivi sites have had recent snow.

"This is the closest." A spot in the middle of nowhere northeast of us. "We should go."

"Think we'll find Hannah there, just like that?" Morgan asks, so horribly hopeful.

I don't want to be the one to crush his hope, but honestly, this is a long shot. "It's the best lead we've got."

"Why take students to these things at all?" he asks.

"That's what I've been trying to figure out. I think it's connected to the break-in on Svalbard. Seems they were after this Finnish relic called the Sampo."

"I've heard of that. Supposed to be super powerful," Morgan says.

"Exactly, and it's somehow connected with making my mom look bad, politically I mean."

Morgan looks away and silence blooms like mold in the space between us. I give myself a mental kick for mentioning it, but now that I've gone and dumped a load of awkwardness between us, I better deal with it.

"I know your mom and my mom have their issues—" I take a deep breath. "But whatever they've got going on doesn't matter right now."

"Agreed" He smiles, and relief douses me like cool lake water after a midsummer sauna. "I don't care if our parents have beef, you're my friend."

For once I'm lost for words while "friend" plays on repeat between my ears.

"Go team." He raises his fist for me to bump and I do. "Okay, so back to the stones and kidnapped kids." He frowns, getting serious again. "What do you think this chaos mage wants with Hannah and the others?"

My brain is gripped by a sudden and terrible thought. I want to ignore it, but it sinks its claws into my mind, making it impossible to shake off.

"What did you do last night, when you took my hand?" I try not to make it sound too much like an interrogation.

"Oh, that..." Morgan tugs at a stray curl and glances at me out of the corner of his eye. "Yeah, we should probably talk about that." He takes a moment and I give him the time he needs. "I'm not supposed to use another person's energy. It can be dangerous."

I keep quiet, giving him space to find the words.

"Using energy like that feels good." Morgan doesn't look up from the book where he's dog-earing the corner of the page. "It feels so damn good, like—I don't know—like landing a flip-kick or your first sip of coffee in the morning. But you can hurt someone if you're not careful. I mean, really hurt them." His gaze snaps up to meet mine. "You can kill someone like that," he says. "I could've killed you."

"But you didn't." I suck in a steadying breath.

"Doesn't make it okay."

"I don't have magic though, so why use me at all?" I regret it instantly when he winces at my careless words.

"Your regular, human energy is plenty. Tapping into someone's magical energy would be..."

"Chaos magic?"

We regard each other for a tense and painful moment.

"Exactly," he says. "Which is why no mage is supposed to take another person's energy. Except"—he hesitates—"except, my family is a little different. Using energy like that hurts us too." He holds his wrists.

"Let me see."

Slowly, he extends his hands toward me, and I push up his sleeve on the right then the left. The skin around his tattoos is blistered and scabbed as if he's been burned.

"Ouch."

"At least it means we can borrow a person's energy without having to worry about going too far. The more we use from another person, the more it hurts us. I could've been charred to the bone. It happened to my uncle once."

"That sounds awful."

"Magic always has its price." He pulls his hands away and gingerly rolls his sleeves over his injured wrists.

"Don't you need a bandage?" *Or antibiotics or a doctor?*

"Better to feel it. I need the reminder that the rush isn't worth the consequence." There's something hard and bleak in the look he gives me, and I know there's no point in arguing.

"So, what if that's what's happening?" I ask. "What if someone is—"

"Siphoning magic out of kids?" Morgan's lips curl in disgust.

"Siphoning?"

"Like when you suck on a straw."

"Oh. Great." Now I can't stop imagining Natalie and Hannah being consumed like magical milkshakes.

"Someone must want a lot of power then," Morgan says. "But for what?"

"It must have something to do with Svalbard. But there's something I'm not seeing." I tap a fist against my forehead, as if it'll help. "Definitely a dog buried here."

"What?" Morgan asks.

"You don't say that? Like when something is suspicious?"

"We say something's fishy."

I make a mental note. Clearly, I need to up my game when it comes to English idioms. "Either way, we have to go to the tonttukivi."

Morgan's jaw twitches like he's chewing over something he doesn't want to say.

"What is it?" I ask.

"It's just...this is pretty dangerous, and you seem ready to take this risk for a friend. I mean, I'd die for my sister but the way you want to take on the world for Natalie, it's—it's a lot to do for a friend." There's a knowing look on his face even with the questioning lift of his eyebrow.

I sigh. "Natalie is more than a friend. Well, to me at least. I've had a crush on her since the day we met in fourth grade, but I ruined things."

"How?"

"I tried to kiss her and messed everything up," I blurt out before I can think better of it. It feels good to finally tell someone. "I thought she'd want to kiss me back, but I guess I got it wrong."

"That sucks," Morgan says. "Did she punch you?"

"No, she walked out of my room and basically didn't speak to me again."

"Lucky. I got punched for trying to kiss my crush." He dabs at his lip as if he's still feeling the hit. "Guess I misread the situation." He shrugs.

"I'm sorry. You didn't deserve that."

"And you didn't deserve the silent treatment."

If that's what I got. When I force myself to think about it—something I've been actively avoiding since it happened—I think it might've been me who went silent first. I was embarrassed, ashamed even. I couldn't bear to face Natalie after that, let alone talk to her. Oh gods, what if I *did* destroy our friendship, just not the way I thought I did?

"We should tell the others about the stones," Morgan says, changing the topic and already reaching for his phone.

He's right, but I don't have to like it.

***

The others rock up a few minutes later. Aysha looks like she stepped off the cover of *Teen Vogue*, immaculately dressed in another designer outfit made that little bit edgy with silver buckles and studs.

Ekaterina arrives bleary-eyed in jeans and a black hoodie featuring a violently jagged word I assume is the name of a band who does more screaming than singing.

"Where's Sini?" I ask.

"Horse riding," Ekaterina answers. "She'll only be back this evening. It's a whole day thing," she adds, as if she can't understand why anyone would get up early on the weekend and head outside with smelly animals.

Quickly, I fill them in about everything. Aysha immediately gives Morgan a hug and unexpected jealousy licks like flames at me when I see him hug her back. It's not like I'm into Morgan, but I don't want him to like her more than me, which of course he will.

Because there's nothing to like about you, the little voice says.

Whatever. Right now, my feelings don't matter half as much as finding Natalie and Hannah.

Ekaterina perches backward on Aoife's desk chair and combs her fingers through her dark-red hair. "This just gets better and better." She presses the heels of her hands against her eyes.

"Did you find out anything about MacCrone?" I ask.

"Some of us needed sleep after that summoning spell. Channeling that much magic is like running a marathon," Ekaterina snaps. "Not that you would know."

"Katya, really." Aysha tsks from where she sits beside Morgan, the pale denim of her knee rubbing against the tattered rift of his. "More like doing too much high-intensity interval training, so yeah, we're tired and no, we haven't found out anything we didn't already know," she continues. "As for other teachers or students with tattoos, we made a list of the ones we know." She pulls a piece of paper out of her pocket, the list written in her perfect cursive.

"That's a lot of names," I say.

"And who knows how many more are keeping their ink hidden. I didn't know about yours until yesterday," Ekaterina says to Morgan with something like respect.

"Yes well, what do we do now?" Aysha asks.

"We go to the tonttukivi," I say. "Are you coming with us?"

"I know I'd feel better going to these stones if we had some backup," Morgan adds, and I grit my teeth.

He means *magical* backup. A hollowness opens up inside me as the jerk inside my head yells *Taika the Talentless, Taika the Useless.* I'm not enough. I'll never be enough.

Aysha glances at Ekaterina, who looks less than enthusiastic about the idea.

"It might not be a great idea for all of us to go," Aysha says. "What if something happens? No one will know where we are or where to look. Maybe it's better if we stay here. We can keep trying to find out more about MacCrone. We'll stay connected of course." She holds up her phone.

Good. Let them chicken out.

"Maybe you're right," Morgan says.

Aysha gives him an angelic smile and Ekaterina exhales in what I think might be relief.

"There's a bus in an hour." I stand up, ready to be anywhere but here. "We'll check in regularly. If you don't hear from us, then we're in trouble."

"Can you find my sister and let her know?" Morgan asks, and Aysha nods.

"And my mom, if you haven't heard from us after two hours," I add.

"Your mom. Are you sure?" Aysha's manicured brows lift.

"No, but I'd rather be in trouble with her than with a chaos mage."

"Got a point." Aysha nods. "And a deal."

They watch while Morgan and I get ready. We pack light, taking only a flashlight, the folklore book with the map, water bottles, a bag of trail mix from Morgan's personal stash, and two bananas from Aoife's.

"Be careful," Aysha says as Morgan shoulders his backpack.

"Ready?" he asks, and I nod, not able to speak around the lump of doubt and worry lodged in my throat.

"Let's do this," he says.

We can do this. For Natalie, for Hannah. We *will* do this!

The scenery sweeps by in a monotonous blur of forest and lakes and fields. Most of the trees have lost their leaves, all the bright reds and golds turning a dull brown like the whole world has a sepia filter over it. At least it isn't raining.

Morgan sits with the book on his lap, reading, while I'm doing my best not to puke thanks to motion sickness.

"Peikko," Morgan says, going through the list of magical creatures native to Finland.

"Troll or goblin." Not that these things always translate very well.

"Mörkö?" His accent adds a dozen extra *r*'s to it.

"Like a bogeyman, a bogle even."

"Keijukaiset?" Morgan has to say it twice before I understand.

"Oh, those are like fairies. Cousins to your Tuatha Dé Danann."

"Hiisi?"

"That one is more complicated, but it's a forest creature. Sort of."

"*Mennin*—okay, I give up with this one." Morgan's Finnish pronunciation isn't great but it's awesome how hard he tries.

"Hey, you ever heard of Tumultua or egregore?" I keep my voice low. The bus is hardly full, but I'd rather not risk anyone overhearing us.

"Egregore. Isn't that an old Enochian thing?" Morgan types the word into his phone and pulls up the definition. "Oh damn." His brow furrows as he starts reading. "'An autonomous psychic entity. A manifested thought form that can influence the collective minds of a group.'"

"Um..."

"Like the Easter Bunny or bogeyman, except in the magical context it implies an ability to take something from the spirit realm and make it corporeal."

"Corporeal? Like a corpse?" I ask.

"More like—fleshy, or something physical. Give it a body." He jiggles his arm.

"Okay, so definitely a chaos magic thing." My nausea gets a little worse. "What about Tumultua?"

Morgan starts typing again. "Not a lot of results, and this comes from a site called the Secrets of Kaos, which they've spelled with a *k*," he says, incredulous. "Might not be the most reliable source, but apparently there's a league of chaos mages called the Order of Louhi— that would make a sick band name."

"Order of Louhi?" I barely get the words out.

"Yeah, apparently the leader was someone called Tumultua." He shows me his screen and the familiar symbol of the chaos star with fiery wings. "Says here she's been held in some sort of secret prison for years."

"Sounds like nonsense." Except it really doesn't.

I don't want to believe an entire group of chaos mages could be practicing forbidden magic given the tight restrictions imposed by the UCMW, but six battle mages were defeated at Svalbard, and someone is using chaos magic at school.

Fear turns my body into a giant castanet, my teeth actually clacking together as I shudder. What chance do two ninth graders stand against a chaos mage let alone an entire league of them? Oh gods, what were we thinking?

"This is a little scary, isn't it?" I say out loud.

"Yeah, it is." Morgan's more serious than I've ever seen him. "But at least we have each other." He cracks a grin. "Just think, this could be the story of your career."

"If we survive."

"We will." He bumps my shoulder. "Gotta stay positive."

"If we do, you could write a song about it."

His smile vanishes and he leans his head back, closing his eyes. "Don't think I'll be writing songs ever again."

"Why not?"

"It's not in the Big Plan," he says, making me think the concept deserves capital letters.

"Whose plan?"

"My parents'. The one they have for me definitely does not involve drums or music."

"Is that what you meant the other day when you said you don't want to do magic?" I try to make my words gentle.

He doesn't answer right away, turning to look out the window and tracing a smudge of grime with his finger before looking back at me.

"Sometimes I envy you, you know," he says. "Sometimes I wish I didn't have any magic at all."

His words make me go numb.

"Then maybe I could do what I wanted to with my life instead of what my parents and my heritage say I have to." He all but spits the last part, clearly bitter.

I don't know what to say to that. I can't even begin to relate. Gods, if only we could swap. What I wouldn't give to have the smallest smidgen of his power. I would gladly trade my unmagical life for his any day, even if that came with the baggage of an inherited destiny. I doubt that's what he wants to hear.

"Sorry, I know that probably makes me sound like an ungrateful jerk." He slides lower in the bus seat, hands stuffed in jacket pockets. "Because I really don't have a crappy life I should be complaining about."

Neither do I, but I think I get what he's trying to say and what's making him feel this way.

"I don't think it's having magic that's the problem," I say, thinking over every word before laying it down. "I think it's about not having a choice. You didn't choose to be a powerful elementalist. You didn't ask for the responsibility that comes with that. Same as me, only the complete opposite, of course. It's the lack of choice that makes me angry. And sad, sometimes."

"Aren't we a pair?" He offers me a brittle smile and I return it as we bump fists.

He naps after that, leaving me alone with my thoughts. It's the first time I've thought about what having no magical path laid out for me really means. I can choose to do anything with my life. Of course, it's the thing I can't have that's what I want. But maybe I'm wrong. Maybe an unmagical life could be a happy one.

After what feels like half of forever, the bus pulls over at a rickety wooden lean-to on the side of a narrow road. It's the official bus stop for Kuusikylä, even if it only sees a bus twice a day. We'll worry about getting home to Myrskyjärvi later.

The bus pulls away and disappears down the lonely road. It's getting dark, and without streetlights, the darkness seems thicker, hanging in gooey curtains between the trees flanking the road. In the west, a sliver of clear sky has spilled purple and orange across the horizon, splotching the ragged clouds with bruises.

"I think it's this way." Morgan holds his phone while I hold the book, comparing the two maps.

He's right. We start walking as twilight closes around us.

After fifty-two minutes, we pause.

"Wow, look at the stars." Morgan looks up and I crane my head back too.

The wind has swept the sky clear, leaving a brilliant smattering of stars as our only source of natural light above the leafless branches. The skinny moon doesn't provide much in terms of illumination. It's also much colder. Clear nights always are. I pull up my hood before shoving the book away and arming myself with the flashlight instead. Morgan continues to wield his phone.

The bare birch branches above us are lined in silver and there, surprisingly, are my crows. Rekku, Musti, and even Kamu. Somehow, they've managed to keep up with the bus and follow me all the way out here. We plunge deeper into the forest. Usually, I don't mind forests because—usually—they're a place of comfort.

Sure, there might be wolves or bears in the woods, but I'd rather deal with a bear than ninety percent of my schoolmates. They aren't the bloodthirsty predators so many stories make them out to be—the bears and wolves, I mean. And yet, out here, my fingers tremble and my bones feel spongy. I can't help wonder if a chaos mage is lurking in the shadows.

"I feel something." Morgan comes to an abrupt halt, leaves squelching beneath his feet. "It's... I don't know. There's something here. This way." He shoves his phone into his pocket and takes off, leaving me to play catch-up through a scraggly copse of birch.

Am I imagining it, or do I feel something too, something more than the prickle of unease from being alone in the dark?

"Shouldn't we keep following the river?" I ask. It's not a river so much as a narrow ribbon of black snaking through the trees.

"No, it's this way. Come on." His words come out in puffs of steam.

I don't argue despite my legs burning with the effort of walking up the hill. I shiver even though I'm sweating; I'm definitely feeling something, like a breath on the back of my neck, but there's no one behind me and my hood is up.

"Hey, slow down," I call out when Morgan disappears over the rise.

"I've found it!" he yells back. "Hurry up, you have to see this."

I force my legs up the steepest part of the slope, annoyed by their shortness, and finally stumble into a glade. And there, right smack in the middle of it, stands the tonttukivi.

My crows *crawk* in warning as they flap a hasty circuit around the stones. Their wings shimmer purple. The flickering light turning the glade blue isn't coming from my flashlight—it's coming from the stones.

A spherical boulder perches on top of a large, rectangular one all gray and brown and boring. It looks like any other bit of stone found in a Finnish forest, except for the fact it's glowing.

Morgan drops to his knees, not seeming to mind the cold and wet seeping through the holes in his jeans. He holds up a bare hand as if he's warming his fingers on an open fire.

"Can you feel it?" he asks, his eyes wide and glassy.

All I can feel are tired legs, my cheeks numbed by the cold, and sweat making swamps of my armpits—wait...and something else too, like there's someone else in the glade with us.

"It's coming from the stones."

Whatever I'm feeling isn't just coming from the tonttukivi. It's in the air and under my skin. I crouch beside him and hold out a hand to the stones. My palm itches.

"I have to concentrate really hard," he says. "It comes and goes. It's pretty weak, actually."

The itch in my palm certainly isn't. I must be developing an allergy to moss or lichen.

The light dims and the stones stop glowing. Seven seconds pass before they flicker on again.

"Hardly any energy left now, but it still feels so good." Morgan peels off his mittens and buries his hands in the fallen leaves up to the tattoos.

"Are your palms itchy?" I ask.

"No, it's nothing like that." After a moment, he frowns and pulls his hands back. "I've only ever felt this kind of energy once before, back home in Ireland. We have a few sacred druid sites, really ancient monuments, like Newgrange, where the energy gets like this at certain times of the year." Tentatively, he brushes his fingertips against the base of the tonttukivi.

"Should you be doing that?" I ask, worried by the glazed look in Morgan's eyes as he presses both hands to the stone.

The blue light instantly glows brighter, igniting beneath his hands and traveling up his fingers in shimmering tendrils. His tattoos light up too, with a sizzle I can only hope isn't the result of burning skin.

Freezing wind whips through the grove, throwing ice crystals into my face in a violent swirl. "What are you doing?"

"Oh, I'm not—it's the stones, they're..." Morgan doesn't finish his sentence. The light flows out of him, back into the stones, and he topples over before I can catch him.

"Morgan?" I shake his shoulder. His wrists are bleeding, spattering red across the frosted ground. "Oh gods, Morgan! Please, wake up!" I shake him harder. Nothing. With trembling fingers, I check his pulse and let out a breath in relief. Just unconscious. He's fine.

Are you sure? The little voice pipes up. *What if he doesn't wake up? What if he ends up like Natalie? It'll be all your fault.*

"Shut up!" I yell out loud and bury my face in my hands. This was my idea. I know it'll be my fault if something bad happens to Morgan—if it hasn't already. It was ridiculous to think we'd find all the answers laid out this easily. I hate myself for even thinking it, but if Aysha and Ekaterina had come along we wouldn't be in this mess. Can I drag Morgan back to the bus stop? I tug on his legs, hoping I can move him.

Light splashes out of the stones again, no longer an eerie blue but a buttery yellow, like sunshine.

I'm dreaming. I have to be.

I dig my nail into my palm and bite my inner cheek until I taste copper. Nope. Definitely not a dream. What I'm seeing has to be real. The tonttukivi is still there, but the stones are shimmering like a watermark, translucent where—right in the middle of the nighttime glade—a stone archway now stands. The itching in my hands intensifies as I step over Morgan and through the rippling portal, staring down a leaf-strewn pathway leading into summer woodland.

The sunshine thaws my skin. The breeze ruffles my hair and carries with it the songs of summer birds. The path looks so inviting, the woodland so friendly and safe, it makes me extra wary.

Everything I've ever read about portals to other worlds always includes a warning about getting trapped by mischievous, magical creatures. Or worse.

Is this where Natalie went? Did the mage open a doorway to this liminal realm, as Morgan called it? What if Hannah is lost in a woodland like this one, waiting for someone to find her? I look over at Morgan, but my mind's made up.

For such a skinny guy, he's surprisingly heavy, and I struggle to haul his body across the threshold. I can't leave him lying in the cold. He'd get hypothermia and then we'd really have a problem. I do, however, leave his left foot in the real world just in case stepping completely into the woodland closes the portal, trapping us in the summer forest forever.

"I'll be back," I tell Morgan, hoping he can hear me. "I promise. I'll be back soon." I repeat it until I believe it, then dust off my knees and take a few steps down the path.

My crows squawk at the threshold, their wings beating at some invisible boundary. They land in a huff of feathers around Morgan's foot. They can't follow me. Interesting, and disconcerting. I'm truly on my own here.

No turning back now though, not when Natalie could be nearby. I leave my crows screeching and follow the path through a forest of birch and pine, oak and ash, and even elm. Blueberry and red currant bushes crowd the edges of the path, tempting me with promises of sweetness. Absolutely no way I'll eat anything in a magical realm. I know better.

The path ends at a wall of spruce, the undergrowth tangled into knots not even someone my size can crawl through. The overwhelming smell of *pihka* hits my nose. The tree sap makes the whole woodland smell like a sauna at midsummer.

The briers move and I step back, expecting to see a rabbit dart out of the undergrowth. No rabbit. The bushes move again, wiggle as if...as if... I scramble back even farther. The wiggling bushes aren't bushes at all but a pair of large and thorny feet.

Now I really must be dreaming.

I drag my gaze up the trunks of two trees, which aren't trees so much as legs.

"Terve?" I offer a tentative greeting.

Branches rustle in response, as if they're laughing at me. I squint up into the shaggy green boughs. Clinging to the higher needles is a face with a beard of moss. If I turn my head even a little, the face disappears, and the spruces are simply trees again.

"Little one," a voice says, "are you lost?" This time I know for sure the voice, as gnarled as old bark, comes from the creature that's somehow also a tree.

Hiisi! Of course! Morgan mentioned it in the bus. I should've realized sooner. This hiisi doesn't sound friendly exactly, but they're not the sort of creatures known to snack on humans either, so I'm probably safe for now.

"I'm—I'm looking for my friend." I think it's best to be honest and direct. "Her name is Natalie. Have you seen her?"

"You shouldn't be here." The creature sounds a little angry.

"I'm sorry," I say. "But I really need to find them. We think they were taken by a chaos mage."

A rustle-snap of branches encourages me to continue. I sit on the forest floor in a puff of leaves and spruce needles and, feeling rather ridiculous, I spill my guts to the tree.

The hiisi remains silent after I finish. The hope drains out of me, a slow melt like winter ice warmed by spring sun.

"This is dangerous business," the hiisi says eventually.

I stare up into the boughs, looking for the face that must be talking. There are only shivering branches.

"Your friends aren't here," the creature continues. "Though there have been others stomping about my glade."

"Others? Do you know why they came here? Who were they? What do they want?" My words all run together, the syllables tripping over each other as they rush off my tongue.

The trees sway, sending another wave of sap-scented air across the glade. Then a branch extends like a finger and grazes my cheek and the itch in my palms becomes a full-body tingle.

"You're a Turunen," the hiisi says. "For centuries, your family has been protecting that which is most sacred, that which is most powerful."

"The Sampo?"

"Indeed. Your ancestors asked for our help, little one. Mervi understood what was at stake. We pledged our lives to protect the Sampo, to uphold the balance, to maintain order in the universe and defeat those who would upend it." The hiisi's voice creaks with such sorrow, I can't help the tears prickling my eyes. "We never believed there'd come a time when we could fail."

"How are you failing?" I get to my feet and take tentative steps toward the tree. The trunk, also a leg, is covered in several nasty gashes. The sap I'm smelling isn't sap at all, but the hiisi's blood. Some asswipe hurt it.

"We aren't strong enough," the hiisi says. "We can no longer defend ourselves from our enemies."

"You mean the chaos mage?"

"There is more than one," the hiisi says, and my chest draws tight, my stomach doing somersaults.

I can't keep denying what's becoming painfully obvious. The Order of Louhi—all this time I thought it was a thing of the past, but the Order must still be active, so there could be a dozen mages searching for the Sampo! *And kidnapping magical kids?* But how could snatching Natalie and the others help the Order in their hunt for the Sampo? Slowly, the puzzle pieces slot into place: the Svalbard break-in, the Sampo not being there—the Sampo being *here*, protected by hiidet beyond the tonttukivi, Natalie and the others kidnapped and taken to the stones.

I study the injury on the tree. A sigil part chaos star and part rune I've never seen before has been carved into the bark. Golden-pink sap leaks from the wound, running like tears down the hiisi's leg.

"What does this mean?" I touch the sigil before removing my scarf and gently binding the cuts on the hiisi's shin. If only I could do more.

"The darkest of spells," the hiisi says. "A spell that cleaves and tears asunder. They will stop at nothing to get what they want."

"Where is the Sampo? How do we stop them from getting it?" I ask.

"With our help, Mervi broke the Sampo. Eight shards hidden in eight sacred glades," the hiisi says. "Once they have the shards, they will make it whole. It will be the end of everything."

The end of everything. No more parents, no more school, no more Natalie or Morgan or even Finland. It doesn't seem possible things could just—end.

"We want to help," I say, fighting how very small and insignificant I feel. "We want to stop whoever is doing this."

"Then you must hurry," the hiisi says. "Five stones have been breached, five shards have been taken.”

"But there are more than a dozen tonttukivi marked on our map,” I say. "How will we stop them if we don’t know where to go?”

"There is an order to these things.” Branches shiver above me. "And the tietäjä knows.”

"A tietäjä?” I suck in a breath. "A *tietäjä* is helping the Order of Louhi?” It doesn’t make sense. It’s anathema, going against everything the tietäjät stand for.

"Only a tietäjä could. The next shard is in Lumikuuro. Perhaps there you’ll find your friends.”

Never heard of the place, but I hadn’t heard of Kuusikylä either and maybe that’s the whole point. "How do we get there?”

"Follow the path.” The branches crackle and creak as the tree trunks groan, drawing back to clear a trail through the woods.

The light changes again from buttery yellow to cold blue as sudden twilight descends over the glade. It’s as if the forest is being swallowed by a humongous mouth full of shadow.

"But there’s so much I need to know,” I say. "Please, you have to help us.” How did the tietäjä get the shards? What do they want with the Sampo? Are they draining Natalie and the others of their magic? The wind gusts, ripping away my pleas.

First things first. I hurry back to Morgan as the stone archway bursts apart like the head of a dandelion. Shielding my face, I bend over Morgan to protect him too. The expected flakes of stone feel more like icy kisses thanks to the wind. When the wind dies down, the archway is gone, and the summer woodland starts vanishing faster than I can haul Morgan to his feet. The pathway is disappearing!

"Wake up!” I yell into his face and shake his shoulders so hard I’m afraid he’ll get whiplash. Finally, his eyes flutter open, and he groans. "We have to hurry. You need to walk.”

Eyes half closed, he manages to stagger to his feet, using me like a crutch under his arm. Left foot, right foot—I force our feet to move along the path that’s now scattered with leaves all fire red and burnished gold.

"Where are we going?” Morgan asks, still groggy but leaning

less heavily on me now.

"Where we need to. Just keep walking."

Autumn slips into winter and still the path winds through the trees. I gulp down mouthful after mouthful of icy air. What if the hiisi was lying? What if this is a trap? I glance over my shoulder. There's nothing behind us except a yawning emptiness swirling with noodles of mist. The woodland has completely disappeared.

"Hey, I think I'm good." Morgan unhooks his arm from my shoulder, and I stand up straight, working the stiffness from my back.

Free of Morgan, I flick on the flashlight. The forest is completely dark now and the beam cuts a strip of yellow through the shadows on the increasingly snowy trail.

"Are we there yet?" Morgan pulls up his hood against the torrent of snow pouring down around us.

"I hope so."

"Want to tell me what happened while I was out?" he asks.

The hiisi's words whip up a tornado inside my mind and I tell Morgan everything.

"I still can't believe a tietäjä could be behind this all."

"And one of our teachers," Morgan adds.

Mom—never!

Dad—no way!

Emmi—hard no. She's far too nice. Besides, she and Mom were friends in university. There's no way she's involved.

Aleksi—possibly.

Miss Kaneda—maybe. It's well-known gossip Kaneda left university before graduating as a tietäjä herself. I never managed to find out exactly why though. According to Mom, it's none of my business. According to Dad, some people just aren't cut out for it. According to Toivo, it's because Miss Kaneda is only half Finnish, which is absolute nonsense and something only my jerk of a brother would believe.

Kaneda, Emmi, and Aleksi were all at the buck building so they couldn't have been the ones to take Hannah. Or could they have slipped away long enough to become a kidnapper? For now, I'll keep them on my list.

That leaves only one more tietäjä at the school.

"Joakim," I say out loud. "It has to be."

"Has he got tattoos?" Morgan asks.

"No idea."

"Think he could be working with MacCrone? The hiisi said there was more than one, right?"

Dammit, yes. I'd forgotten about that. "Joakim with MacCrone as an accomplice—that makes the most sense."

"Wish I'd been awake," Morgan says. "I might've been the only druid alive to have ever seen a Finnish fairy."

"A hiisi isn't really a fairy."

"Close enough."

"You might be the only druid to have ever touched a tonttukivi," I offer instead. "That seemed pretty intense?"

"It felt like I was getting all the energy sucked right out of me." He shudders.

"Like, siphoning?" I say, remembering his word.

"Maybe. It was strange, like the stones wanted something from me, but I didn't know what and then I couldn't control the flow of energy anymore."

"Is that when you opened the doorway?"

"I didn't decide to do it. It just kind of happened," Morgan says. "I don't think I was channeling it right. I just felt all these feelings." He wraps his arms around his stomach. "Sadness, anger, fear. The whole area is hurting."

"I'm not surprised. The chaos mage cut the hiisi," I say.

"Asshole."

"Agreed. But listen, if this is about the Sampo, I think we might be getting in over our heads."

He frowns and I think I must've messed up the phrase again when he says, "You think? I mean, look at where we are?" He gestures to the snow-soaked forest. "Do we even *know* where we are? And we're on the trail of a league of chaos mages. This is kinda crazy, but also kinda epic." A sly grin creeps up the corners of his mouth.

"I just don't want to get you into trouble."

"Tai, please," he says. "I don't care if they expel me."

"I do," I say. "And I care a lot if you die using up too much magic."

"Hey." He puts a hand on my shoulder. "We O'Connors are pretty tough. It'll take more than that to off me. Promise."

I want to believe him, but doubt is starting to erode what little courage I had to begin with.

"Besides, we've come this far." He punches my shoulder lightly. "No point turning back now."

As if we even could if we wanted to.

Despite how fast we're walking, the cold seeps into my bones, making my spine ache and teeth chatter. It hits me smack between the eyes that we could die out here and no one would ever find us.

All the more reason to succeed. I will not die out here and I will not get Morgan killed. I refuse. Turning my attention away from the morbid thoughts circling like vultures, I focus on what Morgan said about the stones and think I'm finally starting to get it.

If opening the portal to the hiisi's forest took so much out of him, no wonder those who are after the Sampo are kidnapping magical kids. What good would it be if opening the doorway left the mage passed out for hours? They could be using Natalie and the others to open the tonttukivi—but that doesn't explain why Natalie became a liekkiö. Or does it?

I study Morgan: his bloodshot eyes and pale, almost gray face. Is he going to start fading and turn into a ghost? I'm trying to decide whether or not to voice this concern when the trail widens, and the wind dies down. So does the flashlight, plunging us into ink-black night.

"Hey, look up!" Morgan nudges me with his elbow.

Above us, a canopy of stars stretches across the patch of sky visible between the leafless branches.

"Whoa, are those the northern lights?" he asks.

"Yeah." Ribbons of color dance above us in shades of green and purple and vibrant pink.

"Damn, this is so sick. I didn't think they could really be those colors. I thought it was some CGI trickery when I saw videos online."

"They're mostly green. This sort of show is pretty rare." I've witnessed the aurora before, but never like this. It's mesmerizing.

"Well, that's one thing I can check off my bucket list." He mimes a check mark with his mittened finger. "What do you call them in Finnish?"

"Revontulet." I repeat the word a few times until Morgan can say it properly. "It means fox's fire."

"Why?" He doesn't take his gaze off the sky.

"Some people believe the northern lights are caused by a fox's tail whipping—no, that's not the right word..." I have to think for a moment, running a search in my mental Finnish-English dictionary. "Whisking? Is that a word?"

"Sure, like when you whisk eggs."

"Yes, like that," I say. "So people used to believe the lights were caused by a fox's tail whisking up the snow."

"That's kinda awesome."

"In some Sámi cultures though, they think the lights are the blood of the dead spilling across the sky." Yeah, great. Really didn't need to bring that up right now.

Morgan looks at me, eyebrows drawn together. "Let's hope not."

With the northern lights glimmering above us, we continue along the pathway until it opens into a glade like the one in Kuusikylä, complete with glowing tonttukivi. Except this time, we aren't the only ones who've found it.

21

Toivo and Aoife stand arguing beside the stones. These ones glow shades of red instead of blue, casting a ruby halo on the snow. Our siblings are both wrapped up against the cold, shouting through their scarves at one another.

Toivo. It can't be him. He's nowhere near a tietäjä yet, but here he is, yelling at Aoife. And...

He had the book on chaos magic.

He knew things about the Sampo.

He's a terrible brother.

So yeah, it has to be him. I'm only a little surprised and mildly disappointed. Mostly I'm relieved it's Toivo and not Mom or Emmi or someone I actually like.

"Let me do it," he says.

"And then what?" Aoife puts her hands on her hips. "What if... I can't do this alone."

"I know, but one of us has." Toivo takes a step forward.

"Get away from her!" I stomp into the glade with Morgan at my side.

He grips my hand, fingers squeezing tight as he pulls me back a little.

"Taika?" Toivo spins around. "What the hell? Where have you been?"

"We've come to stop you," I say, knowing full well I won't be able to do a damn thing if my brother is the evil tietäjä. Can it really be Toivo? He's powerful, but not O'Connor powerful, and he's not even a straight A student. It can't be him.

It could be, the voice chooses now to pipe up. *You know it could be. Maybe you're just jealous he has magic and you've got nothing.*

"What are you talking about?" Aoife asks. "We've been searching for you. Janey Mack, Morgan!" She rushes forward and tugs her brother into a hug, wrenching his hand out of mine, as he sways on his feet.

"I'm fine," Morgan says. "Seriously, stop, okay?"

"But what happened to you?" Aoife demands. "How did you get here? Do you know how worried we've been? You've been gone two days!"

"Two days?" That's not possible. It's only been a few hours, hasn't it?

"You have no idea how freaked out—" Toivo looks like he wants to say more but he shakes his head instead. His cheeks are bright red; I'm unsure whether it's from cold or anger—probably both, considering the glower he's giving me. He looks so much like Mom right now, it's almost creepy.

"Aysha called," he says. "She told us about your ridiculous idea."

"It's not ridiculous." I plant my feet, meeting my brother's furious gaze.

"And then Cludd published your forum post in the *Messenger*. Mom had to deal with hysterical students and even more hysterical parents!" Toivo spits out every syllable as if it tastes rotten.

The blood leaves my body, yanked out of my veins in an

invisible riptide. "He wasn't supposed to do that. I put it in the forum for students only."

"Well, you got the front page you've always wanted," Toivo says. He might as well have flung knives at me.

"I think I'm going to be sick." I press a hand to my stomach, as if that ever helps.

"You two sure created quite a mess," Aoife says. "Some parents came to pick up their kids, others came to lend support. Our parents—" She bites her lip.

"Are they pissed?" Morgan turns even paler.

"What do you think?" she says.

Morgan swallows hard before his face rearranges itself into a punk-rock sneer. "At least we're doing something to find Hannah."

"Where the hell were you?" Aoife asks. "And how are you *here*?"

"We went to the tonttukivi in Kuusikylä," I say, because this idea was mine and Morgan shouldn't take the fall for it. "We know this is where the tietäjä will strike next."

"You shouldn't be here." Toivo points his finger at me, and I fight the urge to break it. "You have no idea the danger you've put Morgan in."

"Stop telling me what to do!" The words erupt out of me. "I'm not the one using chaos magic! I'm not the one hurting hiidet or kids like Hannah!"

"You think—" Toivo stops midsentence, his eyes wide with shock before his forehead creases with... Is that hurt? No way. But the expression is gone, hidden by a fresh coat of anger. His eyes narrow and his lips press into that tight just-like-Mom line.

"I'm not the one doing this," Toivo says. "Really, Taika? Did I go to Svalbard and break into the vault too?"

"But you had the book!"

"Use some common sense." His words sting.

"Your brother has been trying to figure out who's behind all this," Aoife says. "The book isn't about chaos magic." She swings my backpack off her shoulder and pulls out the tome. "It's a battle mage handbook."

"What?" I stare at the chaos star on the cover. "But the symbol, Morgan's allergies—"

"The symbol is completely different," Toivo adds with his usual smugness.

It's not *that* different. Sure, the points are equal length and evenly distributed about the circle, but it still looks an awful lot like a chaos star.

"The reason it's off-limits to most people is because battle and chaos magic are different sides of the same coin," Aoife says. "Look, I've read it. There's a lot in here *about* chaos magic but it isn't a how-to on anything forbidden."

"It literally is," Morgan says quietly. "Unless you're secretly a battle mage?"

Aoife stares at her brother, biting at her lip as if she wants to say something but can't think of a comeback.

"How did you get it?" I direct my question at Toivo.

"Sorin snuck it out of MacCrone's cottage," he says. "Turns out vampires make pretty good thieves what with shape-shifting and all."

"The bogle." I give myself a mental kick for not realizing it sooner. "That was you, wasn't it? You needed to create a distraction."

"Had to make sure MacCrone wouldn't be around when Sorin went to get the book," Toivo admits, looking irritatingly pleased with himself.

"But why?" Morgan teeters beside me, earning a concerned look from Aoife.

"You think you're the only one who noticed things were weird at school? You're not the only one with a missing friend, and I wasn't going to rely on some geriatric battle mage to protect us," Toivo fires back.

"Risto, right?" I ask.

"He was the first to go missing."

How many kids went missing between Risto and Natalie? I was so busy worrying about *Messenger* articles, about not being good enough for Natalie and hating Sini & Co., I completely failed to notice something that should've been super obvious. A true journalist would've seen what was happening long before being found by a liekkiö. I should've done better from the start, but it's not too late for Natalie and Hannah. There's still time to save them all.

"Where's Sorin now?" I ask, my head aching from the sudden deluge of information.

"I'm not sure," Toivo says. "He was supposed to be tracking the use of chaos magic."

"With a Zeiger counter?"

"Those aren't that accurate. We used a spell from the book to enhance his vampiric senses," Toivo says casually, as if working a battle magic spell is no biggie. "And it was working too. Sorin got here before us and sent us the coordinates. Turns out birds travel much faster than trains and buses."

"But we haven't heard from him in hours." Aoife paces a track through the snow.

"The chaos mage might've gotten to him then," I whisper, afraid saying it out loud might make it true.

"Which is why we don't have time to stand here arguing," Aoife says. "We need to open the stones."

"Agreed." Toivo strides toward the tonttukivi.

"Wait!" Morgan's voice is brittle and breathless. "After I touched the ones in Kuusikylä, I passed out for ages—It took a lot out of me."

"What do you mean?" Aoife asks.

"He means—" I ignore the look from Morgan telling me to shut up. Toivo and Aoife need to know. "He means we think maybe Natalie and the others are being used to open the doorways."

"You activated the tonttukivi?" Toivo raises an eyebrow at Morgan.

"It's how we got here. Opened a portal in Kuusikylä, met a hiisi—had a long conversation actually—and got sent down the path that led here." I relish the growing look of bewilderment on my brother's face.

"You have got to be kidding me. You. *You* spoke to a hiisi?" Toivo stares, dumbstruck.

What I wouldn't give to have my phone right now so I could take a photo of his expression. I'd frame it and point to it every time he calls me useless.

Aoife hangs her head, tears coating her lashes before freezing like tiny stalactites. "If Hannah gets hurt, I—I—" She buries her face in her hands.

Toivo shakes off his surprise. "Tietäjät have been using these stones for generations; it's not supposed to be fatal. Besides, a person doesn't become a liekkiö because they channeled too much elemental magic. That only happens when..."

"When they're murdered," I finish for him. "Usually. But Natalie isn't dead yet. She said we still have time."

"So, Morgan will be okay?" Aoife asks.

"To open a tonttukivi, you have to give the stones energy," Toivo says. "So, I guess that depends on the person. It makes sense the chaos mage wouldn't want to use up all their magic opening the stones if they're still going to have to find a shard of the Sampo." He takes a deep breath and straightens his spine. "I've got this."

"Are you sure?" I remain utterly unconvinced by my brother's sudden heroics.

"This is only what I've been training for my entire life."

Yeah, a whole seventeen years—but I keep that to myself. Aoife tsks, sounding as unimpressed as I feel, and loops her arm over Morgan's shoulders in a loving, protective gesture I've never received from my own older sibling.

"Hurry up then," I snap.

Toivo gives me a withering glance before he kneels in front of the tonttukivi and lifts his hands. Slowly he removes one glove and then the other. The stones glow a little brighter when he raises his bare fingers, wiggling them through the light.

He frowns.

"What's wrong?"

"The energy is so weak. I thought there'd be more power out

here. Everything feels so depleted," Toivo says, and a tiny bell rings in my mind, reminding me of Emmi's lecture in Thaumaturgy.

Toivo closes his eyes as he lays his hands on the tonttukivi.

Red threads wind up his fingers like throbbing veins and disappear under the sleeves of his jacket. For a moment, he becomes a supernova before the light washes out of him and back into the stones. He exhales and hunches over.

Again, the wind whips snow into a furious flurry and I shield my eyes from the stinging ice. Toivo breathes heavily as thin streams of blood trickle out of his nose.

"You okay?" I ask, surprised—and maybe a little disappointed—he hasn't keeled over.

"I'm fine." He staggers to his feet and wipes the blood away with the back of his hand. There doesn't appear to be any more.

"Whoa," Morgan says, and I look up expecting to find another archway leading into a summer forest.

An archway appears, but it's made of white marble laced with silver. This time, there's no summer and no inviting woodland. There's only a windswept steppe crusted in snow and punctuated by twisted trees.

"Taika—" Toivo starts, but I don't let him finish.

"No way, we're all going. Morgan and I got this far on our own. We're going too."

"Whatever, I don't have the energy to argue with you." He admits defeat.

Aoife takes the first step across the threshold, her feet kicking up the snow like sand. We follow in single file with Toivo bringing up the rear.

It's much colder on the other side of the archway. Above us, the sky doesn't offer any familiar constellations or pretty displays of northern lights, and there's no moon to help light our way.

There isn't even a path, only tufts of grass marking some sort of track leading through the fields of white. We follow our feet, the plain gradually giving way to scraggly woodland and, finally, clustered forest.

"Oh damn, that's hard-core." Morgan's footsteps crunch to a stop behind me.

I swivel my head to follow his gaze and my breath locks up inside my chest.

"Janey Mack, are those what I think they are?" Aoife points to the weird teardrop-shaped fruit dangling from the branches.

They appear to be seedpods or some sort of insect nests, cocoons even—until they move. That's when I realize a dozen eyeballs are hanging from the frozen trees, and they're all looking right at me.

22

The eyes are blue and brown, gray, green, black, and even red. Some have ordinary round pupils, others have vertical slits like a reptile's, while several have shapes I can't name—shapes no creature in the real world have, that's for sure.

"Why are they looking at me?" I whisper.

"Because you don't belong here," Toivo says, a jerk in any world it seems. "You're the only one without magic. I guess this place can sense it."

Morgan bumps his shoulder against mine and shakes his head. "Ignore it. He's just scared."

"I'm fine." I am most definitely not fine. Scared is an understatement. The eyes keep blinking at me in a weirdly synchronized pattern, as if opening and closing according to a metronome only they can hear. Eyes, hearing? I am losing my mind.

"Why does this feel so different?" I ask out loud, not really expecting an answer. "At the other tonttukivi, the woodland seemed friendly. It didn't feel this—"

"Hostile?" Morgan raises a middle finger at a particularly glaring pair of eyeballs.

"Each tonttukivi is connected to a different hiisi." Toivo comes up beside me. "They're not all friendly, you know." He takes the lead from Aoife, keeping his gaze fixed straight ahead.

"So, the mage uses the kids to open the stones, why not just leave them then?" Aoife asks as we continue our trudge.

"They're collecting the shards of the Sampo," I say. "It's a powerful artifact—"

"I know what it is," Aoife says. "I just don't understand why it's in pieces or why the mage needs my sister."

Toivo starts answering before I can. "The Sampo was too dangerous to keep in the vault on Svalbard. After Mervi, our ancestor, broke it, she hid the pieces at several magical locations around Finland."

"Why not just destroy it?" Aoife asks.

"She tried." Toivo sighs. "It couldn't be done. The shards were kept locked away by forest creatures, protected by numerous layers of powerful spells. Spells not even a chaos mage could break, unless..."

"Unless what?" Aoife grips Toivo's sleeve, spinning him around to face her.

All the eyes open wide, and an army of chills stomp down my spine.

"Unless, the chaos mage absorbed enough raw elemental energy, then they might be able to break the spells. Once they have all the shards, they could put the Sampo back together," Toivo says.

"So, the kidnapped kids—whoever wants the Sampo, they *are* draining Natalie and the others of magic." That's why Natalie is a liekkiö! My suspicions were correct and, just this one time, I wish I hadn't been right.

"Draining magic like that—it can kill a person." Morgan's voice is a hoarse whisper.

"They're still alive." I try not to think of Natalie and the others being used like magical protein shakes. It's an image that's stained my mind. I'll need a bucket of bleach to wash it away. "We still have time." Maybe saying it enough times will make it true.

"And all this for some relic that does what exactly?" Morgan asks.

"Depends who wields it," Toivo says. "But it'll be used for nothing good in the hands of the Order of Louhi."

"So, the league of chaos mages is still active?" Morgan and I share a look of matching raised eyebrows.

"Always have been, just never this openly," Toivo says. "For someone who thinks they know everything, you don't seem to know much at all."

"Did you know all this before you read the battle mage book?" I ask, satisfied when he doesn't have a comeback. "And what about Tumultua? Is she still locked up?"

"There's a theory that her followers might be trying to use the Sampo to free her and bring about a new era of chaos magic," Aoife answers.

"Sounds ridiculous," I say, because it does. Like some twisted fairy tale come to life in all the wrong ways.

"I thought so too, but they seem pretty determined to collect all the shards," Toivo says.

That sends all of us into a brooding silence as the forest continues to thicken around us. The branches, spiked with thorns, snag on our clothes like corpse fingers. It's quiet except for the crunching of our footsteps, as if the entire world is holding its breath, waiting for something.

There it is. A flash of movement between the trees.

"Did you see that?" Morgan steps protectively in front of me.

A child's laughter bounces among the branches, the sound sinister and not at all cheerful.

"Everyone heard that, right?" Morgan casts anxious glances left and right.

Another flash of movement: a figure in red darts across the path.

"That's Hannah!" Aoife takes off after the figure flitting in and out of the trees as it cuts a zigzag across the path.

"No! Don't!" Toivo tries to grab Aoife's hand, but she shakes him off, running faster and screaming her sister's name.

"Stop!" I latch on to Morgan's arm. "It might not be her."

"She has a red jumper just like that. And that's her voice," Morgan says.

"It could be a trick. You have no idea what it might be," Toivo says.

"*It*?" Morgan clenches his jaw. "That's my little sister." He staggers through the snow in pursuit of Aoife.

It's not hard to keep up with him in his weakened state.

"You two, stay together," Toivo says, then curses in Finnish before racing ahead, calling after Aoife who's a smudge of blue jacket and green scarf in the distance.

The laughter continues and a blur of red and brown flies toward me from the left. I reach out, trying to grab the whirling ball of color, but it's too strong, too fast, and it whirls away, leaving me with strands of saliva and clumps of coarse brown hair sticking to my fingers. My whole body is itching and tingling as if an army of fire ants is waging war under my skin.

"Oh, that's gross." I wipe my hand on my leg, and when I look up, all the eyeballs in the forest have closed.

"Morgan, do you—" Morgan isn't beside me anymore. "Morgan! Where are you?" I scream through the gnarled and twisted trees before jogging up the path, searching for signs of Toivo or Aoife.

I'm alone, the wind scrubbing away our footprints. In a few moments it's as if I've always been here alone, all traces of the others erased.

I will not panic.

You're panicking, the little voice provides a helpful rebuttal.

I'll be fine.

You are not fine.

I'll find them.

What if you don't? You'll be stuck here and you'll die and everyone will be glad Taika the Talentless is gone, gone, gone.

Tears blur my vision, but I search the shadows between the branches for any sign of the others. I listen, too, straining my ears to hear beyond the blood thumping through my veins.

To my left, someone screams. I dive into the trees, not caring about the thorns tearing at my clothes and skin. Blue fire erupts all around me, and the trees screech as they burn. The eyeballs melt off the trees, dripping from the branches to form jellied puddles. I swallow down the rising sick. Halloween decorations, that's all they are, I try to convince myself as I tiptoe my way through the steaming globs.

I follow the path the blue fire has charred It smells more like burnt plastic than burning pine. It doesn't take long for me to find the others.

Toivo and Morgan are engaged in battle with what might be mistaken for a human child, if not for the horns protruding from the creature's head and the flash of fangs. Aoife kneels in the snow, blood seeping from a wound in her shoulder where she's been slashed by claws. But the wound doesn't stop her from using her power. Pillars of earth erupt from the ground to shield Toivo and Morgan from attack.

I stand watching. I don't need the little voice to tell me how utterly useless I am.

"We have to run!" Toivo yells.

"Not until we have Hannah," Morgan shouts back before drawing a shimmering shield of air around them using a sigil combining *raido* and *algiz*.

Clearly Toivo has learned more than just history from the battle mage handbook as he sends a ball of fire zipping toward the creature. The monster slaps it away with a hand that looks more like a paw. The orb of energy hits a tree and the whole thing turns into a tower of blue flame.

The tingling in my body becomes a sudden burning, a torrent of heat flaming up through my soul and crisping my skin. Involuntary tears leak from my eyes. The trees aren't the enemy and they're the ones getting hurt.

"Stop burning the trees." No one can hear my breathless sobs.

"We can't help Hannah if we die here," Aoife yells.

"I have to find her." Morgan dodges the creature's claws only to trip over a snarl of burned branches and land on his butt in the snow. His face is flushed and peppered with sweat.

A column of earth shoots out of the ground to his right, stopping the creature from swiping claws through his face.

"I'm almost spent." Aoife clutches her injured shoulder and blood slicks her fingers.

Toivo carves sigils in the air I don't recognize. More battle magic, maybe. The wind rushes in a violent whoosh toward him, which he somehow manages to direct toward the monster In a display that's definitely not basic elementalism where runes can only be used defensively. This is an attack spell.

The wind hits the monster with the force of a high-speed train, knocking it back through the pines. Every tree it hits turns to splinters and I cry out, feeling as if my bones are being shredded.

"Stop hurting the trees!" The scream leaves the taste of copper down the back of my throat.

The others turn toward me as if only now noticing I'm here. "Stop hurting the trees," I say at a more reasonable volume. "You're upsetting the forest and the trees aren't our enemy."

Toivo gives me a perplexed look as he hauls Morgan to his feet, but at least he doesn't argue.

"It wasn't Hannah, was it? She's not here." Morgan sounds so utterly broken.

Aoife staggers over to him, leaving a trail of burgundy in the snow.

"We need to go, right now. Back the way we came. Go!" Toivo says, his gaze riveted on the broken branches as if the monster could jump out any moment.

We retrace our steps as best we can, but the wind has swept away our footprints and the forest keeps shifting. I'm pretty sure the path wasn't so straight the first time we walked it. And I don't remember seeing two spruces laced together like that either, but Toivo stomps ahead as if he knows where he's going. The shadows are thickening again, the darkness pressing against us as if it has substance.

"We should've been at the arch by now." Toivo pauses. He carves more sigils, and a burst of light illuminates our surroundings.

I stare at my brother, able to see him now. Where the heck did my mean, sulky, smug, bookish brother go? Who is this magic-wielding superhero? His jacket hangs in tatters and he's bleeding from a gash above his right eye, although he doesn't seem to notice. He's sweating and breathing hard, a thin trickle of blood snaking out of his nose again.

"Are we lost?" Aoife asks, her face gray and sleeve soaked red.

"It's the forest." Toivo's lights wink out. "I don't think it wants us to leave."

"Why?" I ask.

"Because—" Toivo grimaces, his face screwed up as he smacks his forehead with his hand. "This tietäjä wants magical kids and we walked right into their trap."

I can't argue, but something about that doesn't seem right. There's no way the forest would team up with the chaos mage.

"Do you feel anything?" I whisper to Morgan. "I mean, like you did before at the tonttukivi? The emotions of the place."

"Fear," Morgan says. "Fear and anger and"—he winces—"pain. A lot of pain. Our magic hurt the trees."

"I told you not to burn them." I glare at Toivo.

My brother responds with a twitch of his clenched jaw as he looks away from me.

"We're not going to get out, are we?" Aoife asks.

"Oh, we're getting out," Toivo says. "Even if I have to burn down this whole damn forest and eviscerate every maahinen to do it."

"Burning the trees is a mistake," I say. "I think we're lost because we hurt the forest and it's upset."

"What are you talking about?" Toivo throws his hands up, finally acknowledging my existence.

"I'm the one who spoke with the hiisi, remember? And I'm telling you, you pissed off the forest. Keep hurting the trees and we'll die out here." My words are harsh, too harsh maybe, but I don't think being nice will get my message through Toivo's thick skull.

"Aoife's losing a lot of blood," Morgan says.

"I'm fine." The fact she's swaying on her feet says otherwise.

"Can you help her?" Morgan turns to Toivo, who wipes blood and sweat off his face and shakes his head.

"Well, I'm not a healer either," Morgan says. "But we have to do something."

"*Uruz.*" Aoife names the earth rune used for healing as she staggers, her shoulder knocking eerie tinkling sounds from the dangling, but thankfully closed, eyeballs.

Uruz. Yes, that could work, especially...

"Combine it with *laguz* and *nauthiz.*" I draw the water and air runes for strength and survival in the snow.

"Dude, you're brilliant!" Morgan smiles and gets to work, casting the sigils in the air.

He shoves one hand into the snow and presses the other to Aoife's injured shoulder. His tattoos turn luminescent again, opening up the scabs. Aoife whimpers as the magic takes effect, blinking away tears which freeze instantly on her cheeks. The trees and hanging eyes freeze too. Branches drop off and shatter when they hit the ground. A few pairs of eyes do as well, scattering vitreous glitter across the snow.

After an agonizing ninety seconds, Morgan removes his hand from her shoulder. "I'm sorry, I can't do more." He's trembling. "But I think it's enough to stop the bleeding. If Da were here..."

"It's okay. It's enough," Aoife says.

"You can do more." I offer him my hand right as a howl slices through the air, making all the hairs on the back of my neck stand up.

Before I can scream, a huge gray wolf leaps into the clearing. It stalks toward Aoife, nose quivering, before turning to Toivo with a snarl. Then it rears on its back legs and the wolf disappears in a blur of fur, leaving Sorin standing naked in the snow.

I should look away—I absolutely should—but I'm in shock, my eyes frozen wide open.

"I told you this was dangerous," Sorin says, his voice all lupine growl. He turns his back on Toivo and pads over to Aoife.

She's bleeding. He has fangs. For a moment, I think Aoife

might become the vampire's dinner, but he kneels beside her and gently takes her arm.

"You should be all right." He looks down at her with eyes dark but no longer wolfish. "It's not arterial and"—he pauses to sniff—"the spell is working. Nice work." He nods at Morgan, who has backed away and looks as awkward as I feel.

I mean, I've seen naked people before. It's normal really, considering Finland's sauna culture, but it's not every day you get to see a beautiful vampire transform right in front of you. If I had a body like Sorin's, I wouldn't hide it under baggy clothes. I'm having serious bicep envy and look at his traps! And damn—his deltoids! I tear my gaze away before he notices how hard I'm staring.

Aoife's face flushes bright pink as her gaze seems to land everywhere but on Sorin. Despite being decidedly lacking in the clothing department, he seems unfazed by the cold. If it's a result of his vampire blood, I wish I had a drop or two right about now. It's been ages since I felt my toes or fingers, and I'm pretty sure my nose has frostbite.

"Where have you been?" Toivo asks.

"Stuck here. Same as you," Sorin says. "I tracked the magic north to the stones. Crossed over. Didn't realize it was a one-way ticket."

"We're trapped here?" Morgan asks.

"Seems so. I've been searching for a way out. Haven't found one." Sorin shrugs. "There's strange magic here. Could be a spell or maybe the forest itself. Either way, we're stuck." Sorin might not have fangs anymore, but he still looks like he wants to bite.

"Trapped." Aoife hangs her head between her knees.

"I might not be," I say, before my brain has time to process the thought growing in my head. "Magic doesn't work the same on me. Maybe I can find a way out."

Toivo looks at me for a good long while, his brow furrowed and his hair gathering snow. I don't need his permission to try this, but I want him to acknowledge me and say it's the only chance we've got.

"Might work," he says as if it causes him physical pain, then switches to Finnish so only I understand. "But you have to promise me that if you can get out, you go. Don't wait for us or try to get us out too. If you can find a way, you take it and you get to Mom and Dad as fast as you can. They'll know what to do."

"But we'll all—"

"Taika!" Toivo meets my gaze without any of his usual animosity. "You want to help, right? You want to save Natalie and Hannah, right? Then know this is the best chance we've got."

"Okay, I'll go," I say in English. "And I'll go straight to Mom and Dad." I barely get the words out before the reddish blur barrels into Toivo, knocking him sideways into the snow. The maahinen is back.

"Run, Taika!" Toivo yells.

With a snarl, Sorin leaps after the creature, changing midair into his wolf form. It's breathtaking but I don't have the time to marvel at his shape-shifting abilities.

"Please, get help!" Morgan says.

For a moment, I still hesitate. For a moment, I consider staying just because Toivo wants me to go. But this is it, this is my one chance to do something helpful and not be completely useless.

23

"Please help me," I whisper, not sure who my words are meant for. "Please let me get out. Please let me help my friends." I scream the last bit at the forest.

With a rustle, the trees part and I don't let myself think before running through the gap in the foliage. Whatever power controls this world is letting me go.

Spitting me out, really.

One minute, I'm sprinting along the snowy path between ragged trees, swatting away dangling eyeballs, and the next I'm skidding down a muddy embankment of a river nowhere near the tonttukivi. It's midmorning and weak sunlight streams through ordinary trees in an ordinary forest without any sinister eyeballs.

Having successfully stopped myself from falling into the water by catching hold of some tree roots, I fish Morgan's phone out of my pocket. The battery is dead. Perhaps a trip to a magical realm has fried its electronics. Without GPS, I have no way of telling where I am.

Not in Lumikuuro at least. I think.

Pathetic, the little voice berates me. *The others could be dying and here you are feeling sorry for yourself!*

"Can you help me?" I call out to the trees, feeling rather silly. What am I expecting? Some magical elk or bear to appear and solve my problems? Still, if the forest beyond the stones listened, maybe the trees here will too.

All is quiet except for the murmur of the river and the occasional croak of a crow.

Crows!

"I'm here! Musti, Rekku, Kamu. I'm over here!" I yell until my voice cracks.

Another croak! It could be any crow, but moving toward the sound is as good a plan as any and certainly beats doing nothing. I stomp the mud from my boots then set off in the direction of the birds. I keep the river on my left, navigating my way over slippery roots with careful steps. Last thing I need now is to fall in.

A crow flies into view, sitting on a low branch, fluffing up its chest where it has a smudge of white.

"Musti! You came!"

The bird caws, as if reprimanding me for leaving him behind at the tonttukivi.

"I'm sorry," I say as more crows gather in the trees above, ruffling glossy feathers. Rekku and Kamu are among them.

"Don't just sit there," I shout up at the mangy corvids. "Show me the way home. Come on!"

Musti and the others take off in a flurry of black feathers.

"Wait! Slow down!" I run after them, slipping and falling and not caring about the bruises that'll no doubt litter my legs.

So tired.

So cold.

So *hungry.*

But I keep going.

A black cat with four white socks drops from a branch a few meters ahead and stares at me with yellow eyes.

"Kalma? What are you doing here?" I study the cat, not sure if I'm really looking at Emmi's familiar.

The cat meows and stalks forward, bashing her head against my hand and purring loudly. It must be Kalma.

"Okay, kitty. Can you show me the way?"

With a loud meow, Kalma scampers off between the trees. Limping, I follow, better able to keep up with the cat who keeps doubling back to check on me.

It seems like half of forever before we get to a narrow stream, and I pause to cup the water in my hand. It's flowing and clear and cool, and I don't care. I'm so thirsty I down mouthful after mouthful of earthy water.

"Taika?"

I shoot to my feet and choke back a sob. There, standing amid a crowd of concerned and confused-looking teenagers is Emmi. I almost didn't recognize her dressed in regular hiking clothes instead of her usual Elizabethan theater getup.

"What on earth are you doing here?" Emmi rushes toward me right as my legs give out.

She sits me on a log and wraps her woolen scarf around my shoulders. Kalma purrs and preens, looking very pleased with herself.

"Bring me water." Emmi snaps her fingers, and one of the students offers me a bottle.

I empty it in a few quick swallows.

"All right, back to camp with you," Emmi says. "Nothing to see here."

The students grudgingly edge away, casting curious glances over their shoulders. Luckily, Emmi has a strict no-technology policy on her camping trips otherwise my blundering arrival would probably end up a meme.

"Where am I?" I ask, now that I've got my breath back.

"You're in Repovesi. How in the world did you get here? You've been missing for days!"

Days! Toivo was right. Time must move differently beyond the stones. The camping trip—I'd completely forgotten. Which means it's almost Kekri.

"Are they looking for me?" I ask. "Mom, I mean. Is she mad?"

"Looking for you? Taika, your parents are *beside* themselves. You and Toivo both missing. It's been utter chaos—" Emmi realizes what she's said and bites her lip. "I offered to help, but I was already committed to this trip. But now I've found you! We have to call your mom. I'll drive you back to school myself."

After having explained the situation to the other teachers on the trip, Emmi ushers me to her car. She grabs a pack of chips, empty water bottle, and some books off the passenger seat and tosses them into the back, shoving the books beneath what look like muddy robes. Kalma curls up on the mess in the back seat and I slip into the front.

"Sorry, I wasn't expecting passengers. The others came up by bus from Helsinki," Emmi says as if I care. "You look famished. Here." Emmi hands me a granola bar and I demolish it in four bites.

We've been gone for days! It doesn't seem real. The food makes me feel a little less like I'm on the verge of collapse, but guilty too. Here I am warm and safe while the others are still out in the freezing wilderness fighting for their lives.

"Your article made quite the impression," Emmi says as she pulls out of the parking lot. She frowns, and the lines people call crow's feet form deep grooves at the corners of her eyes. "It created a lot of unnecessary panic."

"Unnecessary?" I've never been in trouble with Emmi before. She's the last person I want to disappoint.

"You claimed a chaos mage was on the loose and stealing children! How did you think people would react?" Emmi arches an eyebrow.

"I just wanted to warn people. To stop it from happening again."

"While that's admirable, I suppose, you need to consider this from all perspectives. A good journalist never takes sides and only reports the facts."

"I didn't take sides. I mean, chaos magic is outlawed. A chaos mage does bad things with bad magic."

"There is no such thing as bad magic," Emmi says, suddenly stern. "A chaos mage isn't inherently evil."

That pretty much goes against everything I've ever been taught about chaos magic—not that we're taught a lot. It's a taboo subject no one talks about beyond saying, "It's not something to be openly discussed." How can something like that be anything other than wrong?

"But our friends were taken. How is that anything but terrible?" I ask.

"Perhaps it would be best not to form an opinion about something without fully understanding it. Perhaps—" It looks as if Emmi is about to say something else, but she squeezes the steering wheel and coughs instead. "All I'm saying is, these things are rarely so black-and-white. Good people can sometimes do terrible things."

"The whole 'end justifies the means' thing?" I ask, remembering the debates we've had in ethics class.

"Yes. Sometimes. It's complicated," she says, like every adult does when they're uncomfortable talking about something they think a teenager is too young to understand.

Whatever. I lean my head back against the seat and close my eyes, resting them for a moment while Emmi's words scuttle around my brain like cockroaches, creating an infestation of doubt. Were we wrong about everything?

Taika the Useless, Taika the Worthless.

No! Natalie was taken. She was scared and hurt, and she's somewhere out there right now running out of time. Whoever took her and Hannah is absolutely not a good person.

"Do you want to tell me where you've been?" Emmi asks gently.

A thousand words shoot through my mind too fast for me to get off my tongue. I want to tell Emmi everything, but I'm so tired I can barely keep my eyes open.

"Maybe after a nap," I manage to say. My lips, face, and whole body are turning numb with exhaustion. Guess the magical jet lag is catching up with me.

"Okay, you rest. I'll give your mom a call and let her know you're safe."

Sleep tugs at every inch of me, sucking my body down into the black hole the worn leather seat has become, while the radiator wraps me in a warm blanket.

Less than three hours later, we pull into the school's parking lot and Emmi shakes me awake. Mom is waiting, arms folded across her chest and a scowl on her face.

24

"You're okay, you're okay." Mom cups my face in her hands, peering into my eyes and then at the rest of me. "Tell me you're okay!"

"I'm fine, Mom."

With a groan of relief, she crushes me in a hug, squeezing me so hard I can barely breathe. After several moments of bone-cracking love, she pulls away and love morphs into anger.

"Where on earth have you been?" Mom gives me a shake, her hands clamped tight on my arms. "What were you thinking? We've been searching for you!" She gestures to the trees, where more crows have joined my usual three in the branches. Her face is haggard, with dark circles like soggy tea bags beneath both her eyes.

Guilt carves up my insides.

"We were at the tonttukivi," I start. "And we crossed into this liminal realm, but we have to hurry. I got out, but the others are still trapped there!" And I napped in the car, when I should've been telling

Emmi. Rescue efforts could've started hours ago! But there's so much more Mom needs to know. Words start tumbling from my mouth, faster than my brain can process.

"Aoife was injured by a maahinen and they're trapped and Toivo—and the forest had eyes and they were burning—and Morgan—and then Sorin—and we know about Tumultua, the Order of Louhi is back—and Natalie was a milkshake and—" Nothing is coming out right.

"Taika, that's enough," Mom says. "Breathe, come on. Take a deep breath. Good. And another. There you go."

"I think they're in shock," Emmi says. "I gave them something to eat and drink in the car, then they fell asleep. They sound delirious and probably need medical attention."

"Thank you, Emmi. I'll take it from here." Mom loops her arm around my shoulders and guides me farther down the path.

"Are you sure you don't want—"

"Emmi, thank you," Mom's words are clipped. "Really, I appreciate all you've done, but don't you have a camp to get back to?"

How can Mom think a camp is more important than rescuing Natalie?

"All right. Call me if you need me." Emmi hesitates before heading toward her car.

Mom turns her back on Emmi, the full force of her attention on me.

"Right young lady, we're going to have a proper chat."

"Mom!" I glower. I know she's angry but that doesn't mean she can misgender me.

For a moment we stand in silence as Mom blinks at me.

"Gods, I'm sorry." She wipes her hand over her face. "I'm sorry, Taika. I've just been so concerned about you."

I bite my tongue to stop myself from saying it's okay. Ten long seconds trickle past as Mom regards me, waiting.

"They're on the other side of the tonttukivi," I say. "In Lumikuuro. We have to save them."

"Not here," Mom whispers and casts a glance up at the trees.

"We don't know who's listening." She takes me by the hand as if I'm some tantrumming toddler and marches me home.

***

Inside, Mom checks all the wards on the windows and casts an additional anti-eavesdropping spell on the kitchen before she says anything.

"Okay, from the beginning. Slowly this time."

I take a deep breath and start again, this time managing to get the words out and all in the correct order.

By the time I get to the part where the crows and Kalma led me to Emmi, I'm ready to pass out from hunger. The granola bar was hardly enough, and I'm parched again from all the talking. I can only imagine how awful Morgan and the others must be feeling.

If they're even alive, the little voice says, ever the ray of sunshine.

Thankfully, while I've been talking, Mom has been bustling around the kitchen and now shoves a plate of sandwiches into my hands. I stuff my face with rye bread and cheese.

"You really spoke to a hiisi?" Mom asks, and I nod. "And you *asked* the forest for help, and it responded?"

"I told you already," I say.

"Incredible, just—I need to call your father."

I finish the sandwiches while Mom speaks to Dad.

"Is he angry with me?" I ask when Mom hangs up.

"Do you have any idea how worried we've been?" Mom takes a seat across the table from me, eyes all shimmery as if she's holding back tears. "We had no idea where you were. Toivo too. And Morgan's parents—" Mom shakes her head and draws a shuddering breath.

The greater consequences of my actions start to dawn on me as I remember what Dad said about how this would reflect poorly on Mom and jeopardize her position with the UCMW.

"We didn't mean to make anyone worry."

"Worry?" Mom laughs, the sound like splintering glass. "We

weren't worried, we were *terrified*. We still are!"

"I'm sorry." I swallow the boulder lodged in my throat. "But that's why it's so important we go back."

"We?" Mom raises her eyebrows and straightens her shoulders, sliding back into principal mode. "Your father is out there right now looking for Toivo and the O'Connors. You have done quite enough."

"We were trying to find Natalie and Hannah." I slump, defeated, my elbows on the table and my head in my hands. I've made a mess of this.

"I understand you're trying to help," Mom says. "But this is serious, Taika. This isn't something you and your friends can be involved in. And it certainly isn't something we needed splashed all over the *Messenger*."

"That wasn't my decision. I didn't ask Cludd to print it. That wasn't my fault." But I knew it could happen and for a moment when I heard it had, I was secretly happy that something I'd written had finally caught everyone's attention. "What happens if the tietäjä gets all the shards of the Sampo? Is the story about Tumultua true?" I ask instead.

"What do you know about Tumultua?" Mom meets my gaze.

There's anger in the tight press of her lips and the frown scrunching up her forehead, but in her eyes there's fear, which makes the sandwiches turn to concrete in my stomach. If one of the best tietäjät in the country is afraid, I guess I should be petrified.

"Only what Toivo read in the battle mage handbook. Did she really survive the Chaos Wars?" I ask.

Mom nods. "Tumultua was young then, a novice practitioner only. The battle mages spared her in an act of mercy. They thought there was hope for her, that she'd join their side and turn away from chaos."

"But she didn't."

"She did, or so it seemed. She became a battle mage, the best they'd ever seen. Then strange deaths started occurring. A few a year, then more. Battle mages were inexplicably dying without any known cause."

"Was Tumultua sucking the magic out of them?" I ask, trying not to think about how Morgan sucked the energy out of me.

"My word, I really do underestimate you, don't I?" For a moment, Mom looks impressed before her forehead creases with concern again. "Yes, Tumultua was draining other mages of their magic. It was how she managed to live so long, feeding off the energy of others. She'd already become immensely powerful. Far more powerful than one person has any right to be. Thankfully, there were enough battle mages left to fight her."

"That's when they imprisoned her?"

"Many wanted her drained of power," Mom says. "Or executed, which would've been the more merciful option according to some."

"Because a life without magic is worse than death?" My voice wobbles and there's a pain stabbing between my ribs like a stitch, only so much worse.

Mom reaches across the table and takes my hand. "For someone that powerful to have her magic ripped away, yes, I imagine it might be worse than dying, but that doesn't mean an unmagical life isn't worth living."

"What happened to Tumultua?" I ask, needing to change the subject as the ache in my chest burrows deeper.

"The battle mages were afraid of what would happen if they tried to drain her power, if they tried to hurt her at all. So they imprisoned her with the help of a tietäjä."

"Mervi the Magnificent." I finally piece it together. "Did she let the battle mages use the Sampo?"

"They had to use more than that to contain Tumultua, and the Sampo was the only object to survive the spell. The others were destroyed by the very magic they were used to channel."

"The Sampo must be very powerful then."

"Indeed," Mom says. "Which is why we've been keeping it safe ever since. Mervi's your grandmother, going back sixteen generations."

That's a whole lot of *great*s. Still, I feel a tingle of pride knowing I'm related to the mage who defeated Tumultua. *Mervi the Magnificent versus Tumultua the Terrible!* Now there's something I'd love to write about.

The grandchild of one of the greatest mages to have ever lived! And not a drop of magic, the little voice says, leaving my momentary pride in tatters.

"Why would a tietäjä want to free Tumultua now?" I ask, hoping the voice'll shut up if I speak over it.

Mom releases my hand and traces protection sigils on the kitchen table with her index finger. "Because some members of the UCMW believe magic wielders should be free to practice as they see fit without having to follow the rules set by the UCMW—rules put in place to protect magic wielders from themselves and unscrupulous others. Not everyone appreciates our safety-first approach, you see. Some tietäjät have forgotten what we stand for."

"Like Morgan's mom, right? She's in opposition to you."

Mom blinks at me. "You really do know far more than I've given you credit for."

I bite my tongue so hard it hurts to keep from saying, "I've been trying to tell you! But you never listen!"

"Do you know who's doing this?" Better to keep digging for answers.

"We have our suspicions, but we don't know for sure yet." Mom pinches the bridge of her nose and closes her eyes for a moment, then shakes her head. "It doesn't matter, as long as we find Natalie and the others." But by the pained look on her face, clearly it matters very much.

Suddenly, I realize why Mom looks so sad. The person responsible might not be a stranger, but someone Mom knows, maybe even someone she counts as a friend—just like the battle mages trusted Tumultua.

"It's someone at the school, isn't it?" I ask.

Mom presses her palms flat against the table, fingers splayed across the sigils. "This is why I don't want you involved. Why you *can't* be involved. What Morgan did," Mom continues, "accessing the tonttukivi like that—"

"We were trying to help. They're running out of time."

"We'll find them," Mom says. "We, the adults." She quickly clarifies.

"With your crows? With the Zeiger counters?"

"Taika, please."

"I want to help."

"You can't," Mom says.

"Because I don't have any magic?" I fling at her with an unexpected bitterness.

Mom hesitates.

"Come *on*! I spoke to a hiisi, and to the forest. I've been beyond the stones, I—"

"No!" Mom slams her fist against the table, making me jump. "Accessing the tonttukivi could've *killed* Morgan. And now? Toivo, Aoife, and Morgan are trapped who knows where because you thought you knew better."

This is all your fault, the voice hisses, the words sweeping through my thoughts like a wrecking ball.

"But spells don't work the same on me, surely I can—"

"You don't have magic, and so you cannot possibly help! Not with this." Mom's words are a shower of splinters, each piercing my skin and working their way in deeper.

"Because I'm useless," I say out loud what the voice in my head has been saying all along.

"You're vulnerable!" Mom throws her hands in the air. "And we have missing children to find and a chaos mage to subdue. I can't be worrying about you as well. I'm sorry you don't have magic and feel left out. I know you want to help, but this time, you really, truly can't."

Tears drip down my cheeks and I don't even try to stop them. She tries to hug me, but I feel numb, my body turned to stone.

"Please try to understand, I want to keep you safe." Mom ushers me up the stairs and deposits me in my bedroom. "You need to stay here, safe behind the wards. When this is all over, then..."

"Then what?" I stand paralyzed while Mom carves sigils in the air. "Then we'll go back to pretending I'm not Taika the Talentless?"

"Oh, kulta." Mom's scowl shatters and I can see the disappointment in her eyes, can see her wondering how the hell a tietäjä of her pedigree ended up with a kid like me. "Please, just—please don't leave this house. Not until I lift this spell. I love you and the last thing I need is to have to worry about you too," Mom says, her voice choked by emotion.

By the time I lift my head to tell her I understand, Mom has already whirled out of my bedroom.

A moment later, the front door slams. I slide to the floor and pull my knees to my chest, hugging myself tight as fresh sobs rock my body.

Blasting the Knock-Knock Jokes does nothing to drown out the little voice screaming at the back of my mind. It sounds an awful lot like Mom now.

Useless!

Worthless!

Taika the Talentless! Taika the Vulnerable, Taika who only gets in the way and makes things worse for everyone.

On and on and on it goes as I pace back and forth across my bedroom, gnawing on my fingernails when I'm not bashing my fists against my head in time with Morgan's bass drum.

So, I can't do magic—but I have to do something. I stop pacing and grab a pen, writing out the names.

MacCrone

Kaneda

Aleksi

Joakim

Emmi

MacCrone's the only person I can scratch off the list since the hiisi said it was a tietäjä. That leaves everyone else. Aleksi and Miss Kaneda might've slipped away from the Kekri buck building long enough to take Hannah on Friday night, but I've seen Aleksi's arms—his sleeves were rolled up while he worked on the buck—and he doesn't have any tattoos. It can't be him. I put a line through his name.

Joakim. Kaneda. Emmi.

Surely a chaos mage would at least try to be a little less disorderly in their daily life? Or would they make it super obvious so no one would suspect them? I hesitate, not quite ready to eliminate Joakim.

Kaneda or Emmi then?

Kaneda. It has to be. A disgraced almost-tietäjä, bitter about never graduating maybe, wanting to get back at my mom somehow. It sort of makes sense, especially since Dad said this all has something to do with Mom's position on the UCMW.

I fish Morgan's dead phone out of my pocket. If I could charge it, I could call—am I really about to call Sini & Co.? Not like I have a lot of other options. I try plugging it in to charge, but of course Morgan's phone is fancy, and my old charger won't fit!

I fling the phone onto my bed and release the scream that's been building up inside me. This is *pointless*. Even if I miraculously manage to figure out who the chaos mage is, I have no way to share my discovery. I am utterly useless here, but out there, in the forest and beyond the tonttukivi—things were different.

I'm deep into a staring contest with my mirror, wondering if I can will myself into being less pathetic, when the doorbell shrills.

The bell keeps ringing until whoever's outside simply holds down the button. I hurry down the stairs to the front door.

Siinä paha missä mainitaan.

Aysha and Ekaterina are standing on my doorstep, visible through the glass insert. No Sini though and I'm not sure whether to be grateful or concerned.

"What are you doing here?" I ask, surprised to see any

students still on the school grounds, especially them.

"Can you let us in?" Aysha shouts from outside.

I try, but Mom's magic makes it impossible for me to even grasp the handle. She knows spells slip off me like water from a duck's wing, so of course she's spelled the house—to keep me in. Perhaps there's a loophole here.

"Um, my mom spelled the house. I can't open the door." Embarrassment heats my cheeks. I hope they can't see how pink I'm turning. "But I think you might be able to open it from the outside."

"With the key you're going to conjure for us?" Ekaterina folds her arms.

"Check under the lavender pot." I point through the glass at Dad's idea of a garden lining the porch stairs.

"As if I know what lavender looks like."

But Aysha strides straight over to a ceramic pot and fishes a grimy key out from under it.

"This is so gross." Still muttering, she fits the key in the lock and jiggles the handle.

For a moment, I think Mom might've added extra locking layers to her spell, but then the door opens.

"Come on." Aysha gestures for me to follow them.

I take a tentative step across the threshold. Just when I think escape is possible, my skin tingles from contact with an invisible barrier all sticky, staticky spiderweb and I stagger back as if someone shoved me.

"That's annoying," Aysha says with a flick of her long, dark hair.

"Do you want to come in?"

"And risk not being able to get out again?" Ekaterina raises an eyebrow at me, and I instantly regret the suggestion.

"Why are you still at school?" I ask. "Thought you'd be halfway around the world by now."

"Some are. A bunch of parents came to fetch their kids on the weekend. Some want your mom to resign. Others want her kicked off the UCMW," Aysha says.

"It got real ugly," Ekaterina adds.

"The O'Connors got involved. So did the Khumalos. Natalie's moms are a mess. I thought it would get magical, but Morgan's mom managed to calm everyone down. *Your* mom is still going to be held responsible for putting us in danger though," Aysha says.

I study my toes, not wanting to think about the consequences my actions might have for my family.

"My parents are here," Aysha continues. "They're staying in town with the Khumalos. But they know running away isn't going to solve the problem. They decided I was safer at school while the adults do what they think is best." She doesn't sound impressed. "MacCrone and some other teachers have been babysitting a few of us at Pilvitalo."

"So, they don't think MacCrone is in on it?" I ask.

"Apparently not," Aysha says. "And since the *Messenger* piece, no one else has gone missing. No one except you and the O'Connors, of course."

I wince but shake it off. It's not too late for me to make things right. "So, where's Sini?"

"She was one of the first to leave," Aysha says. "We text all the time though. She wanted to stay for Natalie, but you know what her mom is like. Actually had a private driver come all the way from Helsinki to pick her up."

Not kidnapped by a chaos mage then. I guess I'm relieved. "What about you?" I ask Ekaterina.

"My dad sent a ticket like he always does." She sounds more bitter than usual. "I should be in Dubai or Monaco or something by now, but I stayed because that's what friends do. We owe it to Natalie."

"So, are you going to tell us what happened?" Aysha stomps her feet against the cold.

"Are you sure you don't want to come inside?" I'm getting cold too.

Aysha huffs, but tentatively inches one foot across the threshold, wavers back and forth a bit, then commits to stepping inside.

Ekaterina hangs back, shaking her head.

"Oh, it's fine. Stop being so dramatic." Aysha grabs Ekaterina by the coat and drags her in.

With the door closed, I tell them everything that's happened, starting with the tonttukivi in Kuusikylä and ending with me being a prisoner in my own home. When I'm done, Aysha and Ekaterina regard each other with wide eyes before turning back to me.

"This is…" Ekaterina struggles to speak. "This is just…"

"So unbelievably cool!" Aysha finishes for her, which is not the reaction I was expecting. "In a bad way. I mean, it's scary—but scary cool. I mean, you're related to Mervi the Magnificent? That's incredible, but then I really don't understand why…um…" Aysha looks everywhere but at me and I know exactly what she's thinking.

"Why I don't have magic?" I say and Aysha continues to look sheepish.

"You did talk to Natalie when none of us could," Ekaterina says.

"And apparently you can talk to trees," Aysha says with a grin. "So maybe you're not completely without talent after all." She gives Ekaterina a sideways glance.

"Guess not." Ekaterina's lips twitch with an almost smile and the glacier inside me sheds a little meltwater.

"Do you know what kind of spell your mom used?" Aysha asks.

"It was sigil based." As a tietäjä, Mom's power comes from knowing the *synty*—the cause or origin—of something. If a tietäjä knows the synty of a thing, they can control it.

"Maybe I can come up with a counterspell," Aysha says.

"You really think you can outspell my mom?"

"Worth a shot." Aysha shrugs then closes her eyes, starting to hum.

I chew on my nails, already bitten to the quick, wondering if this is yet another disastrously bad decision. Mom asked me not to make more trouble. Morgan, Hannah, Natalie—they could all die, and I absolutely don't want to be the reason they do because I distracted my mom from her efforts to save them. Mom was right, I'll only get in the way and make things worse.

"Wait, we shouldn't do this."

"Urgh, what now?" Ekaterina rolls her eyes.

"My parents are handling this. We should let them do what they need to and not get in their way."

Useless, worthless, pathetic—yup, that's me.

"Are you serious?" Aysha glares.

"We stayed home once before and look how that turned out," Ekaterina says. "We're not going to sit back anymore, so if you want to stay, fine. We're going."

"Not without Taika," Aysha says.

"Why?" A dozen different emotions fizz inside me. "It's not like I can do anything anyway."

"Are you kidding?" Aysha stares. "*You* figured out how to summon Natalie. *You* spoke to her. *You* found the stones and spoke to the hiisi and then the forest and—"

"And you really must be dense if you think all of that is nothing," Ekaterina chips in, her words harsh but her mouth pulling up into an actual grin this time.

What is happening? Am I dreaming? I give myself a pinch to be sure, but I'm definitely awake and these two aren't being awful to me.

I'm waiting for the voice in my head to chime in, but it stays silent and in the quiet, new thoughts begin to form. As much as it sucks to admit, I think Aysha and Ekaterina might actually be right.

I spoke to the liekkiö and Natalie asked for *my* help. I did come up with the summoning spell and it was me who spoke to the hiisi and the trees. And more than that, that time with the bogle and when Morgan healed Aoife, I was the one who came up with helpful rune suggestions.

So, I might not be able to cast spells or put any power into sigils, but that doesn't mean I've got nothing to contribute. Maybe I'm not Taika the Talentless all the time.

"But if you're too afraid to actually do something when you can, then you can stay here," Ekaterina says.

"I'm not afraid," I say, surprised to find it's true. I've been to the tonttukivi before, I've walked through that forest of eyeballs and faced off with the maahinen—it can't get much scarier than that and I survived. "I'm not afraid at all, I'm just not sure I can get out." I squint at the door, wishing I could see the strands of Mom's spellweaving and maybe find a loose thread to pull.

"You haven't even tried." Ekaterina opens the door and steps onto the porch, and her shoulders visibly relax. "Well?" She taps her foot at me.

"Come on, Taika." Aysha follows, looking equally relieved to make it across the threshold.

I approach the door and tentatively raise a hand, expecting to feel the same resistance as before.

Ekaterina grabs my hand and, before I can flinch or pull away, she yanks me onto the porch. Musti, Rekku, and Kamu, perched on the eaves, all give me croaks of disapproval.

"What?" I gasp, patting myself down to make sure there aren't any weird side effects—that my limbs are, in fact, all still attached.

"Told you." Ekaterina looks smug, as if this were her doing, but I think I know what broke the spell.

Mom would've used something as the synty, an aspect of who I am that would've kept me and no one else bound in the house. Whatever it was, it must've changed—something in *me* changed so the spell didn't recognize me anymore. It could've been sloppy spellcasting on Mom's behalf—she was in a hurry—but it's the lack of nasty commentary from that little voice in my head that makes me think maybe it was something else.

Regardless, I'm free, and now I have a chance to fix things and save my friends—as soon as I put on my boots and jacket.

26

"We need to get to Lumikuuro," I say as we head up the path. "There's a map of all the tonttukivet on Morgan's phone, but the battery died."

"Watch and learn." Ekaterina plucks the phone from my hands.

Static charge crackles along her fingers, blue bolts of electricity tangling around her hand before zapping the device. A puff of smoke escapes the edges of the phone's red-and-black case and we all cough at the stench of fried electronics.

"See?" Ekaterina hits the power button and, miraculously, the phone starts up.

Moments later, I show them the photo of the map.

"That's so far away," Aysha says. "How are we supposed to get there?"

"Bus then train then—" I'm trying to explain, but Ekaterina interrupts.

"Oh please, there must be a better way, a *magical* way of getting there. I bet whoever took Natalie didn't take public transport."

"You think the chaos mage used a portal?" I mentally kick myself for not thinking of it sooner.

"Makes sense," Aysha says. "They'd definitely be strong enough to open one."

Portals are super hard to control. For a start, the mage has to be able to use runes from all four elements and then feed the portal enough energy to keep it open long enough for someone to cross over—similar to the way a tonttukivi works, only minus the stones. The greater the distance between the entrance and exit of the portal, the more energy it requires, or so Toivo's Sigils and Systems textbook says.

"Could you—we—open our own?" I ask.

"Definitely not," Aysha says so emphatically I think better of pushing the issue.

If only Morgan was here, I bet he'd be able to do it, but he's not and it's my fault, so on to plan B.

"So, we find the portal and hope it's still open, or we take the bus."

"I vote for portal finding." Ekaterina raises her hand. "I mean, you do know how to find one, right?"

"With this?" I hold up the Zeiger counter I stole from Toivo's room. It's our only option without a vampire to sniff out traces left by the chaos mage.

"Is it working?" Aysha asks. "It doesn't seem to be sensing much of anything."

"Maybe there's nothing for it to pick up out here," Ekaterina says. "Should I try?"

Warily, I hand over the device. If Ekaterina fixed the phone, maybe she can fix this too.

Sparks. Smoke. The smell of charred plastic.

Eleven seconds later a very dead Zeiger counter tumbles out of her hands.

"Well, there goes that idea." Aysha nudges the puddle of

electronic remains with the tip of her shoe.

"Dammit. I'm sorry." Ekaterina's voice is all quavery like she might be trying not to cry—surprising, considering her all black clothes and the vicious spikes studding her jacket and boots. "It's hard to control how much power I use," she adds.

"Like that time you blew up the amps in the music room?" I ask gently.

"Yeah. And thanks for writing about that, by the way." She shoves her hands into her pockets.

A pang of guilt needles at me. Maybe I didn't need to write all those articles about students who'd had magical mishaps. Most of them had been about Ekaterina.

"I'm sorry." I meet Ekaterina's gaze, again surprised to see all the hurt brimming in her eyes, which are smudged black and purple with makeup. "That was mean, but it's not like you were particularly nice to me either."

Silence. For a horrifying, heart-stopping moment I think I've said the wrong thing and ruined the tenuous truce between us. Then Aysha sighs.

"You're right," she says. "We owe you an apology too."

I nod at Aysha, momentarily lost for words, then glance at Ekaterina.

"You hurt me." My hand involuntarily grips my wrist where she burned me.

"*That* was an accident," Ekaterina bites out. "I told you, I can't always control my powers, and I was angry with you about the article you wrote. Actually, I kind of hated you."

No kidding.

"You don't know what it's like, living like this." Sparks crackle off her fingers. "I hated you because I was jealous of you not having magic. I still am," Ekaterina says.

How is it possible for these powerful mages to envy my lack of magic? I don't get it. I'd give anything, *anything,* to have a single drop of their power.

"Anyway, I'm sorry too," Ekaterina says, but she refuses to

look at me.

"And I'm sorry about all the articles." I hope she accepts the white flag I'm waving. "I was jealous of you. I am jealous. I'd give anything to have what you do."

"Careful what you wish for, Taika." Ekaterina looks up, her gaze glassy, which is somehow way more disconcerting than if she'd been wearing her usual scowl.

"Think we could all just agree to be kinder to each other from now on?" Aysha asks. "For Natalie's sake? Because if we're serious about saving her we need to work together and put all this stuff behind us."

"Agreed," I say, although it's hard to get the word out around the brand-new lump in my throat. Do they know what happened between me and Natalie? Do they know why she stopped speaking to me? Would they still want to be nicer to me if they knew?

"As long as you stop calling me Ekaterina." Ekaterina gives me a comforting glare. "I prefer Katya."

"Katya, got it." I attempt a grin and Katya's own purple-smeared lips return it.

"So," Aysha says, "we just killed our only way of finding the mage's portal."

"Give me a minute." Maybe there's something else we could use, something else with a sensitivity to magic, that reacts to spells or energy. I've got it!

"Mr. Fotsios!" I pick up the pace, angling toward the school along a shortcut carved through the forest.

Unlike the rest of the faculty, Mr. Fotsios doesn't concern himself with spells and fancy conjurations. Instead, he pours all of his Apollonian power into music. There isn't an instrument he can't play, and he's even built his own.

"What about him?" Aysha asks.

"He has theremins that react to people's auras. I've seen them in the music room. We can use those." I don't tell them how it was Natalie who told me all about them or how we spent four weekends trying to build our own, but never quite got it to work.

"How?" Katya asks.

"They already sense magical energy. We just need to tweak it so that it picks up chaos magic," I say, wondering how on earth we're going to achieve that.

"You know how to do that?" Aysha asks the question I've been dreading.

"Couldn't you hum a modification or something?"

"Or *something*?" Aysha arches an eyebrow.

"Do we have a better idea?" Katya asks. "No? Then I'm with Taika. Let's go." She bursts into a run, and we follow.

27

There are over a dozen theremins lining the shelves in Mr. Fotsios's storeroom. Big ones and small ones, some prickling with odd adornments whose functions I can only guess at.

"This should do." I choose one double the size of a large flashlight and haul it off its shelf. It's heavier than I expected, but I can manage it with two hands.

"I probably shouldn't touch that," Katya says.

"Don't even look at it." Aysha waves her hands and Katya backs up, keeping her distance as I set the instrument on the nearest desk.

"What do I do?" Aysha asks.

"See these two antennae?" I point to the two metal rods sticking out of the theremin, one vertically, one horizontally. "Usually, holding your hand close to this one controls the pitch and the other one controls the volume." I flip the power switch and a crackle of white noise comes from the speaker.

"But with these ones, they react to a person's aura. Like this." I push it closer to Aysha. The device instantly produces a fluting melody.

She steps away and the music grows softer. "That's actually pretty cool."

Katya tries next, stepping cautiously closer to the antennae. The melody changes, becoming more jagged.

"What about you?" Katya asks.

I inch closer and the device falls silent. No tone, no white noise—nothing at all.

"Huh, guess it can't react to what isn't there." And somehow this doesn't bug me quite as much as I thought it would.

"It's reacting to something." Aysha pulls the device away from me and the white noise returns.

Maybe some residue from the liminal realm rubbed off on me, like pollen on a bee's legs, and that's what the theremin is picking up.

"So, Mr. Fotsios can control the flow of energy," I say, getting back to business. "He can create a whole symphony with these."

"How do you know all this?" Katya asks.

"I went to one of his concerts." With Natalie. "It was pretty good."

"Didn't know you were into music."

"Actually, I'm more into rock and punk." I give her a single shoulder shrug.

"You, really?" She stares at me like I've grown two heads.

"Do I not look the type?" I ask. "Because I don't wear all black, shred the knees of my jeans, or paint my nails?" Personally, I consider my style somewhere between everyone-hates-me-anyway-so-why-bother and if-it's-clean-I'll-wear-it, with a preference for stripes and flannel.

"No, it's just—I don't know," Katya says. "I think I had the wrong impression is all."

"How about you leave the fanby'ing over screechy guitars for later, kay?" Aysha says.

Her use of the word *fanby* makes me smile. Katya grins too and I'm pretty sure I can see the ice between us melt a little more.

"Let me see what I can do." Aysha lifts her hands and closes her eyes, then starts to hum, weaving her own song through the melody from the theremin.

Gradually, the harmonies change, the melody jumping wildly before settling on a single note—the same one Aysha is humming. After a few more moments, she opens her eyes and lowers her hands.

"To be honest, I have no idea what I'm doing, but I figured all I needed to do was tune it to elemental magic."

"Makes sense," I say.

"Around us, it should sing like it's doing right now. If there's chaos magic, I have no idea what it'll do, but it won't sound like this."

I pick up the theremin and the instrument falls silent again. Katya and Aysha share a questioning glance.

"Maybe my magic didn't work," Aysha says.

"Guess we'll find out." I tighten my grip on the instrument. "Now to find the portal."

28

We start our search in the school, because why not. For four of five floors, the best we receive are a few weird blips and pings from the theremin, both outside Emmi's and Joakim's rooms, but that's it.

"This is hopeless," Katya says.

"Still got one floor to go." We've been working our way down from the top, which leaves the ground floor. My hopes of finding the chaos mage's portal sink with every step I take down the stairs. It could be anywhere. It could be somewhere out in the forest—somewhere we have no hope of finding. What if this was a waste of time?

"Hey, I think it's working," Aysha says as we cross the foyer near the cafeteria.

The theremin is whining, the sound made all the more eerie in the otherwise silent and deserted building. We continue down the hallway and the whine grows louder, more shrill, driving painful daggers into my ears as we get closer to MacCrone's office.

"Thought you said it wasn't MacCrone." Katya raises an eyebrow at me. "Think it's just reacting to battle magic?"

"Maybe, let's check inside." I hand the theremin to Aysha before opening the door.

It's not locked and hasn't even been shut properly. Not good signs.

Inside, it's as if a tornado has torn through the office. Papers are scattered on the floor along with a smattering of blueberries. Files lie strewn across the desk and the computer's monitor hangs at a lopsided angle from its mount on the wall.

"What happened here?" Aysha asks.

"Clearly nothing good," Katya says.

"But there's no portal. We should keep searching." I want to get out of here and stop the theremin from screeching. Whatever happened with MacCrone, we're too late anyway.

We back away and the whining persists, thankfully at lower decibels.

"It's definitely picking up something." Aysha leads us down the corridor to the emergency exit we only ever use during fire drills.

The exit, like MacCrone's door, is ajar, and several blueberries have been crushed and smeared across the linoleum floor. At least, I hope that's only berries and not blood.

I shove open the door, scanning the twilight forest. This corner of the school cozies right up to the woods, with two paths leading away: one to the faculty parking lot which doubles as the emergency meeting point, the other into the trees, toward MacCrone's cottage. My crows are already there perched on the eaves, restless and croaking their concern.

"There are more blueberries." Katya crouches down on the muddy path. "Claw marks too. It goes this way."

We follow, happy to let Katya with her ability to conjure lightning bolts go first.

The theremin continues to sing dismal notes as we wind through the woods. My crows circle above, performing several low swoops over my head as if trying to stop me. I wave them away and force one foot in front of the other, trying to ignore the cold sweat on the back of my neck and my heart pounding faster than punk-rock drums.

When we reach MacCrone's cottage, the theremin screeches even louder, making the whole instrument vibrate. Aysha drops it and claps her hands over her ears. The theremin gives one final wail before erupting in a shower of sparks. A single black tendril of smoke curls up into the air and then, silence.

"Guess we're in the right place." I turn to face the cottage—not a place I would normally venture if I had the choice.

Claw marks cut grooves into the pebbled pathway leading the last few meters to the house. The door hangs open on a single hinge as if someone or *something* tried to rip the whole thing away. The only light comes from the static charge dancing between Katya's fingers. Aysha hums it into glowing orbs, lighting up the syrupy darkness inside the cottage. Nervously, we approach. Katya holds out a sparking hand, fingers trembling.

I gulp down some air, hoping it'll help me squash the fear bubbling up my throat. I'm the descendant of Väinämöinen! The blood of Mervi the Magnificent runs through my veins, the blood of the tietäjä who saved everyone from the chaos of Tumultua. Mervi certainly wouldn't have been afraid of some shadows in a cottage, and neither am I.

But she had magic, the little voice pipes up, making me grit my teeth. I thought it had gone for good, but I guess not. Well, I might not have magic, but that doesn't mean I can't have courage.

Despite the warning ruckus from my crows, I'm the first to step into MacCrone's cottage.

Feeling along the wall, my hand finds a switch and I flick it, lighting up the carnage. The cottage is in a worse state than the office was. Broken furniture lies scattered in splinters around the tiny living room. Smears of dark red decorate the walls where pictures hang askew. Some have been knocked down altogether, and glass crunches under my boots.

"Holy crap, is that blood?" Aysha clings to me as we survey

the destruction.

I want to lie and say it's just smashed berries, but my words are stuck behind my teeth. Judging by the splatter from wall to ceiling, someone must be badly injured.

"Look at the claw marks." Katya points at deep gouges along the floor and walls. Did Fiona do that or something else? There are far worse things than a maahinen lurking in the in-between spaces, ready to be summoned.

"It's so cold in here." Aysha rubs her arms through her jacket and stamps her feet.

"Is that snow?" Katya nods at a pile of white gathering at the far end of the living room.

Slowly, we pick our way through the wreckage. A cold wind whistles through the cottage, tossing flakes into our faces. Snow—tons of it—lies in a spreading puddle across the living room carpet, with more billowing in from the bedroom.

We stop, our shoes already dusted white. There's a hole in the wall, a haphazard oval, its edges frayed and scorched by whatever magic carved it. The sigils seared into the wallpaper aren't any I know, but they look familiar, like the ones in Toivo's room. Battle magic, or chaos magic then.

The bed has been upended, a snarl of sheets and broken bits in the corner. Several frayed pieces of wool and fluff are snagged on the springs. Wool the same sunshine yellow as Fiona's sweater, and fluff like the fur of the maahinen.

I take careful steps through the wall into the forest beyond, but where there should be leaves and shrubs, only the twisted remains of dead plants and ash remain.

"It's like when we did the summoning, only worse," Aysha says, her voice catching. "Look at the trees!"

Dead. All of them. Gaunt, lopsided, black, and crumbling as energy continues to be sucked out of them toward a shimmer that hangs like a curtain a few centimeters above the ground. It might've been a mirage were it not for the flickers of blue flame licking at its edges.

"A portal," Katya says as another gust of wind flings more snow at our feet.

Even as we watch, the shimmer grows smaller, its edges folding inward as a nearby tree collapses.

"It's closing. We have to hurry." Tentatively, I press a hand into the shimmer and feel the biting cold of the liminal world beyond. Again, my body starts to tingle, then my arm disappears.

"This is it." I gesture for the others to follow me.

Aysha takes my hand, then Katya's and, together, we step between worlds.

29

At least we end up somewhere recognizable.

"Are those—are those *eyes*?" Katya shivers as she stares at the ghoulish decorations dangling from the trees.

"Yip." I shudder and tug my beanie down over my ears. Snow continues to tumble out of the sky in big, sticky chunks. Birch trees moan in the wind, their leafless branches a thick tapestry above our heads. "It means we're in the right place." I flip up the hood of my jacket and start wading through the knee-high drifts.

"We should close the portal," Aysha says. "Otherwise, there might not be any forest when we get back."

"Can you do it?"

"I can try."

"But if we close it, we'll have no way to get home." Katya zips her jacket up to her chin.

All those metal spikes make it look like she's wearing armor. I wish I was.

"Well, we absolutely cannot leave it open and using up all the magic like that. We'll have to figure out another way back." Aysha starts to hum, holding her hands out in front of her a hairbreadth from the shimmer.

With her right hand, she draws the air rune *nauthiz,* using the more destructive side of the symbol to close the portal. It works. After a few more seconds the shimmer snaps shut with a sound like ripping Velcro, disappearing in a flutter of blue flame.

Aysha rests her hands on her knees, breathing hard. Sweat peppers her forehead and soaks the hair around her face.

"I'll be fine," she says before I can ask. "Just need a minute."

Two minutes and forty-two seconds later, we continue on our journey.

"What do you think happened to MacCrone?" Katya asks.

I've been asking myself the same question and don't much like the answers storming through my mind.

"Doesn't matter," I say. "Nothing we can do now except try to find the others. The trail leads this way."

The wind is doing its best to fill up the tracks, but there are still two visible sets of footprints, and a trail of claw marks clearly belonging to Fiona. We can't be that far behind. I lift one foot, then the other, cleaving through the snow.

"What is it?" Aysha asks when she catches me glancing left and right.

"Nothing." My mind is playing tricks on me, fear making me think every flitting shadow might be a monster reaching for my throat.

But there! No, I didn't imagine it. Between the trees, wisps of green flicker and dance, knotting into balls of flame.

Taika, you came... There's still time... Natalie's voice is faint, but it sends a jolt of energy through my cold and tired body.

"Is that Natalie?" Katya asks.

"She's glad we're here. We're close. We can do this." I forge ahead, thighs aching and calves on fire.

This is it. I know it deep down in my bones. This is our last chance to stop the chaos mage and save Natalie, Hannah—all of them.

The memory of Aoife's blood on the snow, of Morgan's terrified face, drives me forward. Six balls of green fire accompany us, zipping ahead through the trees.

"Those eyes are watching us. Are they, like, the mage's security system or something?" Katya asks.

"No. I think…" I pause and stare back at a particularly bright pair of yellow orbs suspended above my head. "I think they belong to the forest. Maybe they're part of the hiisi's security system."

Which gives me an idea. It seems silly to be talking to a pair of eyes, but I've got nothing to lose. Morgan said he felt fear and anger because his magic hurt the forest. Maybe that's why the forest let me go. It wasn't afraid of me and didn't see me as a threat.

"We're not here for the shard," I say in Finnish. "We're here to protect it."

"What are you doing?" Katya asks.

"I'm sorry we hurt you," I continue, ignoring Katya for the moment. "We didn't mean to. We want to stop the tietäjä from getting the Sampo." Gods, I feel ridiculous, but if this works… "We don't want another hiisi to get hurt either. My friends and I, we need to find my brother. Can you help us?" I rest my hand on the nearby trunk of a rowan, not expecting much from the trees or the eyes. Some are actually still dripping, freshly excavated from whatever unlikely creature's skull they used to call home.

As if responding to some secret signal, the eyes all blink and the moaning of the trees grows louder. Instead of an itching in my palm, this time there's a spreading warmth. The moaning turns to creaking and popping as if the branches are being stepped on by very large and heavy feet.

"Taika, what did you do?" Aysha's fingers dig into my arm.

"Watch out!" Katya shoves us both out of the way as a branch crashes to the ground.

The tapestry above us comes apart, the gnarled boughs snapping away from each other like arthritic fingers.

"The forest is showing us the way!"

"It's trying to kill us!" Katya says. "It threw a branch at you."

"Trust me." I push ahead, following the new path.

Wisps of green fire flit above us, pale but present.

"But the footprints," Katya says.

"I trust the trees."

"I hope you know what you're doing." Katya follows, breathing heavily, with Aysha in tow.

It feels like we've been going for hours when I finally spot the familiar distressed denim of Morgan's jacket.

"Morgan!" I yell so hard my voice cracks and my throat burns.

He's slumped against an oak, not moving. Pushing my aching legs to their limit, I sprint the last few meters.

"Morgan? Are you okay?" I give his shoulders a shake.

"Tai?" He opens bloodshot eyes and peers up into my face. "You came back?" He shifts and that's when I notice Aoife lying curled up in his arms, her eyes closed and face corpse-pale.

"Aysha, quick. Aoife is hurt."

Aysha joins me as Morgan unravels his hold on his sister.

"It's her right arm. It won't stop bleeding." He gives Aysha easier access.

Aoife groans and Aysha starts humming, her fingers gently prodding at the site of the injury.

"Where are the others?" I ask.

"Here." Toivo limps into the clearing.

His once blue jeans are stained brown. Aoife's green scarf has been crudely tied around his thigh, but he's bleeding too.

"What the hell are you doing back here? And with them?" He jerks his head at Aysha and Katya.

"If you want me to help with that leg, you'll be a little nicer to your sibling," Aysha snaps.

Toivo folds his arms, wincing, but he quickly covers up the pain with an angry scowl. The gash above his eye has swollen seven different shades of purple and is no doubt infected by whatever diseases the claw of a maahinen might carry.

"You were supposed to get out and stay out," he says.

"Mom and Dad know where we are."

"Then how did you get back here?" Toivo asks.

Katya fills him in, thankfully sparing the bit about how she and Aysha helped bust me out of house arrest.

"Did you find Hannah yet?" I ask when she's done.

"No, we've searched. Feels like we've been walking in circles." Toivo eases himself into the snow as Aysha comes over.

I try not to look at the red spreading beneath his knee.

"We killed the maahinen," Morgan says. "It took everything we had. We're all pretty spent."

He catches my eye and I think I know what he's trying to say. He's used up his own store of energy, but that doesn't mean he can't use someone else's. I give his hand a squeeze, hoping he gets the message I'm sending.

"Elemental mages aren't built to fight like this," Aysha says before she starts humming over Toivo.

"Luckily we've picked up a few tricks from MacCrone's book." Aoife offers my brother a weak smile. I'm a little envious they all know runes I don't, but I'll catch up later when we get out of here. If...

"Time moves faster here," I say. "It's only three days till Kekri in the real world, so we only have a few hours here."

"As the veil gets thinner, the chaos mage is only going to get more powerful. We can't waste any more time." Aoife looks at Toivo, who offers her a stoic nod.

"Good thing we're here, then." Katya holds up her hands, blue sparks dancing between her fingers.

"Not quite good as new, but good enough," Aysha says, and Toivo mumbles a thank-you as he tests his leg. It's not bleeding anymore. Aysha mops more sweat off her forehead. Using her magic this much is going to exhaust her too.

"Don't think we'll be enough to defeat a chaos mage who got the better of MacCrone," Toivo says.

"We have to try." Aoife struggles to her feet with Morgan's help. "Is Sorin back?"

"Not yet." Toivo winces as he puts more weight on his injured leg. "He went out hoping to track down Hannah or the mage, but he's been gone a long time."

"We need to find the hiisi in this liminal realm," I say.

"Is that what we're calling it?" Katya asks, but no one answers.

"We have to stop the mage from getting another shard of the Sampo," I continue.

"But how?" Morgan asks.

"The forest. Every time I've asked for help, it's answered me one way or another." I take a deep breath, very aware of all their gazes on me—especially the glower I'm getting from Toivo. "I don't think it wants to hurt us," I continue. "It's just afraid."

"It *was* afraid, now it's pissed." Morgan shudders. "Really, really pissed."

"You spoke to the forest?" Toivo asks, incredulous. "How?"

"In Finnish. With words." I'd roll my eyes if the situation were less life-threatening.

"That's—that's a form of shamanism," Aoife says, a frown folding across her forehead.

And shamanism is a form of magic. Does that mean—no, I'm not even going to consider it. It'll only set me up for even greater disappointment and humiliation.

"Think you can do it again?" Toivo asks.

I survey the surrounding trees. The eyes are staring at me again, but not in a threatening way, more like they're waiting for something. Waiting for me.

Magic or not, I can do this. I take a deep breath and let it out slowly before finding the words.

"Thank you," I say, switching to Finnish again. "Thank you for leading me to them, but now we *really* need your help to protect the hiisi and the Sampo. Can you help us again?"

The forest remains quiet. The snow has stopped falling and the wind has died down completely. Natalie and the other liekkiöt have vanished. The silence is unnatural, unnerving, and everyone exchanges anxious glances while studying the shadows.

The dangling eyes swivel their gazes away from me, toward a particularly dense patch of darkness. The shadows melt together as if the darkness is liquid. It ripples and shakes, slowly taking form.

Everyone else scrambles away. I stand my ground.

"Is that what I think it is?" Katya's voice quavers.

The forest answers before I can as the shadow beast lumbers forward on four gigantic paws. It opens its mouth and roars.

30

The bear rears up on its hind legs, batting at the air with immense paws that end in scalpel-sharp claws. Its fur is mottled gray, like the very shadows it materialized from. It drops to all fours and stares at me, then at everyone else in turn, as if weighing us up. Its shiny black eyes are far more intelligent than any ordinary bear's, and I can sense it judging us.

"Are we going to die?" Aysha whispers.

"No. It's here to help," I say in a voice much calmer than I feel.

"Are you sure?" Morgan stands beside me, his elbow bumping mine.

"Bears are sacred, and this is no ordinary bear."

Toivo offers his thanks in Finnish to the creature with more reverence than I thought possible from my brother. He even addresses the bear as *Metsän Kuningas*—King of the Forest. The creature exhales a puff of white steam in Toivo's direction before turning on powerful legs and lumbering through the trees.

"We should follow it," I say, and no one argues, limping and leaning on each other for support as we move forward. It's only Katya who looks skeptical. She keeps blue sparks dancing between her fingers, as if that'll be enough to defend us.

It's easier going, walking in the bear's enormous footprints. Toivo, Aoife, and Morgan seem to be gaining more strength, too. They walk a little straighter and aren't leaning so heavily on each other.

"It's this place." Morgan glances down at his feet. "There's more elemental energy here. It's like I'm powering up."

"It's the bear too," Toivo says. "Thank you for that, by the way." He gives me an appreciative nod, which is far more shocking than having a magical bear appear.

My brother has never looked at me with anything other than disdain. I don't think he's ever thanked me for anything in his life, not even for presents on birthdays. Maybe he's starting to hate me a little less now that I've proven myself not completely useless.

But that thought stings too. I've finally started making peace with the fact I'll always be unmagical, and now this happens. Could I really possess some form of shamanic ability?

"What if this isn't magic?" I didn't mean to say it out loud.

"You still helped us, and I still have a reason to be grateful." Toivo's gaze rakes over me as if he can see magical auras and is searching for mine.

Surely if I was suddenly developing powers of my own, I'd feel different, but I feel the same as ever.

A few meters ahead, the bear pauses and rears back on its hind legs again. It growls, a low thunder shaking the trees, showering us with snow.

"There, just ahead." I edge tentatively around the bear, casting a cautious glance at the paws easily twice the size of my skull.

There's a large clearing and, on the far side, a stand of spruce trees similar to the one in the glade where I met the hiisi. There, two figures are fighting, and another lies prone and splattered horrible shades of pink.

Aoife sucks in a sharp breath. Morgan grabs my hand. Aysha and Katya huddle together, mouths open. Toivo stares wide-eyed and I guess I must look much the same.

In front of us, Emmi and MacCrone face off against each other. They're both bleeding—Emmi from claw marks that have cut her sleeves into ribbons. Intricate ink winds up both of her arms. I've never noticed her tattoos before. She certainly doesn't seem the type to be all inked up.

MacCrone bleeds from a gash on her neck, and her clothes are scorched in several places, probably from deflecting spells. Fiona lies in the snow, her tail whipping back and forth in irritation, her front legs cruelly twisted beneath her. Kalma drops from a tree branch, hissing at the dragon, her fur standing on end and her back arched.

"Help me!" Emmi yells as we creep closer. "She's after the Sampo. We have to stop her."

MacCrone? No, that can't be right. Emmi is the tietäjä. It has to be her. But... Emmi has always been so kind to me and was the one to bring me home. It can't be Emmi! Can it?

You know it is, the little voice pipes up, the truth scouring my thoughts.

"That's rubbish and they'll know it," MacCrone wheezes out between gasps. "They'll not believe the likes of you."

"But they'll believe you? A washed-up battle mage turned to chaos just like Tumultua."

"She's your friend, not mine." MacCrone scrawls a sigil in the air and sends it hurtling toward Emmi as if it were a dagger Emmi dodges but the sigil catches her on the shoulder, opening up a tear in her sleeve.

"See?" Emmi says. "She attacked me. She came after me in my classroom wanting to drain me of magic."

"That's not true," Aysha whispers, looking at me and Katya. "We went to Emmi's room. There was no sign of a struggle. She's lying."

My mind whirls, thoughts ricocheting back and forth between possibilities.

"Please, Toivo, Aoife," Emmi says. "I need your help. I can't do this alone." She raises her hand, ready to carve a sigil.

That's when I see it. On her forearm, nestling in the crook of her right elbow—a chaos star with fiery wings, the emblem of the Order of Louhi.

I point at Emmi's arm. "She's the chaos mage."

Emmi glances at the ink on her arm, her expression almost sad as her finger grazes the mark. She doesn't even try to deny it. Instead, the sadness melts away, replaced by grim determination as she lifts her chin and squares her shoulders.

"You're too late to stop me. Balance will be restored," she says.

MacCrone snarls and brings her forearms together, the tattoos on her skin glowing blinding white before sending a burst of energy that sends Emmi skidding backward through the snow toward the trees. She lands heavily on her knees, gasping for breath.

MacCrone advances and for a moment, it seems the fight is about to be over.

But Emmi reaches into the snow, scrabbling at what I thought was a boulder at the base of the spruce behind her. She staggers to her feet, hauling up a small, limp body with one hand. In the other, she holds a dagger.

"Hannah!" Morgan takes a hesitant step toward them, his fists clenched.

Hannah opens her eyes, clearly dazed as she glances about. Her gaze finds Morgan and she starts to cry.

"I'm going to kill you!" Morgan rushes forward, with Katya and Aoife right behind him.

The bear roars and joins the charge. I catch the look of fear flitting over Emmi's face as she takes in the bear surging toward her.

Meanwhile, I'm paralyzed, my thoughts seized in the grip of panic and disbelief. The only teacher I ever liked, who ever liked *me*, is a chaos mage and the one who kidnapped Natalie!

"No, not like this," Toivo says, but no one's listening.

Lightning bolts spark from Katya's fingers, dropping to fizzle in the snow even as she rushes forward. If only Katya knew battle runes, she'd be formidable. As it is, she needs to touch her target before she can unleash her power.

"Don't hurt Hannah!" Aoife screams.

Hannah's eyes widen, her mouth opening and closing as if she's struggling to breathe. Emmi carves sigils in the air with the tip of her blade, sending an invisible fist pummeling into Katya. She goes flying, landing in an explosion of snow several meters away. Aoife and Morgan dive sideways to avoid Emmi's next barrage. Only the bear seems undeterred.

"I see you've brought a friend," Emmi says as the bear nears. She pulls Hannah in front of her like a human shield.

The bear circles, trying to get between her and the trees, one of which must be the hiisi, but Emmi holds her ground.

"Emmi, please, you can stop all of this," Toivo says as he approaches our teacher with his hands up as if he's approaching a cornered dog and not a chaos mage.

"I wish there was another way," Emmi says. "But you wouldn't stop. I tried to tell your mother. I tried to get her to do the right thing, but she and her council friends—no one would listen. Something had to be done."

Tell our mother what? What didn't Mom do?

"Stay back, children," MacCrone orders, one hand pressed to her neck.

Emmi draws a complicated sigil and, muttering in a language I don't recognize, sends MacCrone pirouetting headfirst into the trees. The battle mage falls and doesn't get up.

Oh gods, oh gods, oh gods. We're all going to die.

"I'm sorry," Emmi says. "I'm sorry it has to be this way, but soon you'll understand."

Hannah's eyes roll back in her head, and she collapses as if her bones have turned to water. Emmi drags her closer to the hiisi, dagger at the ready.

The bear attacks.

Kalma springs, tiny claws extended toward the giant creature, her ears pressed flat against her head.

"Protect the trees," my voice is a squeak. I swallow and try again. "The trees! That's where the shard is!"

Toivo gives me a nod and Aysha squeezes my arm.

"We need to save Hannah," Aoife says, picking herself out of the snow.

"Just don't let Emmi touch you," Toivo adds.

"I'm going to kill her." Morgan's face is weirdly blank of any discernible emotion, then a blur of brown careens into him.

"*Varo, maahisia!*" Toivo shouts in warning. "You know how to deal with them. Do it!" he yells at Aoife as another monster hurtles into the clearing.

They aren't the only creatures either. Crows gather in the trees, their harsh cries punctuating the sounds of battle coming from all directions now. The glade lights up with magic—flickers of blue fire and ribbons of green-brown energy. It's so hard to keep track of everybody, but I see Katya set one monster on fire only to get slammed into the snow by another.

Aysha hangs back, staring at the chaos around her. "My magic doesn't work like this." Her voice is thick with tears.

"But you can help people who are injured. Help Katya, help MacCrone!" I say, biting back the *Don't stand there being so damn useless!* because that's exactly what I'm doing.

Useless, worthless, pathetic—what good is being able to talk to trees in a battle like this?

Aysha nods and runs over to help Katya first.

Stop her. You have to stop her! Natalie's voice shrills from above where, once more, balls of green flame cut zigzags across the clearing.

Katya sits up in the snowdrift looking furious. Aysha moves on to MacCrone.

"Do something." I point Katya toward Morgan and Aoife.

Katya smiles as she grabs at the nearest maahinen, lightning dancing between her fingers. The monster screams and retreats to lick its charred wounds, but another tears into the clearing to take its place.

Aysha shouts something incoherent and I turn in time to see a maahinen hurtling toward her. A wolf snarls and leaps in front of her, shredding the monster with enormous fangs.

Sorin finishes off the maahinen and bounds after another, joining Toivo, who's currently embroiled with two of the monsters. The horns twist from their heads at awful angles, their paws slashing at my brother's chest. Then Sorin has one of the creatures by the throat. Bone and cartilage crunch in wolf jaws and my stomach twists as I fight back a wave of nausea.

Morgan turns a maahinen to ice and shatters it with a kick, only to be set upon by yet another.

"*Tiwaz*," I shout to him. The fire rune of victory and strength—the rune for warriors.

Morgan adds my suggestion to the next sigil he draws, waiting for the maahinen to get perilously close before powering up the sigil. It vaporizes the monster. Another maahinen thinks better of attacking and retreats through the trees.

I turn my attention back to Emmi.

Kalma has managed to avoid the bear's claws, dancing nimbly out of the way, springing to land the occasional swat of a paw that couldn't be more than a mosquito bite to the king of the forest.

The bear focuses on Emmi and lands several blows to her body, revealing even more ink. Emmi's blood dapples the snow and tears burn in my eyes. This can't be happening. It's the worst kind of nightmare.

It looks like the bear is going to win. Am I really going to stand here and watch Emmi die?

The bear rears up once more, opening its mouth to reveal long, yellow fangs. It grabs Emmi with its paws. It might've been giving her a hug were it not for her screams. The bear lowers its jaws and I look away. I expect to hear another crunch of bone; instead, there's a terrible silence and then an awful, wet tearing.

I peep between my fingers and watch in disbelief as the bear slumps to the ground. Wisps of shadow peel off its fur, evaporating into nothingness. Emmi remains standing, her arm greased to the shoulder with blood. She has the bear's heart in her hand. Bleeding and clearly tired, she gently lays the heart in the snow, tears streaking her cheeks. The heart smokes for a moment before it, too, vanishes. My heart lurches as I feel the bear's loss like a wound opening inside of me.

Emmi's remorseful gaze meets mine. "You don't understand, I'm doing the right thing. I only want to give back to nature what's been stolen from it."

"The only ones doing any stealing are you and the rest of your order, breaking into the vault on Svalbard and kidnapping kids!" I hurl back at her.

Emmi, still crying, turns to the grove. I have to do something. I can't let her get the Sampo shard.

The trees shudder and shiver, branches snaking out to bat at Emmi's legs and arms. She slashes at the boughs with her blade, and the scent of sap fills the clearing. Emmi steps up to the largest trunk, which has to be the hiisi. I think I just make out its face in the snow-caked branches. Emmi raises her dagger in one hand while grabbing for Hannah with the other.

Stop her, Taika! Voices ring inside my skull—not just Natalie's, but Manami's and Elijah's, Peter's, Risto's, Qendresa's! A chorus yelling at me to do something, *anything*.

I bound across the clearing, aiming straight for Emmi.

Emmi turns and sculpts a sigil in the air. She blows the spell like a kiss. The magic hurtles into me, knocking the breath from my lungs and my legs out from under me. The spell weaves around my limbs like rope. I've never felt magic like this. It hurts, it hurts so much more than I can take. For a panicked moment, I wonder if there are types of magic I might not be resistant to even as I count the seconds. After fifteen, the spell loses power.

After twenty, the burning eases and the magical bonds loosen on my limbs.

Suddenly, Morgan is here and pulling me to my feet.

"You okay?" he asks, breathless.

There are shallow claw marks down his cheek, and the sleeve of his jacket hangs in ragged strips. His face is drawn, and eyes sunk deep in bruised sockets.

"Are you?" I ask.

"Completely out of gas."

"We can stop her. Together." I squeeze his hand.

"I don't—"

"For Hannah," I say, and he leans on me as we make our way toward Emmi.

She's so focused on carving into the hiisi, she doesn't notice us approach.

When we're in range, I feel a tug on my energy as Morgan traces more runes in the air.

Snow tumbles from the branches, forcing Emmi to stop her work with the dagger to deflect the avalanche. That's when Morgan launches a second attack, drawing on my energy to knock Emmi sideways with a blast using *raido* and another rune he must've learned from the battle mage handbook.

He staggers and I catch him before he falls. His wrists are bleeding, and he squeezes his eyes shut as he tries to stay upright. Using my energy is only going to hurt him more. He can't keep doing this.

Emmi stumbles away from Hannah but remains on her feet, her gaze narrowed at Morgan.

"I'm sorry," she says. "Maybe one day you'll understand."

Her fingers flick a sigil into the air and the spell wrenches Morgan out of my grasp, tossing him across the snow as if he's made of paper.

He looks at me, eyes terrified, but he can't move. I know how that feels, only the magic won't slough off Morgan like it did from me. Emmi leaves him paralyzed in the snow and returns to the tree, sinking her blade hilt-deep in the trunk.

My feet move of their own volition, closing the distance between us.

"No!" I kick and punch at her, bite and tear with every last bit of my strength.

Out of the corner of my eye, I see Aysha tending to Morgan. He's coughing, but at least he's breathing and slowly starting to move again. I redouble my assault on Emmi.

"Enough, Taika." She spins, dagger raised, and I freeze.

All I can see is the tip of the blade hovering above my face. I can only watch as the dagger plunges toward me.

31

I watch in frozen fascination as the blade descends.

"I'm sorry," Emmi says, even as the dagger continues its slow-motion trajectory toward my chest.

Toivo charges in from my left, reaching for my shoulders as he dives to cover me. The blade disappears into my brother's back.

We roll, Toivo shoving me away as we go sprawling in the snow. Winded, we both lie still for a moment, only there's a pool of blood spreading out beneath him and I'm uninjured. I crawl over to him, and Morgan joins me.

"Is he dead?" I whisper, barely able to form the words.

"I wouldn't waste his life like that." Emmi looms over us and reaches for the dagger.

A moment later, she's blasted backward by a surge of power that gives me an instant rash of tingles.

"Holy crap, it's your mom," Morgan says.

I peer up through the curtain of tears currently blinding me to see Mom stride into the clearing, a billowing mass of crows flocking around her. They wheel and dart at Emmi.

"Emmi, how could you?" The expression on my mom's face is equal parts rage and astonishment. "You betrayed us. You betrayed everything we stand for, everything that's sacred!"

"You don't understand. You've always been so shortsighted," Emmi snaps while defending herself from the crows.

Several of the birds explode in a shower of black feathers, but more keep coming. Mom continues the barrage of magic against Emmi. The chaos mage is powerful, but she's tired and injured, while my mom is fresh to the fight.

"You have desecrated this sacred place. You have broken our covenant with the forces of nature. You are no tietäjä!" Mom says, every word sharper than Emmi's dagger.

"This is your doing," Emmi spits. "You and your council members took everything from us. You took everything from nature. Did you feel the stones? Can you feel the energy here? We're draining the worlds. It's only a matter of time before natural magic is gone for good, and then what?"

"So, you resort to this?" Mom says. "We could've talked about—"

"We tried!" Emmi yells. "We've been trying for years. For *centuries*, but you're as ignorant as your ancestors."

We. The word sets a dozen alarm bells ringing in my head as I can't help wondering how many more chaos mages there might be, who they are, and if any more lurk at our school.

"Mervi did what she had to to maintain order," Mom says.

"Is that the story they tell you?" Emmi presses a hand to the bloody slashes cut by the bear across her belly. "Mervi was a tyrant. The order you speak of is just an excuse to bleed this world dry of magic."

I don't get it. Nothing she's saying matches with anything I've read. Mervi the Magnificent was a hero, who won the war against the evil of chaos. Of that, I'm sure.

Aoife staggering toward us with Hannah in her arms distracts me from Mom and Emmi's continued argument.

"She's breathing, barely, but she's still with us," Aoife says.

Morgan wraps his arms around his sisters as Sorin limps across the clearing, shaggy and blood-flecked, peering into the shadows of the surrounding forest as if expecting another attack. He glances at my mom, but warily keeps his distance.

Closer to the trees, MacCrone is sitting up, hugging Fiona to her chest. I scan the clearing and see Aysha a little further away, slumped in the snow, her eyes closed.

Katya crouches beside her, only the tiniest of sparks flickering from her fingers—her scowl and four-letter curses all she can offer to the fight now.

Everyone is beyond exhausted.

Mom and Emmi are shouting, talking over each other with fists raised—potential magic swirling like an invisible tornado around them. There's nothing I can do to help my mom, but Toivo...

"My brother," I say, voice cracking.

"I'll do what I can." Aoife lays Hannah down gently to tend to Toivo. She kneels over him, hands trembling.

"Use me." Morgan offers Aoife his hand, blood oozing around the fresh scabs on his wrists.

"No, here." I offer my hand instead.

Aoife's own wrists are raw and bloody too, but she grips my fingers and crafts a healing sigil above Toivo. Morgan squeezes my other hand, drawing the same sigils as Aoife, but adding *uruz* to his for more potent regeneration.

"Together," he says.

Aoife nods and they start chanting in Irish. The air leaves me in a rush, but I'm ready for it this time and know not to panic. It feels awful. It feels like dying, but I can take it, gritting my teeth until Morgan cries out and grips his wrists. They're smoking. Aoife's too. She drops my hand, plunging her hands into the snow.

"We did what we could," she says, and I nod my thanks while I suck in painful breaths.

Taika the Talentless, useless, worthless—the little voice at the back of my mind taunts me, but it's wrong and this time I know it.

I feel the shift in magic before I see my mom raise her hand to carve the first sigil. Her crows screech as my mom releases all her pent-up fury in a barrage of elemental spells. Mom isn't a battle mage so I'm counting on the fact that Emmi is tired and injured to give mom the upper hand.

As I watch though, I start to lose hope. Despite my mom's fresh conjurings, Emmi somehow manages to counter every single one. She might not have the energy to attack, but she's not backing down.

The liekkiöt dance above me, flares of brilliant green. Emmi and the Order of Louhi haven't won yet. This fight isn't over.

Despite how drained I am, I manage to stand and stride through the storm of crows and magic. Mom's spells glance off me. I'm not their intended target so I barely even feel them. I stare at my hands, and then at the branches of the trees behind Emmi.

"Please, help me now. Help me make things right," I whisper to the forest, and I feel something open inside me, as if all the blood is pooling in my feet, spreading like roots, like capillaries through the earth, connecting me to the trees. Warmth rushes through my toes, twining up my legs to curl like spring fronds in the center of my chest.

I raise my hands and the trees respond.

"This will never—" Emmi's words are cut short as the branches move, curling into fingers that make a fist as I ball my own.

My head fills with a sudden buzzing, as if a thousand bees have chosen the inside of my skull for their hive.

The branches reach down and wrap around Emmi, pinning her arms to her sides. She struggles in the forest's grip, then stills and gazes at me with an expression I've never seen on her face before: it's equal parts horror and wonder.

"This stops now." I glare at Emmi and the buzzing gets louder.

"It's over." Mom stands beside me.

"It's over for me," Emmi says. "And it's only right that I should give back to the forest what I've taken from it. But we won't stop—not until balance is restored, or you drain every last drop of magic from this world." She turns her stare on me. "Taika, please. Try to understand."

My fists tighten and the branches squeeze, robbing the chaos mage of breath. Not Emmi, not the teacher who was kind to me, but a chaos mage who hurt Natalie and Hannah, who cut the hiisi, who stole what she had no right to. The mage closes her eyes and I blink the film of tears out of mine.

Mom puts her hands on my shoulders, making me aware of how tense I am. My whole body is rigid as I try not to think about how much I liked Emmi, how I trusted her and believed the care she showed me. I want her gone so she can never hurt anyone ever again.

The forest shivers and a gust of warm wind, ripe with the smell of damp earth, blusters through the clearing. The branches envelop the chaos mage, vines tangling through her hair, around and through her limbs. Now it isn't only sap running in red rivulets down the tree trunks. The smell of copper fills the air and I want to be sick. The buzzing in my head gets louder and louder, until it's so painful I'm sure my head will explode and release an entire stinging swarm.

Thank you, a creaking voice cuts through the buzzing, stilling the frenzy.

"It's okay, Taika," Mom says. "It's over now. The forest has claimed her. You can stop now. Whatever you're doing, it's enough." She peers into my face, stroking sweaty hair off my forehead.

Slowly, I unclench my fists, prying each finger individually from my palm. Gradually, the buzzing in my head fades into a dull tinnitus.

"Your dad is on his way. Everything will be okay now." She pulls me into a hug I'm not sure I'm ready for. I stiffen at first, then relax and wrap my arms around Mom too. I think we're only standing because we're holding each other up.

Taika, hurry! Natalie calls from above, where the liekkiöt still dart through the air. They disappear through the trees, and I pull away from my mom to follow.

"Natalie and the others. This way." I force my feet through the snow.

The trees part for me, showing me a cleared site where a tent like the one Emmi uses every year on the camping trip has been pitched.

The liekkiöt flash and flicker above the tent before flitting inside.

I scrabble with the zip, ripping it open as fast as my frost-nipped fingers will let me.

Natalie and the others are laid out side by side, their faces all covered with a sheen of deathly gray, their eyes closed in dark hollows. None of them appear to be breathing. I kneel beside Natalie and take her hand, pressing my fingers to her papery skin in search of a pulse. I can't find one.

Mom nudges me aside, checking each kid. She stops beside Natalie.

"Is she—?" I can't say it. I don't even want to think it.

Mom bows her head, shoulders sagging. I've never seen my mom so depleted before. She used up everything she had in the fight against Emmi.

"If you use my energy, can you save her?" I ask as I offer her my hand.

"Oh Taika." Tears spill down Mom's cheeks. "I'm so sorry. I was so wrong about you. About everything."

Raised voices prevent me from asking what she means. Dad and Aleksi stick their heads into the tent

"Quick. We need to get them out of here as soon as possible if we want to save them," Mom says.

"Come on, kulta." Dad takes my arm and gently pulls me out of the way.

I don't want to leave Natalie. I don't want this to be the last time I ever get to see her. There's so much I want to say to her.

But I have no more strength to fight against my dad as he guides me back to the others. Everyone sits huddled together under rescue blankets. Morgan wraps one of the blankets around my shoulders and I lean up against him. Dad heads back toward the tent. There are so many people in the clearing now. At least a dozen teachers and parents, only some of whom I recognize.

"Where's Emmi?" Caitlin O'Connor asks as her husband

fusses over Hannah, drawing healing sigils in the air above her.

"Gone," Aoife says.

"The forest took her," Morgan adds.

"She paid for what she did to the hiisi, to Natalie and Hannah," I say.

Caitlin's face pinches with concern as she spins in a circle, scanning the trees.

"She won't be back." Don't think I'll ever be able to scrub the memory of those bloody branches from my mind.

"She's dead?" Caitlin chokes out. "Are you sure?"

I nod and Morgan waves toward the trees where Emmi was taken. There are red smears on the bark. Caitlin says nothing after that, going back to Hannah, but I glance up and catch her giving me a dark and twisted look. It lasts a second at most, but it makes my insides tighten. Of course, she's angry with me. I put Morgan in danger and it's probably my fault Hannah got taken at the buck building too, since I was the one who suggested we sneak away, but—but nothing. I'm just exhausted. I curl tighter into Morgan, letting his warmth soak my side.

Joakim helps MacCrone, who's far more concerned about Fiona than herself. The dragon seems fine, walking on four legs as mended by Aysha, and nuzzling MacCrone for blueberries. Mr. Fotsios drapes his coat over Sorin's shoulders, who sits human and naked in the snow.

"Are you okay?" Morgan asks.

"I don't think so. You?" My teeth are chattering, and I can't feel my toes anymore.

"Not at all," he says. "But we did it. We stopped a chaos mage. Well, you did." A tentative smile quirks up his lips.

"Yeah, you were pretty amazing," Katya says from where she's sitting under a blanket with Aysha.

"Time to get moving." Miss Kaneda directs parents and teachers out of the forest.

Eoin O'Connor carries Hannah, and Caitlin loops an arm around Aoife. Together, Morgan and I struggle to our feet. Aleksi, Joakim, Natalie's moms, my parents, and a few others carry bodies wrapped in blankets.

Please let her be alive. Please please please! I hope the forest hears me and answers my plea one last time.

"Come on, let's go home." Toivo walks stiffly, clearly still in pain despite all healing attempts.

"I want a hot shower," Aysha says.

"I want food. Like, all the food." Katya looks as if she's about to fall asleep on her feet.

"I'd kill for a cup of coffee," Morgan says.

Together, we stagger away from the clearing, a slow procession of exhaustion and cautious optimism.

But... Five shards have been taken. The Order of Louhi has more than half of the Sampo. They won't give up now, not when they're so close to getting what they want.

As we leave the liminal realm and stumble back to the tonttukivi, Emmi's words echo in my head. Despite our victory today, I know this isn't over.

32

Every year, Myrskyjärvi International School for the Magically Gifted celebrates Kekri with a dance. We honor the ancient harvest traditions by serving up a huge buffet complete with reindeer meat and way too much dessert. Everyone stuffs their faces because the food at Kekri is actually good and not at all like what they serve in the cafeteria.

At midnight on Kekri eve, Mom gives a speech and burns the buck—the one we've spent hours making. After that, the Pebbles go back to Kivitalo for hot chocolate while the older kids stay for the real party. Mr. Fotsios cranks up the sound system and everyone dances until the early hours of the morning, shoulder to shoulder with the occasional ghost who manages to cross over when the veil between worlds is thinnest.

This year, Kekri isn't going to be like that.

This year, I dress in black, my heart heavy as lead.

"Are you ready?" Mom asks when I pad into the kitchen.

"As I'll ever be."

All my shock and fear has been replaced by anger. Anger at my parents, at Toivo and MacCrone, and especially at Emmi. We could've saved more lives if someone had listened to me from the start, if they'd bothered to believe me about the liekkiö.

"I know it's going to be difficult for you," Mom says. "It's difficult for all of us. I just hope you know how proud we are of you, and how sorry we are."

Mom's words wash over me, snagging on the prickle of thorns I feel pushing through my skin. I don't want her apologies. Apologies aren't going to bring anyone back from the dead.

"What you did, all of it," Dad says. "That took real courage." He pulls me into a hug, and I wish my thorns were real, so he'd feel some of the pain I do. "You truly are remarkable," he adds.

"Because now I have magic?" Guess I'm finally lovable.

"No. That's not it at all." Mom eases me out of Dad's hug. "Look at me, Taika."

I don't.

She tucks her fingers under my chin and lifts my face until we make eye contact.

"Magic doesn't make the person. Never forget that. You have always been amazing, and I have always loved you. I admit I made mistakes." She sucks in a breath. "I don't expect you to understand or to forgive me for what I said. I was scared, I was trying to keep you safe, and I'm sorry. I should've listened. I should've tried to understand you better."

Are these words really coming out of my mom's mouth? I never expected her to apologize and now that she has, I'm not sure what to do.

"It's okay, Mom."

"No, it's not, but it will be. Recent events have shown me how very special you are in a way that has *nothing* to do with magic, and I know I have a lot to make up for." She hugs me again and tears burn at the back of my eyes and nose. Finally, Mom kisses my forehead and releases my face.

"Now isn't the time for gifts, but we wanted you to have this." Dad hands me a box wrapped in silver paper with white ribbon.

"What? Why?" I ask, even as my fingers rip open the package.

It's a silvery-gray T-shirt marked with the lightning-like *sowelo* rune representing House Aithyr.

Aithyr. My house. My element. Finally, I know where I belong, and everyone else is going to know it too.

"Thank you," I say, although inside I'm being bombarded by a lot of conflicting emotions. "What about Sorin and the others?"

"They'll get their shirts," Mom says. "It's about time we acknowledged all forms of magic at this school."

Carefully, I fold the shirt and leave it lying in the wrapping on the kitchen table. I'll get to wear it soon enough, along with the other six students who have always truly belonged under the Aithyr banner.

"Let's go," Mom says. "Don't want to be late."

Together, we walk up the icy pathway lit at intervals by candles in brown paper bags full of sand. Mom's usual cloud of crows is a little smaller now, but still there, cawing from the treetops. Rekku and Kamu flutter close, letting me know they survived the ordeal on the other side of the stones. Musti didn't and I don't even have their body to bury. I didn't think I'd miss one of my crows this much.

Most of the students have already gathered at the lake, parents too. Candles ring the shore, illuminating dozens of solemn faces. The Kekri buck waits at the water's edge.

This year, no one's in a festive mood.

Six students were taken, only three survived.

The framed photos of the students lost to Emmi have been propped up against boulders, each with their own set of candles and flowers. Risto, Elijah, Manami, all of them smile in the photos, so unaware of what fate had in store for them.

Their families stand nearby. Shoulders hunched, faces drawn and tearstained, eyes staring numbly out at the lake. I can't even begin to imagine what they're going through.

Instead, I search for Morgan. He's with his dad farther up the embankment. This time, he's dressed all in black too, even his boots.

He's wearing a new jacket—black leather slung with a dozen glinting chains. There's a massive red anarchy *a* pinned to the back of it.

Hannah is in the infirmary, which is probably where Morgan's mom is. As suspected, Emmi was draining the magical energy out of the students, using it to fuel not only passage through the stones, but the spell to take the Sampo from the hiisi as well. It'll take weeks—months even—for Hannah to recover—if she ever does. She's still unconscious and no one knows if she'll ever do magic again, if she wakes up. Just have to wait and see.

Toivo stands with Aoife, who has an arm around his waist to prop him up. He's supposed to be in the school's infirmary too. The dagger punctured his lung, narrowly missing his spine. If it wasn't for Aoife's and Morgan's efforts, followed by the potent healing power of Natalie's South African mom, who's an inyanga, Toivo would be dead. He would've died saving my life—a fact I'm still processing.

Sorin is with his own family, all pale-skinned with dark hair and beautiful faces. He keeps glancing over at Aoife, but she doesn't seem to notice.

MacCrone is there too, walking with the aid of a crutch and grumbling constantly. Fiona, wearing a black sweater over her scales, waddles beside her. When MacCrone sees me, she gives me a slow nod.

"Off you go," Mom says. "I've got a speech to make."

I'm traipsing along the shore, heading for Morgan, when four figures block my way—Aysha, Katya, Sini, and, held between them, Natalie. "You're supposed to be in bed," I say before I can think of something better. My heart already thinks I'm running a marathon.

"And miss all the fun? Not a chance." Natalie smiles.

Her cheeks are gaunt, and her brown skin is shiny as if she has a fever, but she's alive and as beautiful as ever. Like Hannah, she was drained of her magic, but thanks to her inyanga mom and her Muspellian genes, she's recovered a lot faster than the others. Though it'll be some kind of miracle if she ever wields fire again. Despite all that, she's here and she's looking at me like there's more she wants to say.

"Hey girls, think we could have a moment?" Natalie says, and the others shrug.

Natalie leans into me. She *takes* my *hand* and I stop breathing, exhaling only when she's led me far enough away, so we have some privacy.

"Thank you," she says. "I'm only alive because of you and—and there's something I should've done..." She teeters toward me, our faces almost touching, and then even that sliver of a gap disappears. Her lips brush against mine. Soft as butterfly wings.

"Is this okay?" she asks. "I mean, it's been a while since—so I'm not sure if—"

The initial shock dissolves and this time I press my lips to hers, my heart about ready to crack my ribs as I wrap my arms around her, holding her up. We kiss and this time, she doesn't pull away.

I do.

I need to catch my breath.

"But why?" I ask. "Last time—I thought I made a mistake and ruined our friendship, that you didn't like me that way. That you..."

An awkward silence hangs between us as I struggle to say what's been gnawing at my mind for months and months and months.

"I thought you stopped liking me because I came out as nonbinary," I continue. "That maybe you only liked girls, or boys, or something."

"No, that wasn't it at all." She grips my hands. "I just—when you kissed me, I wasn't ready. I wasn't sure what I was feeling. It's complicated you know, with my moms. Like they're super supportive. But I didn't want to be the queer daughter of the only queer parent couple at our school."

"That we know of."

"True, and it's silly, but I didn't know it then. I do now. I know how I feel about you, and after all this..." She twirls our hands in the air. "Life is way too short not to admit when you have feelings for someone." Natalie offers me a smile and I swear she hasn't lost her magic at all because the look on her face sets my blood on fire.

"I did try to talk to you about it afterward," she continues. "But you were avoiding me, and I thought maybe you regretted it and didn't know how to tell me, so I just—"

"No! No, never!" I stammer. "I was afraid I'd ruined our friendship and I was so afraid of what you'd say if we did talk in case you hated me. I—I guess I did actually ruin things."

"Ancient history now, though, right?" Natalie says, but I can feel her waiting on me to confirm.

"Ancient history," I say, and she tugs me into a hug.

My chest explodes with a supernova of warm fuzzies as I inhale the scent of her and soak up her warmth. I want to stay like this forever, but our embrace turns into a group hug as Aysha, Katya, and even Sini wrap their arms around us. I brace myself, half expecting to get zapped by Katya, but I don't, and it actually feels kind of nice.

"Okay, enough, enough, I can't breathe," Natalie says, and the hug breaks apart.

I don't have the words in either English or Finnish to express what I'm feeling, but Natalie takes my hand and nothing else matters.

"Aw, he looks lonely." Katya nudges Aysha toward Morgan. "Should we go cheer him up?"

We head over. He sees us coming and meets us halfway.

"Hey." He tugs at a curl escaping the edge of his beanie.

He notices my hand in Natalie's and gives me a sneaky thumbs-up only I see. There are thick bandages on his wrists.

"How you feeling?" Aysha asks.

"Definitely been better, but I'll live," he says, and she gives him the cheesiest grin I've ever seen.

Together, a surprising group of six, we look out over the lake, at the faces of the students who didn't make it.

"If only we'd done what we did sooner," I say. "We might've saved them all and Hannah wouldn't have been hurt."

"We did all we could," Aysha says.

"And we were pretty badass." Morgan bumps me with his elbow. "We fought off monsters and defeated a chaos mage!"

I should feel pride at our victory, but something else niggles inside me. What if Emmi was telling the truth? Natural magic is being destroyed. So, what if finding the shards of the Sampo was the right thing to do?

"I'm sorry I missed it," Sini says, breaking into my thoughts.

Aysha raises her eyebrows.

"Almost," Sini says. "I'm rather happy I did to be honest. And I'm super glad you all survived."

"Thanks to Taika," Katya says.

"How come you were the only one who could hear Natalie?" Sini asks.

"Magic," I answer, and it almost makes me smile. "Not sure exactly what kind yet. Maybe some sort of shamanism, maybe something else. I'm in House Aithyr now. Even got the T-shirt."

"Like Sorin and the shape-shifters?" Morgan asks.

"Yeah, there'll be five houses from now on."

"I thought practicing Aithyr elementalism was too close to chaos magic." Sini glances at me nervously, as if she's a little afraid.

Not going to lie—I quite like the way that makes me feel.

"It's a gray area, a different sort of magic," Aoife answers as she joins us, her arm still around Toivo. "And probably something we all need to understand better."

"You know, Cludd wants to dedicate a full page to Risto, Manami, and Elijah," Sini says. "Want to do it together?" She still looks nervous, thumb poised beneath the elastic on her wrist.

"Definitely," I say. "I'd be honored to share a byline with you." And I'm surprised I actually mean it.

Mom clears her throat, and everyone is quiet.

"Dear guardians, students, and staff of Myrskyjärvi," she begins. "We are gathered here today to remember the lives of three incredible students. To mourn them. To miss them. And to make sure we never forget them. Their lives were taken in an unspeakable act of cruelty and betrayal. We will not rest until *all* those responsible are brought to justice."

I zone out, my gaze on the photos illuminated by flickering candlelight. All the *if onlys* skewer my insides as the procession of twelfth graders sweep around the lake.

They move through the silence like spirits in their white robes.

Carefully, we all pull out slips of paper from our pockets. Earlier, we wrote down our sorrows, all the awful things from the past year we want to get rid of so we can make room for the good stuff coming in the next year.

My paper is pretty full. So is Morgan's, his spidery handwriting scrawled across the back and front. He folds it up before I can read anything and places his paper along with mine in the baskets the twelfth graders are using to collect all the sadness. They take several minutes to place our notes into the twigs, making the buck look as if it's wearing a garland of white flowers.

After, the twelfth graders stand like a rank of ghosts at the water's edge. Mom lights a taper and approaches the Kekri buck. She closes her eyes, uttering words not meant for the crowd's ears. I offer up my own silent words to the dead, knowing the forest is listening.

I'm sorry we didn't help you sooner. I'm sorry you died. I wish I could've done more. And to Mervi, my great-great-great—something—grandmother, despite what Emmi said, I hope I can make you proud of me one day.

You will, a voice definitely not my own whispers at the back of my mind. *You already have.*

Mom lowers the taper and the kindling catches fire, quickly devouring the numerous bundles of sticks so meticulously tied and placed on the buck's frame. We watch our sorrows go up in flames. We watch until there's nothing but ash, ash the wind blows gently into the dark waters of the lake.

"I can't believe they're making us go to class tomorrow," Katya says as the crowd begins to disperse, celebration over. "I thought they'd close the school for at least a couple of weeks. Not to mention the thaumaturgy teacher got eaten by a magical forest."

"We have to get those shards back," Toivo says. "I owe Risto that much."

No one argues.

"At least the Order of Louhi can't release Tumultua unless they have all the shards," Toivo says. "Which means they'll keep trying to get the rest of them."

I listen without saying anything. I don't want the most powerful chaos mage being released, but I need to know more about what Emmi said. I have to consider both sides of the story—it's what good journalists do.

"This time we'll be ready," Aoife says, her words ominous.

Fear-laced dread gathers like a storm cloud above us as we walk along the water's edge, pausing at the photo of Elijah, Manami, and finally Risto. Toivo grits his teeth as he looks at the last photo, and I can only imagine how he feels. Natalie takes my hand again and I am so very grateful her photo isn't here.

"So, what do we do now?" Morgan asks.

"You still have that battle magic book, right?" I ask.

"For now," Aoife answers.

"Then we study it and learn everything we can. We need to know a lot more about everything."

"We're seriously going to take on a league of chaos mages?" Aysha asks.

"They've been defeated before. We can do it again," Toivo says with a bravado I definitely do not share. Not yet.

"We have to try," Natalie says. "I don't want what happened to me to ever happen to anyone else." She shudders and I pull her closer to me.

"We won't let it," Aysha says.

"We'll get back the shards," I say. "And…"

"And save the world?" Morgan offers me a wry grin.

"We can try."

Taika, the little voice at the back of my mind starts up. *Taika the Brave, Taika the Resourceful, Taika whose name means magic*, it whispers, and, this time, what it says is true.

ABOUT THE AUTHOR

Climber, tattoo-enthusiast, and peanut-butter addict, Xan van Rooyen
is a genderqueer non-binary storyteller from South Africa, currently
living in Finland where the heavy metal is soothing and the cold, dark
forests inspiring. Xan has a Master's degree in music, and—when not
teaching—enjoys conjuring strange worlds and creating quirky
characters. You can find their short stories in the likes of Three-Lobed
Burning Eye, Daily Science Fiction, Cast of Wonders, and The Colored
Lens. Xan hangs out on instagram, twitter, and facebook so feel free to
say hi over there.

ACKNOWLEDGMENTS

Whenever it comes time to write this section for a novel, I am always terrified I'll forget to mention someone.

Writing is an often lonely pursuit with hours, days, years spent all up in your own head wrangling your creations into some semblance of coherence. And even when you think you're done, you're really just beginning because writing is rewriting and editing and revising again. And sometimes it's throwing out an entire draft and starting from scratch.

That's what happened with My Name is Magic—more than once.

I began this book more than five years ago. Since its very first iteration, the book has undergone some major changes. It would not be the book in your hands today were it not for some of my earliest readers taking the time to provide insights into plot, character, and all things Finnish. Kiitos paljon Sara, Angelica, and Katja with an extra special thank you to Katja for not only allowing me to borrow her name for a character but for creating some absolutely stunning fanart of Fiona, convincing me to keep my knitwear-sporting Komodo dragon in the story even when it evolved from MG to YA. And a huge shout out to Helinä for answering all my Finnish-language questions—any mistakes are entirely my own!

I owe a lot of thanks to my former agent, Adriann, who was one of the first to believe in this story. She helped me smooth many of my story's sharp edges and working through revisions with her has definitely made me a better writer. To Stephanie, for editorial insights that again helped elevate this book beyond what I ever thought it could be. To Lindsay, my current agent, who has been a tireless fan of and advocate for my work, never once doubting this little story's worth and believing in my vision when I just knew that in order to tell this story authentically, the book needed another overhaul.

To the Helsinki Writer's Group, the Dragon Writers, Skolion crew, and Nine Lives Authors group for always being supportive, championing my efforts, commiserating rejections, and celebrating every little win—I don't think I could keep doing this without the support both IRL and virtually from my writing buddies.

Kiitos Sini (I may have borrowed your name) for always being a champion of my work, making sure to include me in Finnish fan spaces, and ensuring my books are in local libraries. Your support over the years has meant the world to me.

And now, about that cover. I am in awe of the artwork Alex Copemann produced for my book. To be honest, I had my doubts anyone would be able to accurately capture the angrycute (thanks Cat!) vibe of my book, but Alex blew me away. Seeing Taika and Morgan so perfectly rendered on the cover brought me to tears. So, thank you, Alex, for being such an integral part of bringing my book baby to life.

This book wouldn't exist without Josh and the team at Tiny Ghost Press. Thank you so so much for taking a chance on this story. I couldn't have asked for a better home for my book, a home that has loved and nurtured Taika and their crew from the very start. My goal has always been to write the stories I wish I'd had growing up queer and lonely, in the hopes a young reader might pick up one of my books and feel less alone, feel seen, and loved. To this end, I have so much respect and appreciation for Josh and the TGP team who have and continue to put in the work to make this goal a reality. Extra special thanks to Dana for her meticulous attention to detail during copyedits and challenging me to make every sentence the best it could be.

To my readers—I do this for you. Thank you for holding this book in your hands, thank you for wanting to read my stories, thank you for all your love and support.

And finally, to Mark, who has never once questioned why I write and who has only ever been supportive, holding me through tears and disappointments and sharing my elation when the stars align so I might send another book out into the world. Thank you for putting up with my rants about uncooperative characters and annoying plot holes, for always reading my words when I need you to, for respecting the time and space I need to write, and for loving me through all of it.

www.ingramcontent.com/pod-product-compliance
Lightning Source LLC
Chambersburg PA
CBHW011150190726
48288CB00010B/3254